Praise for Steven Manchester

¤ ¤ ¤ ¤

"Steven Manchester has a gift for expressing through his writing the complicated and transcendent beauty of the human experience with poignant clarity."
— Yolanda King, eldest daughter of Dr. Martin Luther King Jr.

"Steven Manchester writes about life as it really is and really could be."
— Crystal Book Reviews

"Steven Manchester has become one of my must-read authors."
— Literary R&R

"I really liked Steven Manchester's poetic writing style and ability to construct such a vivid, exciting, and impassioned story line full of heartbreak, inspiration, hope, love, and faith."
— Book Trib

"Steven Manchester is the Norman Rockwell of literature!"
— Literarily Illumined

"Steven Manchester really knows how to write family . . . I cannot wait to read more by this author!"
— The Grand World of Books

Gooseberry Island

Gooseberry Island

Steven Manchester

THE
STORY PLANT

The Story Plant
Studio Digital CT, LLC
P.O. Box 4331
Stamford, CT 06907

Print ISBN-13 978-1-61188-180-6
E-book ISBN-13 978-1-61188-181-3

Visit our website at www.TheStoryPlant.com

First Story Plant Printing: January 2015
Printed in The United States of America
0 9 8 7 6 5 4 3 2 1

Acknowledgments

◻ ◻ ◻ ◻

First and forever, Jesus Christ, my Lord and Savior. With Him, all things are possible.

To Paula, my beautiful wife, for loving me and being the amazing woman that she is.

To my children—Evan, Jacob, Isabella and Carissa— for inspiring me.

To Mom, Dad, Billy, Randy, Darlene, Jeremy, Jenn, Jason, Philip, Baker, the DeSousa's—my beloved family and foundation on which I stand.

To the Dream Team of Operation Desert Storm.

And to Lou Aronica—my mentor and friend—whom I could never thank enough.

For Marc Susi—rest in peace, brother

Chapter 1

□ □ □ □

It was late dusk, early spring. David was on his fourth date in two weeks with Allison. With the top down, they drove along a coastal highway in his beat-up Mustang convertible, while Allison applied the finishing touches of makeup in the rearview mirror. She smiled at her reflection, obviously pleased with what she saw. David shook his shaved head and readjusted his gaze to the stars above. "What a perfect night to lie on the beach and count the stars," he said, revealing the depth of his thoughts.

Allison was still in the mirror. "David," she blurted, "you said you were taking me dancing."

He never paid her any mind. He was too distracted. "Ever wonder if there's other life out there, Alli," he asked, "you know, maybe even making wishes on our sun?"

Allison finally removed herself from the mirror and shot him a look that asked, *Are you serious?* He never noticed. "Come to think of it, no," she said, cynically. "No, I've never wondered that." She looked down at her nails. "But I have wondered why this nail polish looked red in the store and now it doesn't." She sighed. "This putrid shade of purple doesn't even match my shoes."

David returned to the present and looked at his shallow date. Shaking his head, he scanned the channels until reaching a station playing soft rock. He left it there and looked back toward the sky. Allison finished her makeup, pushed the rearview mirror back toward him and switched the radio to pulsating techno music. He looked at her. She smiled, oblivious to the rude gesture.

"I was thinking it might be nice to spend a quiet night together," he said. "We could talk until the sun came up and really get to know each other." He began daydreaming aloud. "Share our pasts, our dreams... what we really want for the future."

"I'd rather dance," she said.

David was taken aback. "You'd what?"

"You heard me," she said, with equal amounts of vanity and crudeness. She looked at him and attempted compassion. "Truth is, Davey, I hate talking with you. You're too intense and it depresses me."

He was even more shocked. "I'm what?"

She looked the other way and breathed heavily. "I hate this part," she mumbled under her breath, and then turned her body to face him. "Maybe it's good that we have this talk now, before you..."

"Before I what?" he interrupted.

"Before you get too attached." She took another deep breath, and the rest came out in one callous blurt. "It's only been a few dates, but it's not working, Davey. I just want to have fun. I'm young."

He chuckled, cynically. "Young? You're almost thirty."

The comment made her snap. "Fine! But I'm old enough to know that you're worse than a girl."

Steven Manchester

Instinctively, he pulled the car off to the side of the road. The moon shone brightly on them both. "Worse than *a girl*?" he barked.

Her face was incredibly smug. "Well, since I met you, all you ever do is babble about faith and dreams and finding a soul mate." She nodded. "It's true, you're worse than a girl." The pitch of her voice could have turned a popsicle headache into a full brain freeze.

He felt like strangling the conceited wench. Instead, he threw the shifter into drive and sped off.

Allison looked sorry for the last comment, but not enough to remain quiet. "I think we should both play the field and see other people," she suggested.

"Alli," David said, "I'm not sure there's a whole lot of field left for you to play." He snickered. "Besides, I'm leaving in a week and..." He stopped.

She didn't get it and looked at him blankly for an explanation.

David peered at her and, within seconds, his anger was replaced by a smile that took up most of his baby face. A minute later, he felt ready for laughter. *She's just done me the biggest favor ever*, he realized.

Alli clearly didn't know what to make of the change in facial expressions. "I'm sorry," she whispered, nervously.

"Don't be, Alli," he said. "Don't be. You're so right it's actually hilarious." He nodded. "I was hoping we might make a connection before I shipped out, but it didn't happen. Trust me, it's not a big deal."

Allison looked hurt. "Look, I know I'm not the right one for you..." She slid closer to him. "But maybe I could be the right one for tonight?" she whispered.

David pulled the car into her driveway and threw the shifter into park. He looked back toward the sky. "*Tonight* would never be enough for me, Alli." He shrugged. "Take care of yourself, okay?"

Shocked by the sudden breakup, Alli got out of the car and shot him a longing look.

With a sense of relief, David pulled out of the driveway, leaving her to pout like the spoiled brat she was.

¤ ¤ ¤ ¤

David punched a few numbers into his cell phone. "Coley, it's Dave. Where are you?" He grinned and rolled his eyes. "Right. Where else would you be? I'll be there in ten minutes." He listened to his friend and shook his head. "No. Nothing's wrong. I just need to talk." He closed the cell phone and pressed down on the accelerator.

¤ ¤ ¤ ¤

Ten minutes later, David reached the Eagle. As he walked into the busy nightclub, he spotted Coley standing at the bar. His handsome friend was talking to some unsuspecting female victim. David stepped up and yelled his drink order over the loud music, "A Coors Light, please." Coley noticed his friend and whispered something into the girl's ear. She giggled, nodded at David, and then walked away. David looked at Coley and shook his head. Coley smiled. With beers in hand, both men turned and placed their backs against the bar to face the action on the dance floor. David was completely out of his element, while Coley looked right at home.

"What'd you just tell her?" David asked over the thumping music.

Coley grinned. "I said that you and I had business, but once I got rid of you..." He smiled and took a swig of beer. "I'd be back for some serious *business* with her."

David shook his head and took a swig of his suds.

"So what drags you into my dark world?" Coley asked.

David took a look around, unsure whether he should go on. "I don't know, Coley. Maybe I came to the wrong place."

Coley gestured for his friend to follow him. "Come on," he yelled, and started through the crowd toward a quieter corner. David was right behind him. Once there, Coley said, "Trust me, you've come to the right place. Now, go ahead. I'm listening." His grin was contagious.

Reluctantly, David reported, "Alli, that girl I just started dating...I just dropped her off at her house."

"Already?" Coley asked, surprise painting his face. "What happened?"

"For starters, she told me we should both see other people."

Coley smirked. "And that's a problem?"

David scowled at him and took a long draw of his beer. "She implied that we could still hook up, but..."

Coley nearly spit out a mouthful of beer. "You passed?" he asked, confused. "I don't understand."

David shook his head. "Alli loves herself so much that there'd never be room for me...or anyone else, for that matter."

"Well, I can relate to that," Coley muttered.

David glared at his friend. "You're pathetic."

"No, just realistic." There was a pause. "Dave, not everyone feels comfortable swimming at the deep end of the pool. Don't be so judgmental. We each make different choices in life. That doesn't make any of us any better or worse." He smirked. "Maybe just a little less brave?"

David pondered Coley's words and chuckled. "Whoa!" he said. "For someone who can't handle *deep*..."

"I know," Coley interrupted, comically. "It's scaring me too." He smirked. "I think maybe it's you who's the bad influence." Coley looked around the room and caught another pretty girl's attention. "Sad part is," he reported, "they're all the same. You can't trust any of them."

"Hello kettle, this is Coley," David joked. "You're black." After a long chuckle, he shook his head. "I don't know, buddy. I think you're wrong there."

Coley pretended to be annoyed. "Did you come here to tear me up?"

"I'm just messing with you." David laughed. "Seriously, I appreciate your ear."

Coley nodded. "Not a problem, partner," he said, and then searched his friend's face. "For real, are you okay?"

David nodded, convincingly. "I am."

Coley shrugged. "Maybe it's for the best, anyway... with you heading off next weekend?"

"Maybe," David admitted.

Coley looked back toward the dance floor and eyed up the pretty one he'd been talking to at the bar. They exchanged a playful smile. Coley sighed. "In that case, my man, I've done all I can here." He finished his beer. "Wish me luck," he said, grinning. "If you need me, I'll be at the shallow end of the pool." And with a wink, he headed back toward the dance floor.

"Try not to drown yourself," David yelled.

To David's surprise, Coley turned back and stopped. "My point exactly!" he said, smiling. "Not a chance." At that very moment, the swaying crowd swallowed him whole.

David rolled his eyes, thinking, *And this is the help I get?* He finished his beer, scanned the room once and shook his head. *This lifestyle is definitely not for me,* he thought, and stepped out into the dark night.

◻ ◻ ◻ ◻

Lindsey Wood sat on the edge of the couch, watching as her dad fought valiantly—like an old soldier sensing his end.

Denis Wood, the decorated Operation Desert Storm veteran, was nearly rolled into a ball in his worn recliner. Covered in a film of toxic sweat, the man's extremities twitched and convulsed.

He must be replaying an old battle in his mind, she figured.

Denis's breathing became heavy and labored as he shook his head from side-to-side. "No," he moaned, "Oh God, no!"

Lindsey held her breath, hoping that he'd open his eyes soon.

"Marc," Denis screamed. "They're everywhere. We've gotta get out now!"

Please wake up, Dad, she thought, knowing that if she attempted to roust him from his nightmares, there was a very good possibility that he'd attack her—instantly, violently.

Three war cries later, he awoke panting, his chest heaving. His face soaked in tears and mucous, he slowly turned toward her. His squinted eyes were filled with a murderous rage.

Lindsey sat at a safe distance, holding her breath until his distant eyes traveled all the way back to the present. She'd learned when she was much younger—after her mother had finally left them for good—that there was a critical time period that needed to be respected, and it varied. Without even realizing it, her dad would lash out with a terrifying ferocity. On two separate occasions, she'd suffered a black eye and bloody nose, and felt blessed that she'd gotten away so easily each time.

"It's all right, Pop," she whispered. "It was just another bad dream."

"Yeah," he said, gasping for air. "Right. Just a bad dream," he repeated, while his eyes were still making their way home. He shook his head, closed his eyes tight and took a deep breath. "Bad dreams when I'm sleeping and nightmares when I'm awake."

"It's getting bad again?" she asked, the rhetorical question intended to make him share his thoughts and feelings with her.

"Worse than it's ever been, I suppose." He opened his eyes and looked at her. "I'm not sure how much more I can take, Linds." The sorrow in his voice was deep and sincere.

Steven Manchester

"Have you talked to Dr. Alonso about it?" she asked.

"All we do is talk," he answered. He shut his eyes tightly again, trying to block out some of the pain.

"What about your medication? When's the last time you..."

"There's no middle ground there, Linds," he interrupted. "I'm either tortured with old pictures that I can't get out of my head...faces of dead men that keep screaming for me to help save them." He slowly opened his eyes again. "Or I'm a drooling zombie who can't remember to unzip my fly when it's time to take a leak."

"Maybe you should consider checking in to the hospital?"

"For what, another tune-up that won't add up to a piss hole in a snowbank?"

"Anything's better than sitting in that recliner, thinking about different ways of checking out."

His eyes opened wide at her frightened tone. "You sure about that?" he asked.

Her eyes filled, but she never left his gaze. "I am, Dad," she said.

He closed his eyes again and took another deep breath. "Okay then," he muttered, finally surrendering. "Hopefully they've hired better mechanics at that butcher shop they call a hospital."

◻ ◻ ◻ ◻

On the ride to the VA Hospital, Lindsey stole several glances at her father, making her heart ache. Denis Wood was a quiet, heavyset man who lived in a state of emotional catastrophe since returning home from the first Persian Gulf War. For years, he relied on his bitter wife to take care of the smallest details. But by the time Lindsey was twelve years old, the woman had taken enough and packed her things—never to look back.

Without me, he'd be completely lost, Lindsey thought, stealing another sideways look at him. Together, over the years, they'd set up a mundane routine for him— safe and predictable. But he'd become a shell of the man he'd once been and they both knew it.

Before she'd left, Lindsey's mom said that he'd lost his faith. Lindsey knew better. *Mom took his soul with her when she abandoned us both*, she thought. *She'd carried enough magic for the both of them, so when she left, the rest of his light went out.*

◻ ◻ ◻ ◻

The VA Hospital's façade was clean and manicured. Old Glory snapped and popped in the wind out front, while white-painted rocks surrounded the shrine in meticulous military fashion.

Lindsey's father opened his eyes and cringed. "The Nut House," he murmured.

"It'll be fine," Lindsey said, and parked the car. But after dozens of similar trips, they both knew better. This was just part of the vicious cycle that no one knew how to break.

◻ ◻ ◻ ◻

Inside the foyer, the sanitized smell of pine oil competed with the rank stench of urine. The residents— homeless-looking men, their fingers stained yellow and brown from smoking hand-rolled cigarettes down to the very end—loitered at the top of the front stairs. Unshaven and hygienically challenged, these were men who'd once passed inspections, stressing over a single smudge on spit-shined boots or brass insignia. Now half-dressed in clothing and pajamas, each pathetic package was wrapped up in a government-issued, striped cotton robe. Footwear included boots or slippers—with the occasional pair of wing tips thrown in—but anything seemed to work with the ensemble. And although each one of them looked miserable, they still appeared happier than the folks who worked there.

Moans and groans were broken by the occasional whimper. Lindsey dared a look into some of their eyes and, as usual, wished she hadn't. They were filled with such pain, souls lost long ago in trenches and rice paddies and barren deserts.

Most of the patients were numbed by enough chemicals to silence their screams and paralyze their convulsions. *Government-trained killing machines that have been broken and are now stored in red-bricked warehouses*, Lindsey thought.

"Three squares and a cot, and all the pills your liver can process," Lindsey's dad said, breaking her hideous train of thought.

She shook her head but silently agreed. *We're back in the land of the living poltergeists*, she thought, and turned to her father after he'd checked in. "Okay, Pop, I'll call you tomorrow to..."

"Just don't leave me here," he begged, the terror in his eyes making him look like a young, desperate child.

"I won't, Pop."

"Please, Linds," he repeated, his eyes as wide as dinner plates.

"I won't," she promised, and watched as he dragged his feet down a long yellow corridor, only to disappear behind a cold, gray door that she'd never want to visit.

◻ ◻ ◻ ◻

It was David's last Wednesday night on the island when he met Coley for their weekly game of billiards.

"Whose break?" David asked.

"Let's flip for it," Coley said. "I've got heads." He watched his quarter spin end-over-end until it landed tails side up. "Damn it! Every time."

"Didn't you wear that sweater to the eighth grade dance?" David teased Coley, as he broke the rack of balls with one quick jerk of the wrist.

Coley laughed. "Did you hear the story about the guy who got divorced and was court-ordered to pay off his wife with a boatload of money?" he asked.

David shook his head and put the four ball into the corner pocket.

Coley went on. "He used a dump truck to deliver her alimony...in pennies."

David's brow wrinkled in disbelief.

"It's true," Coley said. "She brought him back to court, but there was nothing the judge could do. It was legal tender, and the exact amount he owed her. Now how perfect is that?"

"It figures you'd like that story," David said, and shot the three ball into the side pocket.

Coley smirked. "You're too straight-laced. You were the same way when we were kids."

"Sure, Coley. And if it means anything, you haven't changed either."

Coley started to grin but stopped. "You're right. And I'm never going to change," he vowed. "I can't help that I'm addicted to romance."

"You mean sex, right?"

With a giant smile, Coley nodded.

David couldn't get over it. *Coley's as shallow as a puddle and he still scores big with the ladies.* His childhood friend was always tanned and his hair was perfect. *But inside, his heart's an echo chamber.* Coley always used the same lines on women, and he always brought them on the same date: a walk down the beach, wine, poetry, candlelight. "I want to wait," most would say when it was time to get intimate. Coley would smile. "I like you a lot," he'd whisper, "and I really want this to be something you'll never forget...or regret." *Pathetic*, David thought, *but it works every time.* One woman even told him, "This was the perfect date." Coley never batted an eye. "It should be," he replied. "It's taken me years to perfect it." David just couldn't understand. While women rejected scores of sweet-hearted guys, they loved his soul-less friend. At first, David supposed that sincerity just didn't go over, that perhaps self-centeredness did. He finally decided, though, that women loved a challenge. Every one of them wanted to convert the player into a faithful man.

"How can you beat it when everything is fresh and new and no matter what you do—it's for the first time?" Coley asked.

"But it's only a fleeting phase," David said, sinking his next shot, "no more important or exciting than any other phase. From what I've seen, it's a real relationship only if you have to really work at it."

"You're sad," Coley teased, "didn't I teach you anything? Variety is the spice of life!"

David smiled, eyed up the eight ball and sank it right in the side to take the first win. "Trust me, Coley, the fire that attracts you in the beginning is the same flame that'll burn you in the end."

Through all the conquests, the excuses, and break-ups, the truth always caught up. In the end, Coley could never be what he wasn't. Even his best lies could only buy him temporary joy.

"Whatever," Coley said, racking another game.

"Well said," David teased before smashing the rack of balls to all four corners of the pool table. "I'm going for a long run on North Beach tomorrow. You want to join me?"

"Not a chance," Coley said. "I'm sleeping in."

David missed his next shot and leaned his chin on the pool cue. "Those days are over for me for a while."

Coley nodded solemnly. "Your brother says your going-away party should be one to remember," he said.

"Craig told me," David said. "Hopefully, we can all stay out of jail."

Coley laughed. "I told him to make sure there are plenty of women there."

"That would be nice."

Coley shook his head. "You wouldn't have time for a girl now anyway."

"Trust me," David said, smiling, "I'd make the time."

◻ ◻ ◻ ◻

At the crack of dawn, David pulled up to the North Beach marina in his convertible and parked. Dressed in sweats, he jumped out—his running shoes still unlaced. On the water, a father and his young son were sailing toward the island. For no particular reason, David waved. They both waved back.

On land, with the exception of a few sweater-wearing stragglers strolling along the beach, Captain Eli was the only other person in the world. The old, black sea captain was mending tattered fishing nets aboard his run-down vessel, *Serendipity*. David stepped onto the dock and visited with his old friend at the bow of the boat. "Mornin', Captain."

Captain Eli looked toward the sky. The sun had just awoken, painting the horizon with a warm light. "That it is," he confirmed with a grin.

David grinned and then scanned the vast ocean before them. "Expecting a big catch today?"

Captain Eli never looked up from the net. "You never know what the day might bring." He took a breath. "And you?"

"Three days 'til I ship out," David said, his tone melancholy.

Captain Eli searched his friend's face. "Looks like you're not looking forward to it." He awaited an explanation.

"Actually, I'm proud to be able to fight for my country. I was just hoping I wouldn't have to be alone the entire time I was there," David explained.

"Alone?"

"It would've been nice to have someone to write to...someone to look forward to coming home to." He shrugged. "I guess that's just the story of my life."

"Well David, if the story's that bleak, then maybe it's time to write a new one."

David looked up, surprised. Captain Eli was no longer smiling. David offered a friendly snicker. "And it would be that easy, huh?"

"Why not? It's *your* life." Captain Eli's tone sounded matter-of-fact. "It's *your* story."

David bent to tie his shoes. "I can't seem to find the right woman," he explained.

"Stop looking."

"No such luck," David joked. "That's just me."

Captain Eli still wore his serious face. "No such thing as *luck*," he vowed, with intensity. "It's a matter of *choice*."

The firm tone came as a surprise to David. "What's that?" he asked.

Captain Eli smiled and softened his approach. "David, people who believe in luck don't take any real responsibility for what happens in their lives. I'd rather make my own decisions than leave everything up to random luck."

David stopped tying his shoes. Captain Eli now had his complete attention. "And how would I do that?"

Captain Eli looked toward the horizon. "Well, I've always just thrown my wishes out into the universe and waited for them to come true." He grinned.

"And they have?"

The older man nodded.

David thought for a moment. "So just ask and wait, huh?"

"I'd say it's best to ask, and then give thanks before even getting your answer." He winked. "Now who could deny that type of faith?"

David nodded again, and then finished tying his shoes. He stood and stretched out for the run. "Thanks, Captain. I'll give it a try." As he started to walk away, he turned back to face his mentor. "I hope the fishing's good for you today," he said.

"For both of us," Captain Eli quipped, with another wink.

¤ ¤ ¤ ¤

With his head spinning, David walked toward the beach and stretched out once more. Just before taking his first stride, he paused and looked up toward the dark sky. "Thanks for bringing me the girl of my dreams," he said aloud and, at a jog, started down the beach.

Within minutes, his legs and his breathing picked up pace. He was just starting to find his rhythm when a pretty woman—a brunette with a fit body—appeared in the distance. She was walking a golden retriever on the approach. With David's labored breath building, they finally got close enough to offer each other a smile. David traveled another ten feet toward the girl when a seagull landed on the sand between them. Suddenly, the dog took off after it. David couldn't slow his momentum and tripped over the leash. To his instant humiliation, he was catapulted onto the sand.

The attractive brunette tried to conceal her laughter. David looked up, angry, and his initial reaction was to verbally lash out. His mind quickly changed, though, when he looked into her chocolate-brown eyes. She was smiling. He returned it and then pointed at the dog. "Maybe you should try feeding him dog food," he teased.

"I am *so* sorry!" she said. "Please, let me help you up."

While she struggled to take control of the leashed dog, she offered David her other hand. He took it and stood. His breathing was still labored. A moment passed before she giggled and looked down at her hand. He was still holding it. She shook David's hand. "Nice to meet you too," she said. "I'm Lindsey Wood."

David caught the joke and blushed. He pulled his hand away in embarrassment. "Oh, I'm sorry," he said, smiling. "I'm David...David McClain."

As he brushed himself off, the two locked eyes and remained there for an extended moment. "Well," he managed past the lump in his throat, "thanks." *She's really cute*, he thought, but immediately changed his mind. *No, she's beautiful.*

Although the dog was jerking her around, Lindsey continued to smile—and her eyes never left his. He half-waved at her and turned to resume his run.

"Five-five-five-three-eight-seven-four," she blurted.

He stopped and turned. "What's that?"

She blushed. "Five-five-five-three-eight-seven-four. If you can remember the number, call me and I'll buy you dinner for the trouble we caused." She looked down at the dog and gave him the eye.

David was frozen and didn't speak.

Her smile grew wider. There was definitely a mutual attraction between them. She broke the silence again. "I don't want to keep you from your run..."

"Oh, yeah." He looked down at his clothes and half-shrugged. "Don't worry about that. I just got started." He couldn't stop smiling either.

She nodded. He stepped forward and bent to pet the dog. It growled. Lindsey was shocked. "Simon, stop that!" she yelled at the dog. She looked up at David. "I walk him all the time and he never acts this way," she swore. She jerked the leash once and brought the canine back under control.

David chuckled. "Dinner sounds good," he said, "but maybe we should leave the big boy at home for the first date?"

Lindsey smiled. "Not a problem," she said. "I'm walking him for a friend."

David stepped backward. "I'll call you," he promised.

"I'm counting on it," she said, her eyes sparkling. "Just don't forget the number."

With a giant grin, David took off down the beach. Lindsey never flinched. She stood motionless, watching him as he ran away.

"Five-five-five-three-eight-seven-four," David repeated as he ran. "Five-five-five-three-eight-seven-four." And then it hit him. *I'm leaving on Saturday.* He picked up the pace, panting. "Five-five-five-three-eight-seven-four."

Chapter 2

¤ ¤ ¤ ¤

David picked up the telephone and dialed.

"Hello?" Lindsey answered.

"Hi, Lindsey. It's David."

"Oh hi, I was just thinking about you."

"You were?" He could feel his face start to burn.

"Uh-huh," she muttered. "I was hoping you'd call tonight."

He smiled. "Listen, I have good news and bad news. Which do you want first?"

"Let me guess, you're married and now you're feeling guilty for accepting my dinner invitation so..."

"No, no. Not at all. The good news is that my friends are throwing me a party, and I'd really love it if you'd come as my guest."

"And the bad news?" she asked.

"It's a going-away party."

"You're moving away?"

"For a while, yeah. But I'll be back."

"Where are you..."

"Come to the party and I'll explain everything to you." He took a deep breath. "What do you say?"

"When is it?" she asked, reluctantly.

"Tomorrow night. It's at six-oh-two State Road, and the party starts at six."

There was silence.

"Well?" he asked, hopefully.

She chuckled. "I'm way too curious to say no."

"Great," he said, relieved. "So I'll see you there?"

"You'll see me there."

¤ ¤ ¤ ¤

Lindsey showed up an hour late to the party. The address wasn't hard to find. It was only a few streets over from the beach, music blaring from its yard. As Lindsey drove past the house, there were cars parked everywhere—on both sides of the street, half on lawns—everywhere. She had to park near the beach and walk back toward the house. From the moment she got out of the car, the music screamed to her. *People halfway across the island can probably hear it*, she thought and laughed. *I wonder what this big bash is all about.*

As she reached the front yard, she spotted a large banner reading "*Come Home Safe, David*" strung from the corner of the house to a tall oak tree. *Come home safe?* she wondered and realized that David must be a military man. *Oh boy*, she thought.

After maneuvering through dozens of strangers holding red Solo cups, she finally spotted David. When he turned and saw her, his eyes immediately lit up, making her skip her next few breaths.

He hurried over. "Hey, I was hoping you'd make it!"

"Told you I would," she said, smiling. She pointed toward the massive banner. "Come home safe?"

He nodded. "I'm an Army Ranger and I've been deployed to Afghanistan for the next twelve months." What started off as a proud and excited announcement ended as more of an apology.

"Oh," she said. "I see."

"Can I get you a drink?" he asked, handing her a plastic cup.

"Why not," she said.

While they shared their first beer, David introduced his friend, Coley, his brother, Craig, and a dozen other names Lindsey would never remember. And through it all, he never took his eyes off of her.

He leaned in toward her neck and inhaled. "You smell really good," he said.

"Okay..."

"Take a walk with me to the beach," he blurted, putting down his plastic cup.

Lindsey looked back toward the beach. There was just enough light to paint the sky a rich, deep purple. "What about all your guests?" she asked. "You're just going to leave them?"

David grinned. "The keg's full. Trust me, they're not going anywhere for a while."

"Are you sure?" she asked, considerately.

He nodded. "They'll be here when we get back."

◻ ◻ ◻ ◻

As they walked toward the sound of hissing surf, he asked, "So how are you?"

She grinned. "Life's better than good," she said and looked at him. *I should have guessed*, she thought. "An Army Ranger, huh?"

He nodded. "I'm stationed at Fort Benning, Georgia, Fourth Ranger Battalion."

"Well, that explains the haircut," she teased.

"We're being deployed to Afghanistan for a twelve-month rotation. It's my first combat tour."

Afghanistan, she repeated in her head and cringed. "And you're shipping out..."

"Tomorrow," he said. "I took all my leave, so I've been home for the past four weeks."

"Wow," she said, taken aback. "You'll be away for twelve months?"

"Yup," he said, looking into her eyes. "I've been told by a few of the guys who've already been over there that it can go by quick."

"Wow," she said again—at a loss for any other words.

He picked up on it. "You don't like the military..." he started to ask.

"Just the opposite," she said. "I have nothing but the greatest respect and appreciation for our men and women in uniform."

"Really?" he asked. "You'd never know it by your face."

"It's just that...well...I also understand that freedom comes with a heavy price." She shook her head. "And sometimes that price can be severe."

David studied her. "Your dad?"

She nodded. "He was an infantryman in the first Gulf War," she said solemnly.

"Wow," David said, using her favorite word and not picking up on the melancholy. "Good for him."

"Yeah, good for him," she mumbled, just as they reached the beach.

As though it had been awaiting their arrival, they found a deserted park bench. Cemented into the cobblestone pathway, the bench's brown slats had been beaten relentlessly by a decade of harsh coastal storms and were now faded and smooth.

David gestured for Lindsey to take a seat. As she did, he took his place beside her. For a long while, they sat in silence, quietly paying their respects to the miraculous surroundings.

Together, they watched the sun set. Just as the final sliver went down for the night, David looked at her. "Good show, huh?"

"I can't imagine a better one," she replied.

He smiled. "Me either." Suddenly, the beach was theirs alone.

As the moon took its rightful place in the darkened sky, the tide ran for the shore where it hissed upon landing. Seconds later, it sprinted back into the ocean, rearranging the cinnamon-sugar landscape and creating a beautiful rhythm as it ran its laps. The sea winds picked up, causing patches of elephant grass to bow to Mother Nature and her violent mood swings. The heavily salted air was crisp, heightening the senses. It was as if someone had pulled away an invisible veil, leaving behind the clarity of a blind man gaining his sight for the first time.

"It's really beautiful here," Lindsey whispered.

"I know," David agreed. "It's my favorite place in the whole world."

She looked at him for a long moment. "Mine too," she admitted.

In the distance, that same soothing tide yanked wave after wave into a headlock, throwing each one into the lighthouse that stood guard over the harbor; walls of freezing seawater were being tossed two stories high into the tall, sleek structure. Lindsey pointed toward the stone lighthouse. "Look at that," she said.

Waves charged the gray tower, which appeared to have grown out of a pile of jagged rocks, pounding hard to overtake the medieval-looking fortress. It was like watching an unwanted guest: a missionary peddling religion from door-to-door, refusing to surrender. Above it all, the light—ten thousand candles strong—which had spent a century guiding the way for those who had become disoriented or lost on their journey, illuminated the entire show. As dependable as a loyal friend, that light stayed on in the face of even the foulest weather.

Lindsey tried to imagine what that strong lighthouse had witnessed in its time. *A silent observer to horrible maritime tragedies; migrating souls trying to find their place in the world; a witness to whalers, men of war and countless fishermen, casting their nets in order to keep their children fed.*

"That old lady, Ruth, has manned that lighthouse since I can remember," David said, breaking Lindsey out of her trance. "They say she's saved quite a few souls in that rescue skiff of hers."

"She must be a hearty soul to live such a solitary life," Lindsey said.

"I guess." He thought about it. "I wouldn't mind living there."

"All by yourself?"

He nodded. "Why not? There'd be no one around to bother me." He stared at the lighthouse. "I've met Ruth a few times, and she's not very friendly."

"Well, being antisocial is probably a valuable trait for that kind of work. Can you imagine spending that much time alone, confined to one space? It must change a person."

"I suppose it might," David agreed, "depending on where your head's at."

Lindsey shrugged. "She chose the isolation, I suppose." After a moment, she added, "You're probably right. I've been in a room filled with lots of people and still felt alone."

David looked at her and smiled. "I think you have to feel comfortable being alone with yourself before you truly know who you are and can feel comfortable being yourself with others."

Lindsey nodded. "Old Ruth rows into town every few months to pick up supplies, but she must live on seafood, mostly. Now that I could do."

"Not me," David said. "I've been eating seafood since the day I was born, I think. I could die a happy man if I never ate it again in my life."

Lindsey tensed at the word *die*. "There are folks who've claimed to smell pipe smoke being carried on the winds from that lighthouse. You think she smokes?"

David grinned. "Who knows? There's no one to stop her or complain."

Lindsey laughed, happy to daydream aloud about the mysterious place. "Do you think that lighthouse has ever seen any pirates?" she asked, immediately creating pictures of sea shanties being sung and casks of rum being consumed, all followed by the usual pillaging and plundering.

David laughed. "Drunken men emptying lobster pots that weren't theirs, maybe, but I can't imagine that Blackbeard and his bloodthirsty crew have ever sailed these waters." The closest thing to pirating would have been the local whalers—heavily tattooed, unshaven men from Nantucket and New Bedford—hunting whale bone to create scrimshaw jewelry and ornate pipes.

He's right, Lindsey knew, but it was still fun to imagine it. Just by closing her eyes, she could imagine the sea winds singing in harmony—with gorgeous mermaids trying to seduce seamen into their watery graves or the terrifying howls of invisible sea monsters lurking within the rising swells.

"What do you think it looks like inside there?" David asked, bringing her back to the present once again.

She stared off into the distance and smiled. "I've always imagined a winding staircase at its center and rooms filled with overstuffed bookshelves springing out."

"That sounds nice," he said, happy to jump into her vivid imagination.

They sat in silence again, while moonlight carved out a swath of light across the rolling waves, creating an abandoned, dimly lit highway that stretched out to oblivion. The night sky—like a giant, darkened meadow filled with fireflies—glowed and twinkled, shimmering off of the vast turquoise desert below.

As they gazed up at the constellations together, Lindsey said, "When I was a small girl, my dad used to show me the stars. He'd say that I was the Little Dipper and he was the Big Dipper, looking over me."

"Your dad sounds like a great guy," David said.

Lindsey smiled. "He is," she said, volunteering nothing more.

David looked up and pointed at the North Star. "That looks more like you to me," he said.

"Really?" she asked.

He nodded. "They're all beautiful, but that one shines the brightest."

She looked at him and started to laugh, but he wasn't trying to be funny or cute. *He's serious*, she thought.

David grabbed Lindsey's hand and held on, surprising her.

"Can I help you?" she asked, half-joking.

"I don't want to get lost," he joked.

She looked down at their clasped hands. "You feel safe now?"

He nodded and never let go of her hand.

"What about *your* father?" she asked.

"He's inspired me my whole life," David said.

"Really? That's great."

"Yup, he's always told me I'd never amount to anything."

"And you're going to prove him wrong in Afghanistan, right?" she asked, her body tensing.

"Something like that," he said.

Just then, people began leaving the party, and the musical roar was reduced to the hum of a few stragglers. "The keg must be empty," Lindsey teased.

David smiled. "Must be," he said, with an innocent shrug. After a while he said, "All right, so tell me, what's the one thing about you that no one will ever know but me?"

His grin and dancing eyebrow almost made her laugh. Instead, she gazed at the stars. "I shouldn't tell you this because you're going to war."

"That's exactly why you should tell me," he said.

"I have this incredible fear of dying alone," she admitted. "And sometimes, I feel lost, as if I don't belong here or anywhere else."

David looked shocked by her depth and moved even closer toward her—until their legs touched.

"I know it's silly 'cause I've never been alone," she admitted, her eyes back on the stars. "But I still can't help the way I feel sometimes."

He wrapped his arm around her shoulder and gave it a gentle squeeze. "It's not silly," he whispered. "And I'm glad you shared it with me." He peered into her eyes and smiled.

For Lindsey, it felt like this wasn't the first time they'd ever been together. She turned to face him and completed the hug. For a few wonderful moments, they held each other tightly.

When they finally broke apart, he pointed at the lighthouse. "Look right over there. Whenever you feel lost or alone," he said, "all you have to do is come here. No matter how dark or stormy, that light will always guide you home...back to where you need to be."

While her eyes filled, she wrapped her arms around him again. This time, she kissed his cheek.

"Hey, what'll your boyfriend think?" he teased.

Her body tightened, and he sensed it.

"Please tell me you don't have a boyfriend, Lindsey," he said, his voice now troubled.

She shook her head. "Of course not," she said, "or I wouldn't be here with you right now." She looked into his eyes. "I was with a guy for three years, but we broke up six weeks ago." She half-shrugged. "I caught him cheating."

"Oh," David said. "I'm sorry."

"He keeps telling me it was a mistake, but..."

"I guess there are some people who could make those kind of mistakes," David interrupted, "but I could never do that to someone I love." He shook his head. "Never."

She searched his eyes. *He's not saying it to be cruel,* she thought. *He's just being honest.*

"Sorry," he said. "I shouldn't have said that."

"Yeah, you should have." She squeezed his hand. "What about life after Afghanistan? What are your plans then?"

"I've been in for a while, so after this deployment I can either get out or re-enlist."

"And which way are you leaning?"

He leaned toward her.

She laughed.

"I'm not sure," he said, straightening up. "I love the Army. I do. But being a ranger hasn't left much time for anything else." He paused. "It's not really a job, you know. It's more like a way of life." He looked into her eyes, where he stayed for a long moment. "And I think I want more from life...much more."

She smiled.

"We'll see," he said.

"Yes, we will," she said under her breath.

They sat on that hard bench, talking and laughing until the sun popped its head up in the east.

It's strange how you can meet someone and feel like you've known them your entire life...or maybe even before that, Lindsey thought. She pointed toward the horizon and smiled. "Sorry, but it looks like I've cost you a full night's sleep."

He turned to face her and locked onto her eyes. "Don't you dare be sorry, Lindsey. This was the best night of my life!"

She searched his eyes for the truth again but didn't need to look far. She was an avid reader, and he was an open book that seemed to be written just for her.

"Besides," he added, with a dimpled grin, "I'll get my sleep on the plane." He grabbed her and pulled her to him. "I promised myself I'd be a gentleman," he whispered, "but I don't know if I can stop myself from kissing you."

"David, trust me, you are a gentleman." She pointed to the sunrise. "If you're concerned with time, then this could actually be considered our third date."

At that moment, they both leaned in toward each other. With pursed lips, David took the final plunge. The kiss was tender and passionate and hungry and magical—all at the same time. It felt like a true first kiss, releasing butterflies that began to tickle Lindsey's insides.

As they came up for air in each other's arms, David said, "It figures that I met you now...my last night before shipping out for a year." He searched her eyes again. "But I'm grateful I spent it with you."

She grabbed his hand. "Me too," she whispered, "but..."

"But?"

"I'm not sure I can start a new relationship right now."

"So you think being a pen pal is a risky relationship?" he teased.

She gave him her contact information. "Here's my email address. If you write me, I'll write back."

"I'll write you," he promised.

She smiled. "You'd better."

As he escorted her back to her car, she said, "Whatever you do, David McClain, you come back to Gooseberry Island, okay?"

"I will, Lindsey Wood," he said. "I'll meet you right back here on the bench before you know it. I promise."

◻ ◻ ◻ ◻

With his heart engulfed in the flames of hope, David hurried home to see his mother and father. When he got there, he found his mother in her flowered housecoat sitting at the kitchen table—already crying—and that the old man had left early for work. "He couldn't even wait to say goodbye to me," David complained under his breath.

"Your father left you this," his mother said, wiping her eyes. Betty McClain was a blonde, with tight curls and a figure that time had punished. Pretty and smart, her sad blue eyes spoke volumes so she didn't have to. Though their family lived on final notices from the utility companies, she was forbidden to work. His dad wouldn't have had it any other way. Most days, she never bothered to change out of her pajamas. There wasn't a good enough reason to get dressed.

She picked up a note from the table and handed it to him.

It read, *Keep your head down —Dad.*

"Well, isn't that profound," David commented, sarcastically.

"He loves you, ya know," his mother said, "and he's very proud of you."

"Sure, Ma. I can tell from the note."

She shook her head. "Did you go see your Aunt Jeanne?"

He nodded. "I did, before the party." David's beloved Aunt Jeanne was his father's sister but the polar opposite of the man. She was a caring, compassionate soul who let everyone know just how much she cared about them.

"Oh David," Betty cried, and stood to embrace her son. "I wish you didn't have to go. I'm already sick with worry."

"Please don't worry, Ma," he whispered. "I've been trained by the best. I'll be fine over there."

They hugged for a few solid minutes before she surrendered him to his awaiting brother.

Craig looked like he hadn't slept in days. "That wasn't cool, disappearing from your own party last night. Everyone was..."

"I know. I know," David said, unable to contain his smile. "I couldn't help it."

"That girl, Lindsey?"

"Yup." David smiled. "I can't even explain it."

"And you're not even going to try, are you?"

He thought for a moment and smiled wider. "We sat on a park bench all night and talked until the sun came up."

"You only talked. Yeah right! You got thrown out trying to steal second base, didn't you?"

He punched his brother's arm. "Not quite, Craig."

They laughed for a few minutes until Craig's face turned serious and his eyes misted over. "Davey, I need you to know that..."

"I know," David said and pulled his brother in for a strong hug. "You don't have to say it. I already know."

Craig pushed away and looked into his big brother's eyes. "But I do have to say it."

David nodded.

"I can't tell you how proud I am to call you my brother..."

David's eyes filled.

"And I really don't want to lose you to some..."

"I'm coming home, Craig. You have my word on it." David reached into his pocket, retrieved the keys to his old Mustang convertible and flipped them to his younger brother. "Take good care of her while I'm away, okay?"

His mouth agape, Craig caught the keys. "Are you serious? You're gonna let me drive the sled?"

"Until I get back."

They hugged again—while their mother stood off in the shadows, grieving like she'd already lost her eldest son to the Grim Reaper.

¤ ¤ ¤ ¤

A half hour later, David emerged from his bedroom, a heavy duffel bag slung over one shoulder and a bulging rucksack hanging on the other. He looked at Craig and grinned. "Looks like I need a ride to the airport. We're flying out of Fort Benning tonight."

Craig pulled the Mustang's keys from his pocket and grinned proudly. "Then let's ride."

After another of his mother's tear-stained kisses, David grabbed his father's note, slipped it into his pants cargo pocket and stepped out of the house.

¤ ¤ ¤ ¤

Halfway across the island, Lindsey kept nodding off on her couch, awakening in the clutches of anxiety. She finally sat up, allowing herself to think about David and the tough road ahead of him. *Please keep him safe, God*, she silently prayed. *We only shared one night, but it feels like we're meant for so much more.*

¤ ¤ ¤ ¤

That afternoon, at the Gooseberry Community Art Center, Lindsey beamed with joy as she showed a child how to paint with watercolors.

Her co-worker, Courtney Winters, questioned it. "Someone's happy today. What gives?"

"I had date last night...sort of," Lindsey said. Even through the long yawns, she couldn't stop smiling.

"Sort of a date?" Courtney repeated, looking confused. Eager to know the details, she pulled Lindsey away from her student. "Well, who is he?" she asked. "Where did you meet him?"

"I met him on the beach," Lindsey whispered. "Simon introduced us and it's...it's his eyes. It's like they call to me. "

Courtney shook her head, still unsold. "Linds, you're still new to the dating scene. There are a lot of jerks out there. Just be careful."

Lindsey shook her exhausted head. "I won't need to," she promised. "Not this time." The smile never left her.

Lindsey spent the rest of the day in dreamland, alternating between smiles and fighting off heavy eyelids. When they could finally break away from the children, she and Courtney ran off and spoke in excited whispers like two grade-school girls.

"Okay, I've been dying to hear it," Courtney said, "and I want details."

Still aglow, Lindsey's eyes grew distant. "It was the best night ever."

"What did you guys do? Where did he take you?"

"We went down to the beach, sat on a park bench and talked all night."

Courtney was getting frustrated. "And..."

Lindsey smiled. "And then we talked some more until the sun came up and he had to go."

Courtney shook her head. "I don't get it."

Lindsey's smile vanished, and she shook her head. "There is one problem, though."

"And what's that?"

"He's flying out tonight to fight in Afghanistan." She inhaled deeply. "And he'll be gone for a year."

"You're kidding me, right?"

"I wish I was," Lindsey said and, to the surprise of both of them, her eyes filled. "I wish I was."

¤ ¤ ¤ ¤

Seven hours later—on a black-tarred runway in Fort Benning, Georgia—David turned to face the C-130 military aircraft and took a deep breath. *Time to go to work*, he told himself. As he got closer, he spotted a fellow soldier saying goodbye to his small daughter. The man was on both knees, trying desperately to comfort the young girl and explain things she could never understand. "I'll be home soon, baby," he said, his voice shaky.

"Daddy, don't go! Please...PLEASE!" she screamed, as though he were heading off to the lethal injection room. "PLEASE..."

The man pulled her into his embrace.

"I want you to stay here with me and Mommy," she pleaded. "It'll be fun if you stay. PLEASE! PLEASE! I'll miss you too much." She began to cry uncontrollably. "And what if you *die*..." Her sobs made her entire body tremble and convulse.

The man pulled her in to him until she was flush with his heaving chest. "Oh baby," he whispered, struggling to be strong for her. "I'll come home. I promise."

Tough promise to keep, David thought, and then pictured both Lindsey's and Craig's worried faces. David glanced again at the soldier and his baby girl and could feel his heart start to tear from his chest. He turned away and quickly boarded the windowless plane.

As he made his way toward the canvas sling that he'd be sitting in for nearly sixteen hours, he questioned his own mettle. Then it dawned on him, *I'll be carrying my own weight over there, but at least I don't have to carry that.* He pictured the little girl's tormented eyes one last time, her desperate cries still fresh in his mind. *I'm not sure I could shoulder it,* he thought before tucking it away behind a door in his mind that he had no intentions of ever opening.

◻ ◻ ◻ ◻

One-by-one, David's ranger team took their respective canvas seats within the belly of the giant steel beast.

Lieutenant Kevin Menker, the team's smart, quick-witted leader, sat beside David. "You good to go, McClain?" he asked.

"Hoo-ah," David replied.

Kevin nodded and conducted a final inventory of his own gear.

Corporal Billy Brodeur, the team's baby, entered next. He was a Boston-based kid, who had grown up on the streets. David exchanged nods with him and smiled. *There's tough and then there's trained,* David thought. *When Billy was growing up, I have no doubt he was the toughest kid on his block, and then the Army was crazy enough to train him.*

Corporal Nathan Michaels filed in right behind Billy. Physically, Nate was the runt of the ranger litter. He was a quiet, unassuming guy who could have just as easily passed for a grade-school teacher—as long as his death-inspired tattoos remained concealed. *But he has a heart the size of his head,* David thought. Nate had two sons, so he had more to lose than any of them. David watched Nate take one last look at a family photo before he kissed it and tucked it back into his camouflaged cap.

Sergeant Max Essington, David's best friend in the Army, lugged his gear onboard and grabbed the sling on the other side of David. "You ready for this, brother?" the single father asked, smiling.

David nodded. "Hoo-ah!"

"Hoo-ah," Max repeated.

Tall and lanky, Max was a well-trained medic.

I'm glad he's with us, David thought.

Staff Sergeant Allen Correiro, a mountain of a man from Texas, was the last to board. He busted balls harder than any of them, but he was their weapons expert—*who will probably be faster to the trigger than any of us*, David thought.

"I hope we didn't interrupt anything important, Big Al," Lieutenant Menker yelled to him.

Al grinned. "Actually, it's called *my life*, but I'll get over it."

Everyone laughed—before confident nods were exchanged all around. The C-130's motors fired up and screamed out a terrifying warning. David took a deep breath and closed his eyes. *Time to go to work*, he repeated in his head. A moment later, they were speeding down the runway toward the fight in Afghanistan.

◻ ◻ ◻ ◻

In flight, amid the loud whine of the plane's motors, the same questions kept repeating in David's head. *Am I ready for this?* He then remembered experiencing the same doubts on his first plane ride to Georgia. That's when the real question arose: *Do I have it in me?*

Keeping his eyes closed, the answer came to him in fragmented memories.

For the first week of training, everywhere David and his fellow recruits went, they ran. Monsters wearing drill instructor hats frothed at the mouth, while the boys did enough push-ups to move the state of Georgia right off the map. The camouflaged demons screamed orders that were never understood, though it never mattered anyway. Their game was all about creating chaos and pushing limits.

Private David McClain easily endured the sixteen weeks of torment hosted by Harmony Church, Fort Benning, Georgia and graduated a soldier—an infantryman. Undaunted by the sweltering heat, he stood rigid at attention, while the company commander spoke of "duty, honor and courage." Throughout the speech, David pictured his father's face and thought, *I wish the old man was here to see this.*

When the commander stepped up to him and slipped the light blue infantry cord over his shoulder, David could almost feel the discipline, independence and strong sense of duty that came along with it. His mind continued to churn with thoughts of his dad. *He'd choke on his words for sure.* David expected orders to a regular Army duty station but was surprised to discover that Uncle Sam had other plans.

After graduating in the top five per-cent of his class and making the com-mander's list, the options for further training remained open. *Why not?* he thought. *Jump school is only three weeks long. How hard can it be?*

Satan himself barked orders, while David and his comrades ran a mara-thon straight through hell's kitchen. David never minded. In fact, he enjoyed most of it. There were con-stant opportunities for an eighteen-year-old man to test his mettle and David never let himself down. Some called it heart. David laughed. It was more of an attitude. He refused to quit and would rather have curled up and died on the side of a road than be sent home to Gooseberry Island a failure. Stubbornness played a much bigger part than heart.

As required, David made the five jumps but figured each one took two solid years off his life. The whole experience was a rush, combining raw excitement with paralyzing fear.

The night jump was a hairy one. No one could tell how fast the ground was coming or when it was time to tuck and roll. A few of the boys miscalculated and were forced to trade in their parachutes for crutches. Still, that fear didn't com-pare to the first time David tested the Earth's gravity by stepping out onto a cloud. *The first time was definitely the most terrifying,* he thought.

Thousands of feet above a checker-board of green and brown, the jump master's mouth snapped open and shut, while his words were stolen by the C-130's whining engines. It didn't matter. They'd gone over each detail a thousand times on the ground. That was one of the joys of being in the Army. Everything was done with relentless repetition, leaving little need for the human thought pro-cess. As practiced, everybody stood, hooked their chutes to the static line and shuffled one step closer toward the door. "The first step is the hard-est," the jump master joked. David quickly discovered he wasn't kidding.

Some guys needed a size twelve right in the backside to help them along, but David was determined to see him-self out. When his turn came, he hung his toes over the lip and anxiously awaited the green light. The few sec-onds it took to get the signal was just enough time to pick out one of the million thoughts that raced through his mind.

Ironically, he pictured one of those infamous Army commercials where decorated veterans marched in a patriotic parade. It was the one where older men from earlier wars stood and saluted from the sidelines, while small children by their sides waved the red, white and blue. "Courage is simply a matter of placing fear aside to get the job done!" claimed the narrator. *Unfortunately, he never went on to define the intensity of such fears.*

With that last thought, David became a screaming eagle and, with only one step, found more freedom than anyone could ever want.

Not five months from entering America's Big Green Machine, David graduated a second time. This time brought even more pride, along with the same picture of his negative father. As the commander pinned wings onto the line of graduates, David awaited his turn. Finally, the stern commander stood squared before him and pinned the wings above his left breast pocket. David tried not to smile. *I'm airborne now*, he thought, "Death From Above" as they called them, and the commander had sealed it with a firm handshake. *I can't wait to show Dad*, he thought. Those in the Airborne Infantry were an elite breed of soldiers and Private David McClain was now one of them. *Hoo-ah!*

A few years rolled by when the 101st came in from two months of field-training exercises. They showered, grabbed some hot chow and headed out to drink every beer ever brewed. On the way to the Enlisted Men's Club, Corporal David McClain halted his pack to make way for a more lethal band of soldiers—the Rangers.

A battalion of Airborne Rangers was on the last leg of a death march and stumbled past them, a convoy of ambulances following in their wake. Out of sheer respect and sincere pity, David and the boys applauded. The death marches were legendary within the ranger units. They were the ultimate gut check. Lasting countless hours, men marched under the weight of full packs until eventually collapsing from total body shutdown. It was considered shameful to drop out. Though rare, there were commanders who showed mercy on their troops. This march didn't appear to be one of those. Their commander looked tougher than any one of them. David cheered the last of them on. *I wish I were right there with them, walking in their footsteps*, he thought, and leaked his wish to one of his buddies.

"McClain, you're as crazy as a Billy goat," the southerner commented. "Do you realize what those guys have to go through?"

David's eyes lit up. "I do."

◻ ◻ ◻ ◻

David emerged from his daydream, thinking, *Of course I have it in me.* He snickered. *I actually asked for this.*

A moment later, he wasn't surprised when his thoughts landed on Lindsey Wood again. *My God, what is it with this girl?* he thought. *It was only one night.* He thought about it some more and smiled. *But what a perfect night.*

For the next few hours, he ignored his exhaustion and allowed himself to bask in every last detail he could recall.

Chapter 3

◻ ◻ ◻ ◻

David and his team were assigned to Camp Phoenix in the Kabul Province. Camp Phoenix...rising from the ashes, David thought, reading the sign at the heavily fortified entrance. As their convoy sped into the barbed-wire complex, they zigzagged past one cement Jersey barrier after the next. *Big-time security,* he thought. *This place must be surrounded by unfriendlies.* With one quick scan, David took it all in—there was a makeshift memorial to a fallen brother; a tattered Afghan flag that had been claimed by someone along the way; laundry hanging outside long concrete bunkers that clearly served as housing. *Well, at least we're not in tents,* he thought.

After the first formation and roll call, David located his assigned billets. Inside the concrete shelter, small rooms were divided by thin sheets of graffiti-laden plywood. *This could be a long twelve months,* he thought and shook his head. He threw his gear onto his bunk and headed out to find a phone or a PC where he could email Lindsey.

The communications building was packed with soldiers seated around two dozen tables containing three computers on each. David stepped through the heavy scent of mildew, locating an unoccupied PC in the back corner. After logging into his email account, he wrote:

Hi Lindsey,

Miss me yet? I hope so because I don't mean to scare you away, but I can't get you out of my head. And trust me, I'm not complaining. Anyway, I wanted to let you know that we landed safely. The flight attendant wore a five o'clock shadow, and it would have been better had they fed us bags of peanuts for the entire flight. But we made it. And you'll be happy to know that I didn't even have to jump out of this plane. They were good enough to land it for us.

I'll be getting my living quarters set up and learning my way around the camp for the next few days. At that point, I imagine that they'll put me to work. I'll contact you again just as soon as I get my bearings.

Lindsey, thank you for giving me something so amazing to think about on that long flight and for the days ahead.

It feels strange that fewer than twenty-four hours ago, I was sitting on a park bench with you, trying to picture what the inside of a lighthouse looks like. And now I'm in Afghanistan, where there appears to be nothing but rugged mountains and goat villages. Bizarre!

Anyway, please think of me, and trust that I'll be thinking of you over here. We'll have to sync up our schedules soon so we can Skype. Let me know what times work for you. And please keep me updated on how the Red Sox are doing.

Talk soon.

David

Wearing his finest smile, he logged off and headed to the chow hall to recharge his batteries.

Two plates of tasteless chicken cacciatore later, he hurried back to the communications building, hoping Lindsey's response might be waiting. When he logged back into his account, he was so thrilled that he had to pretend an excited squeal was nothing but a strange-sounding cough. Three fake coughs later, he read:

Hi handsome,

Yes, I do miss you. And I can't believe I'm telling you this, but I've missed you from the moment we left that park bench. (It's much easier to be brave over email, isn't it?) Although it was much too brief, I really enjoyed our night together. I loved being with you and can't begin to explain how incredible your lips felt on mine and how awesome it was to be in your arms.

Thank you for the flowers you sent before you left. They're still making me smile.

I'm so happy to hear that you arrived safely. See, my first prayer for you has already been answered!

There's not a whole lot to report on your Red Sox, as you've only been gone a day. But I'll keep you updated.

David, although I'll definitely miss you, I want you to know that what you're doing over there is incredibly selfless and I'm very proud of you. You have ALL my support, respect and admiration for doing what you do. Please stay strong and stay focused.

Can't wait to Skype with you! I'm sure my schedule is a lot more flexible than yours. Any night from 5:00 p.m. on (my time) will work for me. I hope it works for you. I can't wait to see your face again and hear your voice.

That's about it for now. Please be safe and remember, life is better than good.

Lindsey

David left the rancid-smelling building and had to be careful not to skip across the camp back to his billets. *No matter how happy or excited*, he thought, *Army Rangers don't skip.*

⌗ ⌗ ⌗ ⌗

At Camp Phoenix, David and his team spent the first few days trying to establish a routine: breakfast at the mess tent, followed by a morning debrief in the headquarters or HQ tent. This was when they received an account of the previous night's events. At that point, missions were assigned by the command staff. It was all standard protocol. What surprised David, however, was the number of men who volunteered for the dangerous missions. Some of those raised hands belonged to soldiers who wanted to play the cowboy and exact justice; others were attached to wanna-be heroes, who enjoyed kicking in doors in order to kick asses. And then there were those who volunteered just to break up the boredom.

Without an assigned mission, morning briefings were followed by physical training, lunch, laundry and letters, dinner, hygiene and a long night of nothingness.

David and his team weren't in-country for a full week—barely settled in—and they were already anxious to get into the action. Besides writing letters home to Coley, Craig, Captain Eli, Aunt Jeanne and his mom, David had been staring up at the bunker's corrugated steel ceiling and couldn't bear it a minute longer.

On the upside, thanks to Skype, communication with Lindsey was turned up a notch.

◻ ◻ ◻ ◻

When David's baby face first appeared on her computer screen, Lindsey lost her breath. He smiled and, if she didn't know better, his eyes misted over with raw emotion.

"Hi beautiful," he said, excitement oozing from his voice. "It's so good to see you. How are you?"

A moment passed before she replied. Between his voice and face, she was taking it all in.

"I'm great now," she said honestly—and feeling just as courageous over Skype. "More importantly, how's it going over there?"

"Truthfully?"

"Ummm, yeah. You wouldn't lie to me, would you?"

He laughed. "It's been unbelievably boring. I've heard a few horror stories from some of the guys who've seen action, but I haven't seen a whole lot worth reporting myself."

"That's a good thing, right?"

"I guess."

"You guess?" She leaned in toward the PC's camera. "You'd better not be trying to play the hero over there because I want..." She stopped.

During her awkward pause, he asked, "Yeah? You want..."

"I want you to stay safe," she cleverly recovered.

He lowered his tone. "Is that all you were going to say, Lindsey Wood?"

"Nope. Not at all. But unless you stay safe, David McClain, you'll never find out, will you?"

"Good answer," he said.

"I thought so," she teased as she studied every crease that his smile sculpted on his face.

"How's the food over there?" she asked.

"Horrendous. What I wouldn't do for a decent plate of pasta or real bacon and eggs. Oh yeah, and some sweets."

"You have a sweet tooth?" she asked.

"Unlike anything you've ever seen. It's terrible. Thank God I like to run and work out, or I'd be a very large boy."

She laughed. "Good to know. I'll start baking tonight."

"Because you like fat guys or..." His attention was completely on her. It felt like he was sitting right there with her.

"Because I like *you*," she blurted.

Even though they were thousands of miles apart, she could see him swallow hard. "That's so mutual, you can't even imagine it," he said, his voice somewhat muffled.

She felt her face blush.

After they stared at each other for a few moments more, he asked, "What about you? You like sweets?"

Nudged from her wonderful trance, she grinned. "Sometimes, but I'm definitely more of a food eater."

He laughed.

"I love hummus, tabouli, anything vibrantly healthy," she volunteered. "I'm a seafood-eating vegetarian who loves my food to be colorful."

He moved closer to the computer screen, wrinkling his nose and making her heart flutter.

"I like clams and calamari, and I really like fruit," she added, "especially strawberries and melon."

"That seems random," he joked. "So meat's completely off the menu for you?"

"Well, I probably won't eat meat, except maybe a piece of General Tso's chicken once in a while because it's a million miles removed from meat."

He laughed hard, lost in the moment. He then looked down at his watch, and his smile was erased. "Listen, I hate to run, but I need to get going. There's a special briefing in HQ in ten minutes. With any luck, they'll break up this boredom and put me to work."

"Is there time for one last question?" she asked.

"Of course. Shoot."

She grinned. "Where would you be right now, if you could be anywhere in the entire world?"

He smiled and cleared his throat. "Well, let's see, my favorite place in the whole world is on the beach at sunset in the arms of someone who really, really likes me."

She giggled under her breath; it came out as a mousy squeak.

"And you?" he asked.

"I have a bunch of favorite places," she said, teasing him. "Reading in my big puffy chair. Sitting on my porch just as the sun comes up, drinking a cup of my favorite tea." She stopped and grinned. "Oh yeah, and sitting on a park bench with someone who likes me even more."

He laughed.

"Spending time with you right now hasn't been all that bad either," she added.

"I know," he said. "I wish we could talk for hours."

"We will," she said. "I'm planning on it."

"Good."

She took a deep breath. "So when can we talk again?"

"Tonight," he said, "in my dreams. Will you meet me there?"

"I'd love to," she whispered.

"Don't worry. You'll be there."

"I want to know the details."

"I'll call you when I can and let you know what we talked about."

She giggled. "Be safe, David...please." It was one degree shy of begging.

"I will."

Driven by the immediate need to share her heart, she leaned in close to the computer screen. "David, if I could be there with you, I would," she said, as if it were a final confession. "But since that isn't possible, please know that I'll be with you in spirit the entire time." She paused. "Concentrate on what you're doing over there because there's nothing on Gooseberry Island that can't wait, okay?" She smiled. "Hint...hint."

"Good to know," he said, happily.

"I'm serious," she said. "Stay focused and please be safe."

"I will," he promised. "Please don't worry."

"Oh, and one last thing," she blurted.

"Yeah?"

"Your Red Sox are on a winning streak. They've taken two in a row."

"That's a winning streak?" he asked, laughing.

"If you're a positive thinker like I am, it is," she said.

"That works for me." He peered longingly at her. "I'll miss you, Lindsey. Bye."

She placed her hand flush to the screen just as their connection was severed.

❑ ❑ ❑ ❑

At the conclusion of the debriefing, David asked to speak to his first sergeant alone. The request was granted, and they stepped off to the side.

"Top, when are you going to assign my team to one of the patrols?"

The older man studied David. "Things have been heating up this past week, lots of insurgents out there looking to even the score. You boys are still..." He stopped.

"Anything would be better than losing our minds cooped up here," David said, shrugging.

"Listen, I'll tell you the same thing I told Lieutenant Menker an hour ago. You boys are being brought into the rotation in the next day or two."

"Good!" David said.

The man studied him some more. "You're still young, G.I., but you'd better start watching what you wish for." He grinned. "In my experience, it usually ends in a steaming pile of crap."

G.I. stood for Government Issue, but whenever David heard the acronym it made him think of home—of Gooseberry Island. As David walked out of the HQ tent, he also wondered whether he'd just made a fool's request. *But we're trained for this, right?* His mind immediately flashed back to the intense training he'd received only a few years before.

Chosen from the best, David was selected a U.S. Army Ranger School candidate and began preparing for the sixty-one most grueling days ever concocted by man. The majority who dared test everything inside of them flunked out and reported it was like living a nightmare without ever falling asleep. David was confident in his physical condition, but it was the mental hardness he questioned. *No man really knows if he has it in him before putting all he has to the Army's harshest test.*

The main objective of each recruit was to perform effectively as small unit leaders in a realistic tactical environment under incredible physical and mental stress. They were exposed to conditions and situations usually exceeding those found in war. Factors such as reduced sleep, hunger, reaction to frequent and unexpected enemy contact, difficult terrain and operating under the pressures of restrictive time limits were all thrown out at once. Graduation depended on quick, sound decisions, as well as the demonstration of calm, forceful leadership under such distress.

The first instructor at Ranger School—a man who had been cheated out of a neck at birth—picked up a stick and threw it over his shoulder. Turning toward the group, he grinned. "The toughest of you will return that weapon to me."

There was one sudden surge, while men punched, kicked, scratched and even bit for the coveted prize. The instructor finally reached in and plucked it from their bloodied hands.

From there, he ordered the group to form teams of six. Gesturing toward a pile of telephone poles, he ordered, "Each team will shoulder a pole, three men per side, and commence running." After reaching a destination of a mile and a half out, they switched shoulders and ran the heavy burden back.

On the first day, the teamwork theme became brutally clear. After twenty-six of the most strenuous hours David had ever endured, they were allowed to sleep. Two recruits had already dropped out, while one was informed it would be best for everyone that he leave. In shame, he did. David felt ill with exhaustion but thought, *I can't imagine what it would take for them to be rid of me.* He fell asleep comforted by the thought. Three hours later, he was violently tossed from his bunk. It was time to do it again.

For twenty solid days, averaging twenty hours per day, they built stamina, mental endurance and confidence. The combat scenarios created seemed so real that the deepest fears were brought to the surface—to either be folded into or overcome. David stayed strong. *All it took was to be constantly and completely abused,* he thought, and through it all David hung tough. He continually reminded his tired mind that he'd volunteered. He had asked to be trained to move farther, faster and fight harder than any other soldier—and he refused to embarrass himself with failure. *Quitting is not an option,* he vowed. Though he never let on, it was more pride than intestinal fortitude. It didn't make a difference. Whatever it was inside him, he decided, *I'm going all the way.*

◻ ◻ ◻ ◻

As promised, the first patrol assignment in Afghanistan took place the following day. David's team was dropped, via deuce and a half, six miles out from camp. Known as "the projects," South Kabul was reputed to be one of the most violent areas on their grid. Sergeant Scott Gervasio, who'd been in-country for months, was assigned to tag along and show them the ropes.

Max, a gifted navigator with the natural instincts of an Apache scout, took point. With every sense heightened to complete vigilance, the team swept from house to house, interviewing locals, checking out any suspicious activity and essentially acting as human lures for concealed Taliban.

The day was uneventful, or as uneventful as it could be when kicking in doors in downtown Kabul.

As the day progressed, a level of confidence and comfort worked its way into their efforts. "We've gone over this back at camp," Lieutenant Menker said. "We cannot fire at the Hodgie's unless fired upon."

"And I'll say it again," Max replied. "It's better to be tried by twelve than carried by six."

Big Al stared at him. "I swear, your family must have too much chlorine in its gene pool."

Everyone laughed.

"And that's coming from a guy who likes to work from twelve to one, with an hour off for lunch," Max countered.

Everyone laughed more.

After debating the rules of engagement and what would and would not land them in Leavenworth Federal Penitentiary, they took Max's hint and located a secure area to eat lunch. Canteen water and dehydrated MREs caused even more comical griping. "We should just grab one of these wandering goats and roast it," Nate suggested.

"Then we'd definitely have a firefight on our hands," Lieutenant Menker said, grinning.

David laughed but remained quiet. He was content with absorbing his foreign surroundings and taking it all in.

Five hours later, the patrol was on its final leg back to camp, tired but satisfied with their effort.

"Another day, another dollar," Nathan called out.

"Yeah, before taxes," Big Al joked, poking fun at their menial pay.

David pulled his father's note out of his pants cargo pocket and read it a few times, while the team walked the six miles back to camp and reported the day's events—*without incident.*

□ □ □ □

After a few days of consecutive foot patrols—and thinking about Lindsey whenever he wasn't scanning for those who preferred him dead—David jumped on Skype again to meet her and continue their long-distance courtship.

"Miss me?" he asked.

"Nope," she said, grinning.

"No?" he asked, surprised.

"How can I miss you when you're always with me... in my heart and mind every minute of the day?"

"In that case," he said, matching her smile, "I haven't missed you either."

She laughed. "Good."

"Lindsey, I've already had a lot of time to think over here, and I've been doing a lot of thinking about the night we spent together on that bench. I have to tell you..."

"Yeah?"

As if he'd waited forever to confess it, he said, "From the moment I first saw you, I felt an attraction that I've never known before. Though I think you're beautiful, this chemistry I feel for you is more than just physical. I honestly think it's a spiritual connection we share. There were times that night on the bench when I looked at you and swore that you saw everything inside of me. And..." He stopped, embarrassed.

"Go on," she whispered.

He smiled. "And that kiss...that was unlike anything I've ever experienced. I know I'm..."

"David," she quickly interrupted, "I've done nothing but think about you since you left, and I honestly can't wait to be with you again." She took a deep breath. "I know it may seem strange to some people, but I've always tried to follow my heart rather than my head. I realize there are people who might call that foolish, but I say life's too short for anything else, especially regret. I don't want to have any regrets the day I die." She shrugged. "I don't want to feel like I should have done something, or worse, deal with the 'what ifs...'"

"I'm just sorry that the timing is bad for us," he cut in.

"It's not so bad," she said firmly. "I'm not going anywhere."

He smiled. "Good." He stared at her for a moment, memorizing her face. "How's your dad doing?" he asked.

"Oh, he's fine. Yours?"

"No idea," he said honestly.

After David babbled on about the details of his recent missions—careful to leave out anything that might be disturbing—the conversation eventually slowed and touched on several random topics.

Finally, Lindsey returned to the one and only subject that they both wanted to discuss. "David, before you have to go I want to tell you...I'm trying really hard to keep myself in check and not let myself get too carried away with you," she said.

"And how's that working out?" he asked, smiling.

"Not good," she admitted. "There are so many things I wish I could share with you right now, but I know I can't. Well, not yet anyway."

"We will," he whispered.

"It's not easy, but I really am trying to keep things in perspective." She stopped, staring at him for a few moments. "I know you can't make me any promises and I understand that, but it's not easy trying to pretend that I don't miss you like crazy...wishing I could be with you right now."

"It'll be worth the wait," he said.

"Oh, I'm sure of it! In the meantime, I want to be able to share everything I'm thinking and feeling with you without putting any pressure on you. That's not my intention. I'm just trying to follow my heart and believe that we'll have a chance. We have to."

"Are you kidding me? I don't feel any pressure at all," he said. "Trust me, I appreciate the openness between us, and I want you to share everything with me. I want to know everything, so please don't ever hold back with me. As I've said before, my biggest fear is our timing. I just don't want anything to happen that'll jeopardize a real chance of us being together. Please trust that I want you at least as much as you want me. I think about you nonstop and..."

"And?"

"And I realize it hasn't been all that long since we met, but I've grown to really care for you, Lindsey."

"We've both grown," she whispered.

They sat in silence for a while—a wonderfully comfortable silence spent studying each other's faces—before Lindsey provided David with his Red

Sox update. "Okay, final report for the day: The Sox lost to Baltimore on Saturday, two to four, but won on Sunday, twelve to ten. They're facing off with Seattle for their next outing. Looks like they're still four out of first place, but I predict that the Yankees are going to slow down and the momentum's going to shift to the Sox. David Ortiz had a great game on Sunday with two home runs, so I think the boys have a breath of fresh air to hopefully get their second wind for a pennant run."

"Wow, listen to you," David said. "You could start working for NESN." He looked at his watch. "Oh man... I hate to run, beautiful, but I have to get prepared for another day at the office." He stared into the computer screen. "Keep smiling, Lindsey. The world's a much prettier place when you do."

She smiled. "Be safe, David," she said. "It'll be over before we both know it."

He winked at her just as the computer screen went blank.

¤ ¤ ¤ ¤

Denis Wood, Lindsey's dad, walked out of the VA Hospital, signing himself out weeks earlier than promised. He was holding a plastic grocery bag filled with his personal belongings.

Lindsey sat in her car, waiting for him in the parking lot. As usual, they drove away from the large complex in silence—no questions asked about the time he'd spent there, no information volunteered—just the way the broken man demanded. Denis never talked about his actual service—ever. The jagged scar above his left eye and a missing index finger spoke volumes even though he wouldn't.

On the way home, Denis finally cleared his throat and spoke. "Joe, one of the regulars on the looney ward, knows a guy..."

"...who knows a guy," Lindsey teased.

He grinned. "...who can get us tickets to the NASCAR race up in New Hampshire, smart ass."

"That's great, Dad," she said, unimpressed.

"What do you say? We could take the ferry over and drive to New Hampshire."

Lindsey was shocked he was asking her to go.

"It could be a great time," he continued to pitch. "A bunch of guys are going..."

"Sure, Dad," she finally consented. "Sounds like fun."

"Great! I want to get up there early, so I'll ride up with Ruggie. You can meet us there in time for the race."

Early, huh? she thought, but decided not to question it.

¤ ¤ ¤ ¤

Late Saturday morning, Lindsey crossed the New Hampshire border and came to a stop. The line of traffic stretched out as far as the eye could see. Pickup trucks inched along, blaring country music. Like a massive trailer park serpent, each car or truck looked like it was attached to the bumper in front of it. People were friendly and yelled out their vulgar greetings. Lindsey was tempted a few times to holler back but didn't. Instead, she spent the time thinking about David. *I wonder what he's doing right now.*

Once she reached the parking lot, Lindsey was amazed at how NASCAR had evolved into such a colossal event. Her dad never missed a race on TV, but it was quite different to see it in person. There were thousands of fans setting up their tailgate camps, each smiling face waiting for the green flag to drop. As she pulled in, she had to drive around the long lines at the port-o-johns.

Their agreed-upon rally area was a campsite that had been set up by some friends from home. It took Lindsey nearly twenty minutes to find it, but she finally did. Everyone else had already gotten comfortable. They'd arrived a day early and would be leaving for home a day after everyone else. In the meantime, they lounged back, got drunk and did some serious people watching. There was no better spot, as thousands of characters walked past their site.

And then she spotted her dad. He was sitting beside his friend, Ruggie, as well as a stack of coolers that were strapped into a red wagon by bungee cords. And, he was already drunk. *Oh no*, she thought, and approached him. "Hi Dad," she said, kissing his bright red cheek.

"Took you long enough," he said.

She ignored the comment and took a seat beside him. When she finally caught his attention, she whispered, "Don't you think you should take it easy?" She pointed at his beer. "It's still kind of early, right?"

"What?" he said at a roar, making everyone look over. "We're here to have fun, and I don't need a nervous Nellie watching over me!"

Lindsey nodded, while everyone else looked away. Denis Wood didn't have a drinking problem, or at least that's what he believed. His drinking was everyone else's problem, especially Lindsey's. Since her mother had left, the bottle had become his soul mate, and he couldn't survive without it.

After an embarrassing start, the next few hours were filled with a strange nostalgia.

"Remember that first race I took you to at Seekonk Speedway?" Denis asked Lindsey, reminiscing about days gone by.

"I do," she said, remembering that very day with a hazy sense of terror. "After the races were over, it took me an hour before I finally found you in the parking lot."

He laughed. "You're crazy! An hour."

She shook her head, deciding to laugh it off as well.

Everyone was in good spirits. And the faster the beer flowed, the more her dad talked; it was an old tradition.

After some more drinking, Lindsey, Ruggie and her dad started up the throughway toward the main gate. It was like a carnival, with both sides of the fairway lined with vendors selling everything from sausages to T-shirts. Lindsey looked back. Her dad was already lagging behind, swinging a heavy cooler with each staggering step. It wasn't even noon and his Dale Earnhardt ball cap was already sitting crooked on his head. *This is going to be a long day*, Lindsey thought.

Ruggie pulled, her dad pushed, and Lindsey carried whatever the wagon couldn't bear. For the first ten steps, it worked well. Then, one of the bungee cords snapped and gouged a hole into Ruggie's hand. Denis laughed. "I didn't think that would hold," he admitted, his words already slurred. As Lindsey wrapped Ruggie's bloodied hand, they restacked the beer coolers and marched on.

Like cattle, thousands filed through the gates. The track was huge. They spotted their seats but decided to check out the fairways inside. It was worth the tour. Tractor trailer trucks of souvenirs lined the black tar trail. Each famous driver had his own and from the lines formed, there was no question that they were raking in the dough. Denis pulled out a wad of cash. As if she were a little kid, he bought Lindsey a T-shirt and hat before they started back to their seats. The crowd was so thick, it was impossible not to bounce off of every third person.

There wasn't a cloud in the sky. Ruggie sat on one of the hard aluminum seats. Lindsey followed, and then her dad sat beside her. Each one of them slid a cooler beneath their seat. With the exception of two bottles of water, Lindsey's cooler was also filled with cold beer. It was her dad and Ruggie's reserve stock. The old man told her, "You should have something to drink. It's going to be a hot one."

The opening ceremonies were incredible, almost spiritual. The celebrity drivers were announced and, two-by-two, the pairs came whipping by in the back of brand-new pickup trucks. The crowd cheered for each one. Then the national anthem played loudly over giant speakers. *I pray you're safe, David,* Lindsey thought.

At the end of the song, two Air Force jets roared directly overhead, leaving Lindsey with an arm full of goose bumps and hair standing on the back of her neck. It was an amazing thing to see. Denis offered Lindsey his first drunken elbow. "Ain't that something?" he asked.

She nodded, knowing that the day promised plenty more elbows. *What fun.*

The row of cars circled the track and then lined up. The green flag was dropped, and they roared by with a fury unlike anything on God's green earth. The sound was humbling. It gave Lindsey more goose bumps. Denis threw his second elbow. "Unbelievable, huh?" he said.

You have no idea, she thought.

As the sun beat down on them, the lead car got a five-car jump and stayed there for almost two hours. For every ten laps completed, Denis replaced another "dead soldier" with a full beer, making Lindsey cringe. It didn't take long before he was through his cooler and already into the one under Lindsey's seat. The elbows started flying faster than the stock cars.

Just like basketball, the race was going to be decided in the last few minutes. It was exciting. People got to their feet. Denis swayed. Seconds later, it was over. Jeff Gordon won—mass exodus.

As they left the stadium, Denis stumbled along like a blue crab, skirting sideways until hitting something that would right his bearings. Somehow, they all made it back to the campsite.

The grills were fired up, and everyone settled in. They got caught up with their old friends, while Denis slurred his words beyond recognition. It would have been humiliating, but everyone knew Denis Wood. As marinated venison smoked, the conversation led to drugs and alcohol. Someone should have steered it in a different direction.

Denis screamed, "So you're saying that if a man had one year to retire and the poor bastard tested positive for drugs, you'd get rid of him?"

His words were so garbled that Lindsey could hardly make them out. "I'm saying that there are rules, Dad, and as long as everyone knows the rules, everyone should be held accountable," she answered, surprised that she was arguing with the same man who'd raised her. The role reversal felt very uncomfortable. Lindsey only talked to him like this because he was loaded and wasn't going to remember a word of it.

The old man went off. "What the hell..."

Lindsey stood. "Dad, let's talk about this when you're sober," she said and headed off. *A quick walk might help me get through the rest of this nightmare.*

When Lindsey returned to the site, everything appeared to be the way she'd left it. The grill was smoking. Seven different conversations were going on at once. The radio blared with country twang. Then she saw him. Her dad was sitting alone on a fold-out chair. He had a plate of food in his lap, but his head was down. A sick feeling gnawed at her gut. She approached him. "Dad, are you all right?" she asked. When the old man lifted his head, Lindsey lost whatever air was left in her lungs.

Denis's face was blue, and his eyes were bulging out of his head. He tried to speak, but nothing would come out. Instead, saliva oozed out of the corner of his mouth. He looked at Lindsey. Even though he was completely obliterated with alcohol, his eyes were struck with terror.

He's choking to death! she realized and scrambled to get behind him. She started yelling, trying to get everyone else's attention, while she wrapped her arms around him and gave one squeeze into his gut from the seated position. *No good*, she thought, while a sense of panic was quickly filling her. Tony, the only other sober one in the bunch, hurried over. The rest of the drunks stood paralyzed, staring. Tony and Lindsey yanked Denis to his feet. Lindsey got her hands interlocked under his rib cage and gave another thrust. *Still nothing.* She did it again. The old man's legs turned to rubber under him, and Lindsey felt her panic overflow; she was losing her father in her arms. *Oh God, please...* She jammed his abdomen hard again and heard him let out a slight gag. As he tried to reclaim his feet, she looked down and noticed a chunk of chicken marinated in saliva and mucous lying on the ground. *We got it out!* she realized and felt her own legs go limp.

Lindsey spun in front of her father to watch two feet of snot swing from his nose to his knees. He gagged and choked, but he took in air. He coughed up a few more pieces of the dinner that had been lodged in his throat. His bloodshot eyes looked like they might actually explode. She patted his back twice more. Her head felt light and her legs began to quiver. *He's just erased two years from my life*, she thought and took a seat.

Her father, on the other hand, cleared his throat and spoke for the first time. "That was the best damn chicken I've ever tasted," he joked, trying to reclaim some of his dignity.

Everyone laughed—everyone but Lindsey. This grown child of a violent alcoholic understood that while they all froze, she and Tony were the only ones sober enough to take action. For that reason alone, her father still lived. For the first time that day, she thought, *Thank God I was here.*

"Want something to eat?" Lindsey's friends asked, but she couldn't. Her hands were shaking too much. Instead, she dumped out the rest of her father's meal and told him, "You're all done drinking for the day." Everyone froze again. No one could have said that to Denis Wood unless his life depended on it. For the first time in Lindsey's life, the old man didnt' argue. He nodded once, grabbed a bottle of water and took a sip, trying to get rid of that bad feeling in his gizzard.

Lindsey thought, *My father gave me life, and I've repaid the gift by giving him a second life.* Part of her wished they were even. She looked at him and felt equal amounts of love and hatred. *But we'll never be even*, she realized. *We're family.*

It was decided that Ruggie would stay the night at the campsite and sleep his buzz off, while Denis would go home with Lindsey.

"That was fun," Denis said on the ride home, trying to make light of his recent brush with death.

Lindsey never replied. *You're just lucky I was there*, she thought, and then filed the nightmare away with the rest of them.

A few miles up the road, she thought, *I hope there's an email from David waiting for me at home.* While the rest of the trip was traveled in silence, she directed her thoughts to dwell on more hopeful relationships.

¤ ¤ ¤ ¤

The following day, Ruggie called Lindsey to apologize.

"It's okay," she told him, letting him off the hook.

"I just got off the phone with your dad," he said. "He says he can't remember too much of what happened. He doesn't remember choking, and he only knows that you saved his life because I just told him."

There was silence. They both knew. Along with a couple thousand brain cells, the old man's *life and death* lesson had been lost in an ocean of beer.

"Great," Lindsey said, "I can't wait 'til the next time we do a little family bonding." Spending time with her father was like showering with a cheese grater—it got more painful each time.

Ruggie laughed. "Next year, I'll stay sober," he said, "and you can get drunk."

"Then you'd better get your CPR card updated," she joked.

"Nah, your dad says he probably choked because he was sitting down. Next year, he says he'll stand up... if he even eats at all."

They both stopped laughing. *The old man isn't kidding,* Lindsey thought.

◻ ◻ ◻ ◻

The telephone rang again an hour later. Lindsey picked up.

"Miss me, beautiful?" David asked.

"It's you!" she said, excited. "I didn't know you could call home!"

"It's like getting locked up. We only get one call, and you were it."

"Good. Now where do I go to bail you out?"

"I wish," he said. "But you never answered my question. Do you miss me?"

"Not at all," she said, giggling.

"Good. I don't miss you either."

"I went to a race yesterday with my dad," she told him. "A NASCAR race."

"How was it?" he asked.

"Interesting," she said, sparing him the stupid details. *He has enough to worry about*, she thought. "Jeff Groban won."

"Jeff Gordon or Josh Groban?" he asked, chuckling.

"Yeah, one of them," she joked. "They put on quite the patriotic show. You can't believe how many people are behind you guys."

"That's good to hear." He paused. "More than you can imagine."

"Still bored over there?" she asked.

"I wouldn't call it bored...just monotonous. We're on patrols almost every day. It's gotten so that I'm beginning to know the locals. They even wave at us as we search through their neighborhoods."

"Are you being nice to them?" she asked.

"Of course I am."

"Any bad guys?" she asked.

"A bunch of them," he said, "but thankfully, they're on our side."

She laughed. "I'm glad it's going well, David, but please be safe."

"I will." He paused. "So the Sox look like they're out of the race, huh?"

"Yeah. Unfortunately, the math doesn't work anymore for them to get into the playoffs."

"That stinks."

"There are worse tragedies."

"Very true," he mumbled.

"I put your care package in the mail a few days ago. I hope the postal service is kind enough to deliver it in one piece."

"That's awesome. Thank you so much. Any sweets?"

"Of course, plus a few books, some of my favorite music, a juicy love letter…"

"A love letter?" he asked, interrupting.

"Yup," she said, "and you'll have to wait to read what's in it."

"That's not fair."

"Well, from what I hear, life's not fair."

"I thought you said that life was *better than good*."

"Exactly! See, now you're getting it. It's all about attitude, and I'd rather choose a positive one."

"Good attitude," he teased.

"I hope you like the books I sent. You like to read, right?"

"I do. In fact, I was just thinking about all those bookshelves inside the lighthouse."

She giggled. "So what else do you like?"

"I like all types of music, especially 'The Dance' by Garth Brooks. And I also enjoy all types of movies."

"Now who's being random?" she teased. "I was hoping you would say me."

"You," he said.

She laughed. "Good."

"What's your favorite song?" he asked.

"I have lots of favorite songs, but Sarah McLachlan's 'Angel' is my best favoritest."

"Best favoritest?" he repeated.

"Well, it is," she said and laughed.

There was a pause. "I hate this part as much as you, beautiful," he said, "but I gotta go."

"Don't go far," she whispered.

"Not where you can't reach me," he said. "And I'll stay safe, okay?"

"Above all else," she said. "And thanks so much for calling me. It was great to hear your voice."

"Thanks for answering," he said. "Bye, beautiful."

Chapter 4

□ □ □ □

Unlike the weather, which had turned bitterly cold, the daily foot patrols were starting to get comfortable. David was even taking the lead on some of them now, searching out anyone who might like to greet them with a rocket-propelled grenade.

"What are your plans after we're done over here?" Billy asked Lieutenant Menker.

"I'll be getting into the family business," Kevin answered nonchalantly.

"And what's that?" Billy followed up.

"I come from a long line of cops, and that's the next stop for me."

David nodded. *Makes sense*, he thought. *Kevin's the perfect backup when the world gets all dark and scary.*

"What about you?" Kevin asked Billy.

Billy laughed. "I'd like to do another tour right here."

Everyone looked over at the young buck, cross-eyed.

"Where else can you lay down a beating like we do and get paid for it?" he asked.

Shaking heads traveled down the line.

David glanced over at Nathan, who was looking at the photograph of his sons—and trying to conceal it from the rest of them. *That sucks*, David thought.

"Not me," Max chimed in. "I want to get home to Max Jr. I've missed that kid something terrible from the moment we left."

"I hear that," Nathan agreed, tucking his photograph back into his cap.

David shook his head in sympathy. *Both Nate and Max have been tortured every minute we've been here.*

The patrol walked quietly for a while and, as he occasionally did, David pulled his father's note out of his pants cargo pocket and read it. *Keep your head down?* He shook his head, thinking, *I'm not sure that's such great advice, Pop.* Fifty yards down the road, his thoughts of home shifted to Lindsey's beautiful face, and he recounted their most recent communication.

¤ ¤ ¤ ¤

"How was lunch with my mom?" David asked.

"Great," Lindsey said. "She's such a sweet person, but..."

"But?"

"Considering that you and I only had one date before you left, I..."

"I've been writing my mother about you for weeks, Lindsey," he interrupted.

"That's exactly what she said. Believe me, I didn't have a problem getting together with her, but I was worried about what she would think of me."

"And?" he asked.

"We hit it off very well."

"I knew you guys would."

"We've made a pact to share any information we get about you," she added.

"Not everything, I hope?" he teased.

"Well, not the good stuff of course," she said, giggling.

◻ ◻ ◻ ◻

Back in the present, David smiled and began to tally his own options, once his twelve-month tour was wrapped up.

I decided long ago that the military life suits me fine, he thought. While others complained about the early wake-up calls, along with the work that followed, he was content with all of it. "You probably just signed 'cause you wanted to wear shoes," they'd joke, but David only laughed.

You have no idea, he thought. His desire to join the service had gnawed at him since his first walk down Sesame Street. It was a yearning that had always needed to be fulfilled. *If not for me, then to prove my father wrong. Either way, I needed to do it.*

But Lindsey's not in the military with me, he thought, challenging his earlier convictions. *She's home on Gooseberry Island.*

The friendships made in the Army were forged from sharing hard times with others. David cherished the camaraderie created by those experiences. There were three squares a day, a warm bunk and few choices that needed to be made. The Army would even decide when a man should relieve himself. Besides breakfast, dinner and supper, David's favorite time was mail call.

Mom, Craig and Aunt Jeanne would write, keeping him up on everything that he wasn't missing on Gooseberry Island. Occasionally, even Captain Eli's chicken scratch showed up in the pile. David responded to each one.

But I'd rather be sitting beside Lindsey, talking with her—instead of looking at her on a computer screen, or hearing her voice through a telephone receiver.

On top of that, the Army can be a lonely life with too much drinking, he thought. From the foxholes he'd dug, there were few opportunities to see the world his recruiter had promised. Worst of all, he was also required to dive from a perfectly good airplane once a month to maintain his jump status. *Still, I feel blessed I joined because when you get right down to it, the military isn't for people who can't do better—it's for those who won't settle for less.* It offered the greatest gift in life—*a sense of purpose.* This was most obvious every time the Fourth Ranger Battalion marched. In no other walk of life did sixty, a hundred, even a thousand soldiers simultaneously step in sync—each devoted to the same cause, each serving something larger than themselves. David couldn't imagine a finer job than to awaken every morning to defend a country. Above all else, military service provided meaning to young men and women who still believed in duty, honor and courage.

But something's changed, he thought, and smiled. *Lindsey.* He felt closest to her at night when he looked into the sky, the North Star shining brightly. *It's like she's right here with me,* he thought, *but still far enough away to be safe.* He felt a strange comfort knowing that they still shared the same constellations to gaze into. On the nights that were overcast—the stars blocked out by gray hovering clouds—he actually felt alone. *Strange*, he thought.

◻ ◻ ◻ ◻

When David awoke from his daydream, he thought, *But Lindsey's home on Gooseberry Island, where I should be.* Shaking his head, he quickly pushed the thought out of his mind and focused on the present. *But for now, I need to get my head back in the game*, he told himself, and checked that his loaded weapon's selector switch was still on safe.

◻ ◻ ◻ ◻

Upon returning to camp from Kabul-land, David hurried to the afternoon mail call. The Supply Sergeant picked up the final package and called out, "McClain."

David quickly approached the grumpy man and claimed the stained cardboard box. The heavy package—half crushed from its long trip—was addressed to *Sergeant David McClain* in black Sharpie.

As David walked back to the formation, he immediately detected a sweet flowery scent. *It's the same perfume Lindsey wore that night on the bench*, he thought, and remembered her promise of a "love letter." He went to one knee and tore the cardboard package open.

Sifting through the snacks and books and other surprises, David located a white envelope, marked, *Handsome*. Smiling, he brought the envelope up to his nose and inhaled deeply a few times. *Wow*, he thought and opened it.

There were only a few paragraphs, but the letter contained enough to sustain him through two wars.

Dear David,

Thank you so much for your recent calls. The sound of your voice completely melts me. Trust that I feel everything you do. I want to be with you more than anything in this world and to share everything with you. I've had lots of trouble not getting lost in my daydreams of us.

I'm ready for you and wish you were here right now. Please try to believe in us the way I do because I believe with all my heart. I can't wait to kiss you again.

I'll be thinking of you tonight and every night after.

Life is better than good.

Love,
Lindsey

Love Lindsey? he pondered and got lost for a few moments in the possible meaning. He hurried off to the privacy of his bunk where he could read—and smell—his love letter without being razzed.

¤ ¤ ¤ ¤

Saturday morning found David's ranger team on just another ordinary foot patrol. With Lindsey's love letter in one cargo pocket and his father's note in the other, David walked right flank in the middle of the staggered patrol, thinking about his brothers and their service.

Fourth Ranger Battalion isn't just a band of tough guys. It's a battalion of trained soldiers, which is much more dangerous. Unlike the ragged Taliban, we have dominant firepower as well as superior training and leadership.

Being here is justified—all of it, he thought. *We have a duty, a mission that we've been trained for and sworn to carry out—defending democracy.* He nodded. *As soldiers, we don't have the luxury to question politics. We don't see things the way civilians do. Our world is black and white, and any shade of gray can prove fatal. Words like* honor *and* duty *and* brotherhood *are our lifeblood, not just catch phrases.* He looked down the line at his brothers and smiled. *We depend on each other completely, like a well-oiled machine with every part working in sync, the whole so much greater than each individual part.*

It was a selfless purpose they served, with a need to have faith in God and a belief that good could and would defeat evil. These were men who stood up for those who couldn't stand up for themselves—against the world's most vicious bullies. Young and naïve, they faced paralyzing fear requiring extraordinary courage—heroes born in the moment out of the love for their fellow soldiers—hell-bent to take a stand and fight.

We understand that the ultimate sacrifice may be asked at any time, David thought, *though we'd much rather our enemy be the one to make that sacrifice.*

Their only requests from home were prayers and gratitude. *Home,* David thought; it was now a distant place that was safely kept in the heart but better stricken from the mind. *Family now means those who wear the same uniform.*

It's kill or be killed over here, he thought, *not a real difficult game to understand*—although the mind was challenged and often sabotaged by the most basic fight-or-flight instincts. And being labeled a coward, especially in one's own mind, was a fate worse than death. *I'd accept anything but that*, David thought.

◻ ◻ ◻ ◻

Nodding proudly, David returned to the present and the dangerous task at hand. As usual, the boys were smoking and joking.

"You want a cigarette, G.I.?" Max asked Big Al, who was walking the position right behind David.

Gooseberry Island, David instantly thought. *I really miss Lindsey.*

"Thanks anyway," Al said, "but I just quit. It was killing my marathon times."

Everyone laughed.

"Aren't you ever serious?" Lieutenant Menker asked.

Big Al nodded. "I used to be, until my dad told me to dance like no one was watching." He grinned. "I tried it at the mall a few months ago, and they asked me to leave. I'm not sure..."

There was a loud bang, high above the laughter. David spun to see a cloud of dirt and dust where Big Al had just stood. David did a double-take. Al was lying on the ground, his right leg severed clean above the knee. David sprinted toward the man, sliding on his knees to attend to his friend.

Half the patrol immediately established a perimeter—a quartering party to provide security on all sides—in case this was an ambush. In that brief time, Al had already removed his belt and begun to apply a tourniquet to his own leg. Still trying to process the grisly scene, David looked into Al's eyes. They were distant, in shock, and struggling to focus on the painful task at hand. Al moaned, but never uttered a word. David looked at his friend's other leg: it was a heap of raw hamburger, with splinters of white bone protruding from his bloodied pants. David applied a tourniquet to Al's second leg, while Max administered a field IV. Billy Brodeur called in a medivac. "We need it now!" he screamed.

"Inbound in five mikes," the radio announced, the garbled message barely understood through the heavy static.

David finished the tourniquet and placed his hand on Al's shoulder. "Relax, brother. The flyboys are on their way."

Al nodded, but he'd already lost a lot of blood. His face had turned ashen.

David quickly assessed the scene of the crime. It didn't take a whole lot of investigative skills to put the puzzle together.

It was an improvised explosive device that three rangers had stepped on, myself included, David thought, his short hair standing on end. *But we're all smaller than Big Al, so we didn't have enough body weight to trigger the pressure plate.* David looked back at Al, who had just slipped into unconsciousness. *Looks like Big Al tripped enough explosives to rip apart a Humvee.*

David then gave more thought about stepping on the IED. *I almost broke my word to Craig,* he thought, *and all those promises to Lindsey.* He felt lightheaded.

The buzz of an incoming chopper could be heard in the distance. Lieutenant Menker popped a canister of green smoke and threw it just outside their perimeter, indicating a secure landing zone. Max had grabbed the radio from Billy and was talking to the flying medics, providing vitals. "He needs more fluids," Max reported. "He's lost a ton of blood."

The shadows of the chopper blades cutting across the sun danced on the dirt road, whining loudly and kicking up a tornado of dust. Everything seemed to happen in slow motion at that point. *It's like we're in a movie,* David thought.

The Blackhawk chopper, with a .50 caliber machine gunner hanging out of the side door, touched down. Two medics ran a green litter out to Al, where he was carefully but quickly loaded—the old IV swapped out for a new one. Four men, David included, lifted the heavy litter and ran it back to the chopper, trying to duck as they went.

David felt a hand on his shoulder. He looked back. It was the patrol leader, Kevin Menker, screaming into his ear. "Go with him, McClain, and report back to us ASAP!"

David nodded.

"And make sure you keep talking to him."

David nodded again and jumped into the helicopter. He took a knee beside Al and grabbed the man's massive hand.

As the chopper took to the air, it kicked up another hurricane of debris—bending the ranger patrol at their waists and making them shield their eyes. Fifty feet off the deck, David watched as the patrol was on their way again, with nasty Billy Brodeur leading the way. *But now they're pissed*, David thought. *And someone's going to pay dearly for this.*

The chopper banked sideways and picked up speed. Even though there was no way Al could have ever heard him over the deafening blades, David talked to his friend, doing all he could to comfort Al's subconscious. "Hang in there, brother. They're going to patch you up good and get you home to that beautiful family of yours." Al's gruesome wounds were already emitting the most ungodly smells.

David gagged and looked back out the door for some air. *Wow*, he thought, surprised at this new perspective of the disappearing world below. *This place is beautiful.*

He looked back at Big Al and squeezed the giant's hand. "You keep fighting, ranger. There's a little guy waiting for you back home." He then looked down at the raw meat that was once his friend's legs and shook his head. *Maybe Top was right*, he thought. *Maybe we should have watched what we wished for.*

□ □ □ □

Just as soon as his schedule allowed for it, David visited Big Al in the evac hospital.

When he entered the sanitized room, Al was lying beneath a white sheet that was pulled tightly over his large body, clearly revealing that he would never walk again on the legs God had given him.

"My boy, Jack, thinks I'm a superhero...out here fighting all the bad guys," Al explained, his eyes filling. "So when I called home yesterday, I told him that I had good news and bad news."

David sat on the edge of his friend's bed, waiting for the payoff.

"I told him that I lost my legs in a fight..."

"Oh man," David moaned, picturing the young boy getting the devastating news. He fought off the emotion that threatened to embarrass them both.

"...but that the Army was making me legs just like Optimus Prime."

David swallowed hard. He nodded but didn't dare respond.

"Jack loves the Transformers, so he was real excited to hear it. 'Really, Dad?' he kept saying. 'Just like Optimus? That's soooo cool!'"

David placed his hand on Al's arm. "You're one of the best men I know," he managed, though it sounded like he pushed it past a mouthful of cotton candy.

Big Al smiled and then looked out the window, giving them both a break before they broke down and cried.

◻ ◻ ◻ ◻

A half hour later, David walked out of the hospital, where he stepped off into the shadows and allowed himself to cry. He was willing to do anything to push off the elephant that was lying on his chest.

Eventually composing himself, he pulled his father's tattered note out of his pants cargo pocket and read it. Shaking his head, he crumpled up the note and threw it into the wind. *What bullshit!* he thought. He then felt for Lindsey's letter in his other pocket. *Still there*, he thought, and left it right where it was safe.

◻ ◻ ◻ ◻

Nearly a week passed before David dared to log onto Skype again. Lindsey was already connected—as she must have been each night since their last cyber date—waiting patiently. Her eyes lit up when she saw him. "Hey stranger, everything okay? I've been really worried. It's been almost a week since..."

"I'm sorry," he said sadly.

Her excitement faded, replaced by serious concern. "How's work been?" she asked gently.

He hesitated. "Okay, I guess. Same old stuff." It was less than convincing, and they both knew it.

"David, what happened?" she asked, looking like she was ready to cry.

"Nothing," he said. "Really, I'm fine." But his voice was as distant as his mind. "Everything okay with you?" he asked, trying to deflect and avoid sharing any details of their recent missions.

She sighed. "Fine," she said. "But if you need to talk about anything then..."

"Lindsey, honestly, I'm fine," he repeated, this time much more confidently. "It's been a stressful week, that's all."

"You sure?" she asked.

"I'm sure." He paused, forcing a smile. "Let's talk about us. I've really missed *us*."

Her excitement returned, and she smiled. "I have to admit, sometimes sharing the little bits and pieces of each other...a phone call every few days and the stolen moments over a computer screen...can be tough. I keep imagining a real fairy tale for you and me." The pitch in her voice rose. "...that you would throw everything you need into a duffel bag and come to me, sweep me off my feet and promise me that we'll be okay, forever. Although I know you can't just yet, a girl can dream right?"

"A boy can dream too," he said, trying hard to appear just as excited.

"Oh David," she said, "I can't wait for you to lean across the table at a crowded restaurant and plant a big, wet kiss on me." She stopped and grinned. "Don't you wish I was there with you right now?" she asked.

"Absolutely not!" he snapped. "I'd never want you here, Lindsey." He took a deep breath and softened his voice. "Anywhere but here," he whispered. "I'd want to be with you anywhere but here."

"Are you sure everything's okay?" she asked. "Remember, you said you'd never lie to me."

True, he thought, *but I never said I'd share this nightmare with you.* He tried to clear his throat but could feel the elephant climbing back onto his chest. "Like I said, I just had a few tough days and I'm really tired."

"Should I let you go?" she asked.

"Do you mind?" he asked, bringing a surprised look to her face.

There was a pause. "Of course not. When can we talk again?"

"Soon," he promised, discreetly trying to calm his breathing.

"Do you still like me, David McClain?" she whispered.

"I more than like you, Lindsey Wood. I love you," he said. "But listen, I gotta run. We'll talk soon." And then the PC screen went black.

◻ ◻ ◻ ◻

Lindsey sat staring at the blank monitor. *I love you too*, she thought, but felt really confused over the strange exchange. After a moment, she shook her head. *Something happened*, she concluded, *something bad*.

◻ ◻ ◻ ◻

Girls' Night Out, also known as the Thursday Night Club, had evolved from a book club into a movie club and then into poker night—dealer's choice. Regardless of the night's events, dinner was always pot luck, washed down by bottles and bottles of inexpensive wine. *We should just be honest with ourselves and call it The Wine Club*, Lindsey thought. But no one cared for the negative stereotype.

The club's active members included Lindsey, Courtney, Paula, Ana, Tonia, Sandi, and Christine. Boys were strictly prohibited, as there was always some significant man bashing to be had. As of late, though, Lindsey's loving glow had been the main topic. Most of the women were happy to share in Lindsey's love drunk stupor, remembering that they'd all felt the same way at one time in their lives.

Lindsey sat beside Tonia and Ana on the couch. Tonia was an older, gray-haired woman who was recently divorced—and happily inebriated as a result. Ana was much younger, pretty with light hair and eyes.

But she was already a man-hater and very angry at the world.

"My ex never even called our son for his birthday," Tonia said with a venomous tone.

Lindsey sipped her wine and grinned. "For someone who swears she doesn't care about her ex, you spend an awful lot of time talking about him, Tonia."

Tonia's eyes lit up, and a smile quickly replaced her sour puss. "Some habits are easier to break than others I suppose," she said, sighing heavily. "To tell you the truth, girls, I'm not sure you can ever stop caring for someone, especially when you've shared a love as deep as mine and Ron's." She smiled. "For now, though, it's a lot more fun to hate him."

The three women shared a laugh. Lindsey stared off into space for a moment, her thoughts consumed with worry over David. Her expression changed from humorous to concern. Tonia immediately picked up on it. "Since it's confession time," the older woman said, "why don't you tell us what's bothering you?"

"David's amazing," Lindsey said, "but..."

"But?" Tonia asked.

Just then, Courtney, Christine and Sandi joined the girls on the couch.

Lindsey shrugged. "I don't know. It might be nothing. It's just that something was different with David the last time we talked."

"Different how?" Courtney asked.

Lindsey shrugged again. "He wasn't his usual funny and attentive self. I tried asking him what was wrong, but he dodged my questions and ended the call very quickly."

"But I thought you guys..." Sandi said.

"Geez, Linds," Christine jumped in, "I wonder what could be wrong? Maybe it has something to do with him fighting a terrible war in Afghanistan?"

Lindsey's eyes filled. "I know that," she said. "I'm just not sure what might have happened to him, and I've been worried sick."

"We shouldn't be over there anyway," Ana mumbled under her breath.

Lindsey's head snapped around, and she shot Ana a look that mirrored Denis Wood's murderous rage. "You don't have to support the cause to support our troops over there!" she hissed defensively.

"I know," Ana said nervously.

"I hope so," Lindsey said, looking away.

A thick silence fell over the group. Tonia finally placed her hand on Lindsey's leg. "Just be there for David and listen. Don't push."

"Yeah," Sandi said, "he'll talk to you when he's ready to share."

Ana snickered and shook her head, drawing everyone's attention. "Either that," she said, "or he's just a typical man, who's completely inconsiderate and self-absorbed."

The others brushed off the bitter comment as though it had never been spoken.

"Take it from me, sweetie," Tonia added, trying to quell Lindsey's growing fears. "Men can be just as mysterious as us. I wouldn't worry, though. From everything you've told us, David's a good man." She looked at Ana, browbeating her into silence. "I second Sandi's advice. Just be patient with him and he'll come around." She winked. "As long as there's communication, respect and trust, love will always find its way."

Christine grabbed Lindsey's arm. "I have to tell you, though, Linds...you also have to be sure that your boyfriend's life doesn't completely consume all of you."

"Precisely!" Ana interrupted. "To hell with any man who thinks he can just..."

Lindsey stood and shook her head. "Thanks for the advice, ladies," she said and then looked at Ana. "And you...you really need to get a new hobby."

Everyone laughed. While Ana's forehead wrinkled in thought, Tonia was happy to partake in some more ex-husband bashing. Lindsey grabbed Courtney. "Let's go find another bottle of Riesling."

"And let's drink it alone in the kitchen," Courtney said.

They both laughed.

¤ ¤ ¤ ¤

Lindsey sifted through a stack of mail and was excited to find a letter from *Sergeant David McClain*. She quickly opened it.

> Dear Lindsey,
>
> I hope this letter finds you well. We just got done Skyping, but I never feel like I've said everything I need to say.
>
> As you can imagine, some days can get really rough over here. I suppose it's hard to witness the things I've seen and not be affected. Whenever I seem quiet or distant, please don't ever think that it has anything to do with you or us. I'm just trying to get

through this tour the only way I know how. And I know that it can be frustrating for you when I don't share the details of what's going on over here. But trust me, Lindsey, you don't want to know most of it.

I miss you like crazy, and I love you even more.

Please keep the emails and letters coming. They're the one and only thing I look forward to.

Love you,
David

Lindsey read the letter two more times before putting it back into the envelope. *But I do want to know everything that's going on, David,* she thought and shook her head. *It has to be even worse over there than I thought.*

◻ ◻ ◻ ◻

Hard weeks turned into long months. David and Lindsey talked on the phone, over Skype and via email whenever they could. They even resurrected the lost art of letter writing. Although many of their exchanges were melancholy, Lindsey had become David's only ray of light in the darkness.

After another foot patrol, which had become much more serious since the IED attack, David was summoned to the HQ tent by the company First Sergeant.

David stood at parade rest before the large man, curious about the rare invitation.

The man looked up from an olive drab folder. "You're being plucked from your patrol for a special assignment, Sergeant McClain."

"Really?" David blurted, surprised. "What's the gig, Top?"

"I looked over your scores on the shooting range. Very impressive."

David nodded.

"We need a man with your skills, your eye, to take out a tier-one target."

David steeled himself and waited to hear more.

The First Sergeant opened a second green folder and revealed a black-and-white photo of a bearded Taliban fighter. "His name's Mullah Abdul Raqeeb. Over the past six months, the son-of-a-bitch and his men have caused us one too many heartaches. In fact, we believe he's directly responsible for the deaths of four American soldiers in an ambush that took place three weeks ago."

David leaned in to hear more. *Four Americans*, he thought, and felt a surge of adrenaline rush through his bloodstream. "I remember that," he said.

"Our latest intel puts Raqeeb at the same location, his mother's flat, every Saturday night. So we'll need you on a rooftop across from that flat. You'll go in under the cover of darkness, twenty-three hundred hours on Wednesday."

"Wednesday?"

"Yeah, you'll need a few days to get settled in and learn the environment."

David nodded, continuing to study the photo and burn his enemy's face into his spinning mind.

"You'll draw an SR-25 from the armorer. He's expecting you."

David nodded again. "Got it, Top."

"And you're being assigned Corporal Michaels as your spotter. He'll carry your ammo and whatnot."

"Perfect. Nate's a good man," David said, and he was right. For whatever reason, Nathan Michaels had proven himself to be unusually talented when sniffing out bad guys.

"Given the location, I was tempted to send you in there alone," the First Sergeant admitted.

"Because two men means twice the risk of getting caught?"

The First Sergeant nodded. "Exactly. This mission's going to require as much stealth as you can muster, so you boys will have to pull off a quick hit and run." This meant they'd be stripped of any identification and, if caught, they were pretty much on their own.

"Understood, Top," David said.

"Son, Raqeeb is a real bad guy. Who knows how many American lives you'll be saving if you can bag him."

"If Raqeeb shows his face, I'll do my job. You have my word on it."

He searched David's face. "Remember, McClain, your mission is to ascertain the target and remove the threat—nothing more, nothing less. It's imperative to keep any and all emotion out of it. Emotions jeopardize missions and put our lives in harm's way. You understand?"

"I do, Top. One shot, one kill."

"Good. And if you and Michaels can slip out right away, great. If not, you'll need to wait it out until the right opportunity presents itself."

"So no backup on this one then?"

"We're rangers, McClain. Obviously, if the shit really hits the fan, we won't leave you out there for dead. But for the most part, you boys will be on your own. It's up to you to get out of there." He peered hard into David's eyes. "You up for this, son? I realize it's a lot to ask. But you're our best chance at..."

"I got this, Top. Like I said, I'll do my job."

The First Sergeant smiled and placed his hand on David's shoulder. "Hoo-ah," he said.

"Hoo-ah," David echoed.

¤ ¤ ¤ ¤

David sprinted down to the communications tent and logged onto his email account. He was happy to find that he had a message from Lindsey in his inbox:

> Hi handsome,
>
> Just been thinking about you and wanted to drop you a quick line to let you know that you're not alone, even if it might feel like you are sometimes over there.
>
> Keep your attitude positive and strong, David, and know that you're in my prayers.
>
> Love,
> Lindsey

Love, he repeated in his head and grinned. These whispers from home made all the difference in his darkened world. He hit reply and wrote:

Beautiful,

I've been thinking of you too—always! I'll be in touch in a few days. Getting farmed out to another unit. No big deal. Just work. I'll be dreaming about you the whole time.

Love you,
David

Chapter 5

□ □ □ □

Dressed as Afghan locals, David and Nate slithered through several back alleyways, moving quickly within the shadows. As though they'd been residents all their lives, they reached their location, accessed the building and ascended the stairs. Once they reached the rooftop, they chalked the door so that no one could follow in their quiet footsteps. *The downside,* David thought, *is that we're trapped like rats.*

While David put in his ear piece and checked that his microphone was strapped to his neck where it could pick up the slightest whisper, Nate conducted a communications check over a secured net. *Seems odd,* David thought, *considering we've been told we're pretty much on our own out here.* He looked at Nate, thinking, *No matter how this goes down, the cavalry isn't coming for a while.*

The radio stuttered one last time. The commo check was successful, and both soldiers went silent.

The mission was specific and clear; he and Nate were tasked to remove one target, a high-ranking official within the Taliban ranks. According to current military intelligence reports, Mullah Abdul Raqeeb visited his mother in the neighborhood, though the frequency varied from weekly to once a month. It didn't matter. Their job was to secure a position—unseen—and remain there until they could obtain their target and complete the mission. *One shot, one kill,* David told himself again. A second shot might give away their position as the enemy would be looking for muzzle flashes, echoed sounds, or movement. *Movement is our greatest enemy,* David reminded himself. And they'd do whatever they had to do to get out of there alive; *either get out right away or wait for as long as needed.* This took discipline and minds that could wander to kinder places without giving away their position.

From the moment they lay prone on the rooftop, David went through the checklist—an invisible range card—in his head. Methodically scanning the street below, he studied left to right and back again; it was an invisible grid that covered every inch. *Rooftops, no movement,* he mentally checked off. *Her windows, nothing. Southwest corner, no one. Street is clear. Southeast corner, no one.*

He and Nate needed to become quickly acclimated to their new environment. It could mean the difference between success and failure, life and death. David was cast into a heightened vigilance that teetered on sheer panic. The sounds from the street below were so foreign and frightening at first. His heart beating hard in his ears, he told himself, *Control your breathing...and do your job!* These words had been pounded into his head since the first day of training: controlled breathing was critical to success. He took three deep breaths and resumed his scan. *Rooftops, no movement. Her windows, nothing. Southwest corner, no one. Street is clear. Southeast corner, no one.* He took more deep breaths. *Slow down,* he told himself, firmly. *Relax.*

Night crawled into day, but neither he nor Nathan was able to sleep.

◻ ◻ ◻ ◻

In the morning, David went through his usual checklist as he'd conducted hundreds of times already. *Rooftops, no movement. Her windows, nothing. Southwest corner, no one. Street is clear. Southeast corner, no one.* He looked sideways toward Nate, who was going through the same relentless scan. Their job was to pick up movement or anything out of the ordinary. When the environment and everything in it became normal—which didn't take as long as David once thought—the intense vigilance was driven by a deep-seated training, which proved just as effective.

The position of the blinding sun, as well as shadows creeping up the walls, were just some of the things to be taken into account. Besides wind and elevation, these would be factored in before taking a shot. The trick was to be three chess moves ahead of an enemy that only knew how to play checkers.

With the hot wind whistling over the black rooftop, the sounds from the street below soon became familiar. Each one was distinct in its own right: a vendor hawking his wares in his foreign tongue; window shutters opening and closing at the same time each day by an old woman hanging out the day's wash; children playing soccer; an old man with a limp, dragging his dead foot behind him. Even civilian vehicles began to sound very different from military vehicles.

Rooftops, no movement. Her windows, nothing, David checked off. *Southwest corner, no one. Street is clear. Southeast corner, no one.*

To help pass the time, David eventually created a backstory for each of these people; *the old man's a war hero, the limp a souvenir from an incoming mortar round.* David also imagined several of the kids playing professional soccer as adults.

And then there was always Lindsey. *I wonder what she's doing right now,* he thought.

□ □ □ □

With her motion sickness wristband fastened securely, Lindsey met Courtney and Christine on the dock a half hour early for the whale watch and checked in.

A preoccupied teenager shuffled them onto the boat where they met an earthy, crunchy naturalist. "I'm Jenna," she said. "Our captain for today is George Cournoyer, and Randy will be our first mate."

"What does the first mate do?" Christine asked, ready to get the day underway.

"You'll see him preparing the boat to depart and dock. He fixes things, helps in the galley...pretty much everything." She sized up the two women and smiled. "Now tell me what your jobs are today."

They stared blankly.

"To listen, be safe and have fun."

"Fun, fun," Christine repeated, being a smart ass.

Watching the whales along Stellwagen Bank promised to be the experience of a lifetime. Cape Cod was the feeding ground for the world's largest mammals— majestic creatures that could measure up to seventy feet long and weigh sixty-five tons. With her Red Sox ball cap pulled down tightly, Lindsey felt excited.

As they moved across the bay, the harbor slowly faded away and the shores of Cape Cod became visible. They could make out the tip of the Cape by the Provincetown monument and the Race Point Lighthouse. The weather was so clear, Jenna pointed out the crest of the Boston skyline.

The sea conditions were fair. After Courtney concluded her tough line of questioning, the three ladies sat back and enjoyed the smooth ride on the open deck. There was no better place.

"How's David?" Christine asked Lindsey.

"He's good," Lindsey quickly replied.

"At least that's the story she's sticking with," Courtney said, half-joking.

"He's fine," Lindsey said, trying to convince herself just as much as her friends.

Their cruise out to the whales took all of an hour. As Jenna was describing the maritime colleges on the Cape, one of the giants surfaced, blew a stream of water straight into the air and looked at them. Jenna went right to work. "If everyone will look on the right side of the boat, you'll see our friend the fin whale."

People quickly shifted positions.

"Weighing up to sixty tons, the fin whale is the second largest of the great whales and can reach a maximum length of about eighty feet. It's one of the fastest of the great whales and has even been called the 'Greyhound of the Seas.' As you can see, fin whales are black on the right side of their lower jaw and white on the left. The reasons for this are unknown, but it may have something to do with their feeding habits."

The loner whale submerged itself and disappeared.

"The finner eats small fish as well as krill. Fin whales used to be hunted in the Antarctic, but their numbers became so few that they're now protected."

"Did you see that?" Lindsey asked the girls, excitedly.

"How could we miss it?" Courtney asked.

"And we're just getting started," Jenna added.

Twenty minutes later, three more monsters swam alongside the boat. "These are minke whales," Jenna explained. "At a maximum of thirty feet, the minke is the smallest of the grooved whales. There are northern and southern minkes. The northern minke can be distinguished by a broad white stripe on its flipper that does not appear in the southern breed."

"Which are these?" Christine asked.

"These are our northern friends coming by to say hello."

Some of the kids on the boat waved at the threesome. Suddenly, two more appeared and then another five. *We're in the middle of a herd*, Lindsey thought.

Caught up in the moment and forgetting themselves, Courtney and Christine started waving until the first whale headed in a different direction, leading the rest away from the boat. Lindsey saw this and laughed.

After an hour of scanning the water, someone yelled out that they'd spotted something off the port side. Jenna hurried over and surveyed the scene. "Those are Atlantic white-sided dolphins, also known as jumpers. They're sometimes found in herds that can number into the hundreds. They're cautious around boats and won't swim in bow waves."

One of them leaped from the water and was followed by another. And then they went under and were gone.

"These two look like stragglers," Jenna said. "They feed on squid and fish, and it's believed that dolphins can communicate with each other by making sounds like barks, groans, chirps, and whistles. They also communicate by means of body posture and by slapping their flukes on the water's surface."

Lindsey inhaled deeply and looked around. She exhaled in a purr, feeling such peace among all the natural beauty that surrounded them. *It's so amazing*, she thought, *I really have to share this with David when he gets home.*

¤ ¤ ¤ ¤

I have to pee, David thought, still lying on the rooftop and looking through the cross hairs of a sniper scope. He slowly placed his arm beneath his prone chest and checked his wristwatch. *Two hours 'til dark*. He pulled his arm back out and placed it back on his rifle. *You don't have to pee that bad*, he lied to himself. *And worse case, just go in place.* He smiled. *I'm guessing that Nate's already pissed himself a few times anyway.*

It took real discipline to suspend all movement and noise—even heavy breathing. For those who smoked, they couldn't. For those who snored, they couldn't sleep—or it could spell death.

It was human nature for people to take even the smallest things for granted, and David and Nate quickly learned that deprivation was the greatest teacher of appreciation. Three hots and a cot had been replaced by vacuum-sealed dehydrated meals and seated cat naps. Squatting now took the place of sitting comfortably on a toilet, followed by waste retrieval in a Ziploc bag. There could be no evidence of their presence left behind—none.

For David, a sweet kiss and warm hug were replaced by daydreams and a longing for Lindsey, until he could no longer afford the bittersweet luxury while carrying out their mission.

When the scan became subconscious—like driving a car home without knowing how you got there—David's thoughts could safely drift to home, all the way back to Lindsey. *I wonder what's she's doing right now,* he wondered. *Rooftops, no movement. Southwest corner, no one. I bet she's at the beach, looking up at the stars and thinking of me. Southeast corner, no one.* And then David allowed his mind a brief glimpse of a happier time in a much safer place.

David and Lindsey sat on their bench, watching as the moonlight illuminated the amazing canvas before them. While the waves kept rhythm to the pulse of life, the night sky was filled with a million stars keeping watch over all of it.

Lindsey lay with her head on his shoulder, the two of them gazing up in quiet reflection.

"Are you afraid, David?" Lindsey asked out of the blue.

He nodded. "I am," he admitted. "Every time I look at you for too long, I'm scared that I'll never remember what life was like before I met you."

"Good answer," she said, playfully slapping his arm. "What I meant was, are you afraid of going over there to Afghanistan?" She locked onto his eyes.

He never hesitated. "Absolutely not," he said confidently.

"Not even a little?" she asked, surprised.

He shook his head. "Long ago, I made a habit of not fearing what I don't know," he explained. "And as a soldier, fear is your worst enemy. My job is to focus on the task at hand, the mission, and trust that my training and the men I serve with will get me to the other side of whatever I have to face."

She looked back into the night sky, thinking about what he'd just said, and then nodded. "Good," she whispered.

"That makes me feel better."

"Good," he repeated, grinning.

And then Lindsey's smile passed much too quickly from his mind. Out of the corner of his eye, David spotted movement on a rooftop adjacent to their location, one story higher. While focusing on their frontal scan, David and Nate had nearly been caught and didn't even realize it.

Oh shit, David thought, and threw a pebble at Nathan to get his attention.

Nate looked his way. David slowly pointed at the Afghan local on the next rooftop. Nate low-crawled to David's position, where they covered themselves in the thick black tarp they'd brought along for such a situation, camouflaging their position.

Within seconds, David began to sweat profusely, while his breathing quickened. *I'm cooking in my own juices*, he thought, but realized that he needed to remain calm if they were going to survive in the heavy boiler bag. *Survival depends on a man's ability to control panic*, David told himself. *A thinking man has a better chance of living another day.*

He could feel Nate lying next to him, trying to calm his own breathing. David recited the Rangers Creed in his head, followed by several "Our Fathers."

Remember your training, David told himself. *Revert back to your training...*

> After conquering dangerous obstacle courses, twelve-mile foot marches, night and day land-navigation tests and combat water-survival training,

which literally taught each man what
it felt like to drown, David's company completed Phase One of Ranger
School. Through attrition, their numbers had been nearly cut in half.

Taking one hour to get haircuts and
purchase any sundry items needed,
they were off to the mountains. David
enjoyed the uncomfortable rest the
flight provided. He welcomed Phase
Two and told his friends, "Follow me
boys!" Minutes later, they were jump-
ing into the smallest, most rugged
drop zone David had ever seen. Many
claimed Phase Two was the most difficult. Sergeant David McClain was the
first to land.

For three more torturous weeks, with
even less sleep, each ranger candidate
gauged his capabilities, as well as his
limitations. Both day and night, they
completed combat missions.

As one day blurred into the next,
David and his comrades completed
Phase Two of Ranger School and
found themselves on a plane heading
to Florida. There were still seventeen
days to go and, as each of them had
been told from the beginning, "those
who flunk out of Phase Three will
have to return to day one." With that
threat in mind, David envisioned his

greatest fear.

From a picture-perfect sky, they assaulted the Sunshine State. By this point, the class of ranger recruits had dwindled to fewer than one half of the number that began the training. Those that remained had reached far beyond their nerves and were now functioning off sheer conviction. Seemingly the most practical of all exercises, they engaged a well-trained, sophisticated enemy. Food was conveniently made more scarce, and the most primitive instincts of survival were brought into play. David hated the grubs, but he ate them. They were the best source of protein, and he desperately needed the energy. No sooner would the recruits close their eyes than the enemy would reappear through sniper fire, keeping them awake and moving.

On the final day of his tour, David discovered one of his men had been taken captive. Leading his small unit on a daring rescue mission, they eventually got pinned down by heavy smal- arms fire. They were courageously continuing to fight toward their objective when David heard a click. It was the distinct metallic click of an M16 A1 rifle. He looked up. It was one of the instructors sitting in a tree, apparently out of ammunition. David shouldered his weapon, took the man directly in his sights and squeezed off a blank. The man jumped from the tree and approached the young team leader. "You would risk all your men for the life of one?" he asked.

David was delirious with exhaustion but responded by quoting his favorite lines of the Ranger Creed. "Energetically, I will meet the enemies of my country. I shall defeat them on the battlefield for I am better trained and will fight with all my might. *Surrender* is not a ranger word. I will never leave a fallen comrade to fall into the hands of the enemy and under no circumstances will I ever embarrass my country."

The man smiled wide, reached into his pocket and offered David and his brothers each a cigarette. Taking a seat on a moss-covered stump, he took two deep drags and looked up. "Good job, ranger," he said.

David lit his own cigarette and cried. They all cried. "We made it," David said. "We're Airborne Rangers."

The graduation lasted no more than an hour, and though families congratulated their sons, husbands and brothers with hugs, David stood alone once again. It didn't matter. *The Rangers are my family now*, he thought. *Nobody back home could ever understand what*

*I've gone through anyway. There's no way
they could.*

Unsure whether the Afghan was still on the other
rooftop—and whether Nate had nodded off—David lay
completely still, allowing his mind to travel to another
place—to Gooseberry Island, where Lindsey was still
waiting for him.

The moon sat directly above Gooseberry Island, illuminating a hypnotic
tide, while the salty winds sang in
the elephant grass. David inhaled
deeply—feeling a wave of serenity roll
through his entire body. He looked to
his left, and that sense of peace was
joined by excitement.

"It's so beautiful here," Lindsey said.

And so are you, he thought, nodding.
"It's my favorite place in the whole
world," he said.

She looked at him, making his heart
skip a beat. "Mine too," she said. After
a moment, she pointed toward the old
stone lighthouse. "Look at that," she
said.

It took everything he had to peel his
eyes away from Lindsey and redirect
his attention to the tall gray beacon.
"They say old Ruth has saved quite a

few souls from these waters."

Lindsey smiled. "She must be a strong woman to live such a solitary life."

He half-shrugged and teased, "I guess I wouldn't mind living there."

"By yourself?" she asked, surprised.

He nodded. "Why not? There'd be no one around to bother me." He struggled to conceal his grin, thinking, *Though I wouldn't mind you visiting me.*

"Can you imagine spending that much time alone?" she asked. "It must change a person."

"I guess it might," he agreed and thought about it for a moment, "depending on where your head's at."

Lindsey shrugged. "You're probably right. I've been around lots of people and still felt alone."

David looked into her eyes and felt his heart flutter again. "I think you have to feel comfortable being alone with yourself before you can feel comfortable being yourself with others."

Oh Lindsey, David thought, *to hell with being alone.* When he emerged from the daydream, he was lying in a puddle of sweat—both his and Nate's. He slowed his breathing again and listened carefully. *Nothing.* Then, like a butterfly emerging from its cocoon, he slowly peeked out. Nothing was more painstaking than trying to camouflage movement. The man on the adjacent rooftop was gone. *Amen.* David squirmed out from under the hefty tarp and reached for his canteen, where he emptied it in two long gulps. The hot wind felt like an air conditioner, waking Nathan from his slumber as well.

Close call, David thought, still not sure how they didn't get spotted. While Nate slithered back to his position, David returned to his rifle, hoping that they hadn't missed their target during the episode.

Rooftops, no movement. Her windows, nothing. Southwest corner, no one. Street is clear. Southeast corner, no one. And then it dawned on him. *Or maybe we did get caught and they're on their way?*

He looked over at Nate, who was now looking back at the chalked door behind them.

Suddenly, there was movement three hundred yards out on the street below. *Unusual*, David thought. It was a teenage boy, maybe fourteen, carrying a burlap bag and quickly making his way home before dark. *Never seen him before*, David thought and smiled. *Back home, he'd be looking forward to getting his driver's permit and dreaming about his first date.*

In a flash, a man—a Taliban fighter—jumped out of the shadows and grabbed the boy's arm, pulling him to the street and spilling the contents of his sack. As the teenager yelled for help, another Taliban soldier emerged from the darkness. The boy screamed louder, but not a single soul came to his aid.

David watched as both Taliban fighters began interrogating the boy. *They might be looking for us*, David thought. The teenage boy shook his head a few times.

Loud yells quickly turned to open hand slaps. The boy fell to the street, where both fighters pounced on him to inflict a vicious, inhumane beating.

While listening to the thud of boots smashing into the boy's skull, David took a deep breath to control his anger while using his thumb to take his rifle off safe. He placed his finger into the trigger guard, sighted in the first aggressor's head and broke radio silence. "Papa Bear," he whispered, pressing the microphone into his neck. "This is Gray Ghost. I've got a young boy at my ten o'clock being beaten to death by two Taliban. I've got the shot. Requesting green light. Over."

The boy's shrills were ear-piercing. Still, no one on the ground came to his aid.

I'll take the first one out, David thought, *and by the time the second animal watches his buddy hit the deck, he'll be on his way to Allah too...right behind him.*

"Negative," Command responded.

"I say again, they're killing the boy," David whispered. "Over."

By this time, the teenager had been beaten so badly he'd quit fighting back.

"Read you, Lima Charlie," Command replied. "I say again, stand down. Will dispatch ground troops to that location. Do not compromise your position." There was a snowy pause. "How copy? Over."

David's oath as a soldier was in direct conflict with his innate decency as a human being, his heart and mind locked in mortal combat. His mind raced, searching for an option that would allow him to save the boy while still fulfilling his duty and successfully carrying out their mission. There was Option A—take out both Taliban and save the boy, while causing the mission to fail immediately, in turn, placing countless American soldiers and marines at fatal risk; or Option B—stick to the mission and forfeit the boy, along with a piece of his own soul. There was no Option C.

"Received," David hissed, choosing Option B, before looking sideways to Nate.

The laughter of both Taliban soldiers drifted up to their rooftop.

Nate slowly shook his head. From the look in his eyes, he was obviously experiencing the same rage and helplessness.

With tears streaming down his chapped cheeks— like the good soldier he'd been trained to be—David shifted his scope and scanned the building before him. He wished with everything inside him that he could silence the boy's desperate pleas, as the teenager continued to beg for his life in his foreign tongue.

Rooftops, no movement. Her windows, nothing. Southwest corner, no one. As David scanned his grid to acquire his one and only target, he skipped over the gruesome scene on the street below.

This pathetic distraction, however, did nothing to mask the boy's terrified howls for help. David's stomach flipped a few times, sending a wave of acid up his esophagus, burning a path straight to the back of his constricted throat. *Breathe....breathe...*he told himself, fighting off the urge to vomit.

The abuse only took three minutes but lasted an eternity. The boy's shrieks were suddenly quieted to mournful sobs. David drummed up enough courage to place his scope back on the teenager. His attackers were gone, but the damage they'd inflicted was evident. The boy was covered in blood—his face already purple and swollen—and rolled into the fetal position, lying completely motionless.

They killed him, David thought. *They beat him to death.* Tears streamed faster down David's face. *I'm so sorry,* he told the boy in his mind. *Please forgive me.*

As an old Afghan man emerged from one of the houses and pulled the bloodied body off the street, David returned to his scan, his eyes blurred with stinging tears. *Rooftops, no movement. Her windows, nothing. Southwest corner, no one. Southeast corner, no one.* He felt like he was breathing through a crimped straw.

¤ ¤ ¤ ¤

By early Sunday morning, the tier-one target never presented itself, and the mission was aborted.

"Gray Ghost," David heard in his ear piece, "this is Papa Bear. Abort mission."

David pressed the microphone on his neck. "Say again, Papa Bear?"

"Abort mission, Gray Ghost." There was static, followed by another squelch. "Battalion confirmed that our intel was bad."

"Received," David hissed, and looked over at Nate—who was already shaking his head. "We'll bug out at dark."

I could have saved that poor kid, David thought, the real war now waged within his heart and mind. His eyes filled with tears. *I could have saved him.* The reality of it poured into his soul like ten tons of concrete, and the same heart that allowed him to stand up and fight also made him cry—quietly.

For another sixteen hours, David lay on the rooftop in the prone position like a wounded slug, watching the world through the limited viewpoint of a sniper's scope. It was way too much time for his thoughts not to wander into the darkness. Whenever Lindsey's pretty face appeared in his mind's eye, he pushed it out of his head as fast as it appeared. Mostly, he just tried to keep breathing without passing out.

Once it got dark, David looked up at the constellations and saw the North Star shining brightly. *Sorry Lindsey,* he thought, *but there's no place for you in this hell hole.*

Slowly and with each movement being completely deliberate, David and Nate packed up and slithered out the same way they'd slithered in—undetected.

Chapter 6

¤ ¤ ¤ ¤

Lindsey was down in her basement, finishing the week's laundry, when she spotted the corner of an old drab green Army trunk buried beneath boxes of Christmas decorations. Curious, she dug the trunk out and dragged it to the open floor, where she took a knee. Among other war souvenirs—a British uniform and beret with desert rat patches, a boot knife with a broken tip, yellow-eared photos—she discovered a stack of old letters bound by an old rubber band. She looked at the stack, realizing they had been mailed to her father from her mother in 1991. He'd been stationed on the front lines of Iraq, Seventh Corps, First Light Infantry.

As Lindsey removed the top letter, the rubber band snapped. She lifted the envelope closer to her nose, detecting the faint scent of perfume. She took a seat, pulled the letter from the yellowed envelope and read:

> My Dearest,
>
> Thank you for your many letters. I can't tell you how much they mean to

me to know that you're safe.

Denis, I love you so much that it hurts.
As I try to go about my daily routine,
I can't think about anything but you.
I sit in front of the TV day and night,
watching what you guys are doing
over there. So brave! I'm so proud of
you that I could scream.

I can't wait to see you again...to hold
you and kiss you and make love to you
over and over.

Lindsey cringed at the thought of her parents together
like that, though she understood what her mother had
been feeling.

There's nothing new on this end. I
saw your mother at the market and we
shared updates about you. Lee Green-
wood's song, "God Bless the USA,"
plays over and over on the radio, and
it makes me think of you every time.

I daydream about the future we'll have
together. Getting married, buying a
house, having children and growing
old together.

Lindsey snorted at the final thought. "Three out of
four isn't bad, Mom," she muttered, sarcastically, and
returned to the letter.

I love you so much that it aches. Think

of me and please stay safe.

All My Love,
Anita

Lindsey dropped the letter and sat in the middle of the dirty floor, thinking. *It's exactly what I'm feeling... what I'm living right now.* She shook her head. *Mom and Dad were definitely in love back then, but in the end look how it turned out.* She shook her head again. *Either their love died, or it wasn't strong enough to overcome everything they were forced to face together after the war.* The truth of it made her shiver.

She threw the letters back into the trunk and kicked it into the corner. Grabbing the laundry basket, she shut off the light and walked up the stairs—knowing that the letter would haunt her, challenging the innocent hope she had for a future with David.

Lindsey made a beeline to her PC and wrote David:

David,

Things are good on this end. I've been thinking about you every day. But as you know, you're not missing anything here—except me.

Please write or call and tell me when it looks like you'll be coming home. It's getting closer every day, and I cannot wait to see you. You have no idea how proud I am (we all are) of you.

I love you.

Lindsey

¤ ¤ ¤ ¤

Halfway around the world, David stared at the computer screen like a drooling zombie, his chest constricted and his breathing shallow. *That night on the park bench was a lifetime ago,* he thought. *So much has changed. I've changed.* And he knew it wasn't for the better.

There were times when he struggled to picture Lindsey's face now—the way she'd looked at him when they gazed up at the stars that night.

I could destroy this before we ever have a chance, he thought.

Still, he wrote:

> Lindsey,
>
> You've taught me that someone doesn't have to be there in person to really be there for someone. Thanks for walking with me every step of the way. Your letters have honestly helped me get through this.
>
> All My Love,
> David

◻ ◻ ◻ ◻

One month before shipping home, David was summoned to the chaplain's tent. Upon arrival, he found the white-haired major sitting at a small, portable desk.

"You called for me, sir?" David asked in the tent flap.

The man turned. "McClain?" he asked, smiling.

David nodded.

"Come in. Come in, please." He gestured for David to take a seat on his cot.

Reluctantly, David sat on the edge. "What can I do for you, sir?" he asked.

The man retrieved an envelope and turned to face David, his eyes now solemn. "I'm sorry to tell you, son, but we've received word from the Red Cross that your dad has passed away. We..."

"What?" David interrupted. "My father died?" he asked, the shock numbing his senses.

The older man took a seat beside David. "He did, son," he confirmed, handing him the letter. "Seems he had a massive heart attack at work and they couldn't revive him."

David stared at the opened letter—unable to read a word of it—while his mind spiraled with a thousand negative thoughts. *But he never said goodbye to me...I never showed him he was wrong...Oh God, Mom must be a mess.* His emotions were even more fractured and bizarre.

The chaplain placed his hand on David's shoulder. "There will be no actual funeral, just a cremation followed by a private burial. I've already taken the liberty of talking to your company commander about you taking bereavement R & R and..."

"That won't be necessary," David said, still dry-eyed and in shock.

"Grief can be a funny thing, G.I."

"Please don't ever call me that," David snapped instinctively.

The man slowly nodded. "Okay, son, but if you want to..."

"I'll be fine," David interrupted, "really."

The man searched his eyes. "Would you like me to pray with you?"

Shaking his head, David stood. "I appreciate that, but I need to call home and talk to my mother. She must be taking it hard."

"Of course. Of course." The chaplain also stood and extended his hand. "My deepest sympathies for your loss. If you change your mind about going home or would just like to come by and talk, my door is always open."

"Thank you, sir. I appreciate that." He thought for a moment. "Knowing my father, he would have wanted me to stay right here and do my job."

The chaplain looked unsure about how to take the last comment. "I hope to see you at service on Sunday."

David nodded again. "Sure, if I'm not out shooting at bad guys."

The older man's eyes went wide.

With the letter in hand, David quickly exited the tent, confused by his overwhelming emotions. *Dad was a real bastard*, he thought, *but at least he was always there.* He shook his head. *I just wish I'd had the chance to face him and tell him what I really thought.*

Although David expected a physical response to follow—gasping breaths, tightening of the chest—he felt nothing of the sort. *Strange*, he thought.

¤ ¤ ¤ ¤

Lindsey approached her car after a long day at work. Joe, her ex-boyfriend, was waiting by her driver's side door. "Hi sexy," he said. "Miss me?"

Joe was tall, bronze and chiseled. With aqua blue eyes and raven black hair, to say that he was good looking would have been a gross understatement. At one time, Lindsey was just another notch in his long line of conquests. He'd cast a spell on her, and she dove headfirst into his winning smile. *But that was a long time ago*, she thought.

"No," she said honestly. "There's nothing worse than being with someone and always wondering who else they're with." *He smells good though*, Lindsey thought, *and it looks like he's been working out*. She snickered to herself. *But a dog dressed in a tuxedo is still a dog.*

Joe shook his head. "I had no idea things would turn out the way they did. But I needed to come see you and tell you what I've been thinking and feeling..."

She started to object when he continued. "Lindsey, you're so incredibly irresistible. You're funny and smart."

His words sounded more sincere than anything he'd ever fabricated, but she could tell he was lying because his lips were still moving. No matter how challenging the game, it was all about the thrill of the chase for Joe, and he kept his eyes on the prize.

"I don't mean to put pressure on you," he said, "but I can't help it. I wish, even for a moment, that you could come away with me. Then you'd understand how real this is for me and how desperately I want you...all of you."

"Joe, please don't..."

He took a step closer and locked onto her eyes. "I could kiss you for hours, Linds, and never stop. All I want is the opportunity to turn your world upside down." He reached for her hand.

She pulled it away.

"When we were together, I felt really comfortable with you. I just wish it didn't end the way it did."

"With you cheating on me with every skank on the island?" she finally asked, breaking her silence.

"I told you, I made a mistake."

"More than one," she said, surprised that she was still angry about it.

"We've both learned that life can change," he said and then grinned. "But I can also see that the attraction between us hasn't changed."

"Life can change," she agreed, "but people are who they are. And you're a cheat, Joe. You'll always be a cheat."

"Listen..." he said, waving off her last comment like she hadn't meant it. "I have a good job, a nice house... it's all good. But there's something missing. One big giant piece of the puzzle is missing. I now know what it is or what I want. I want you, Lindsey."

She tried to stop him again.

"Please Lindsey, at least let me finish." An actual tear formed in the corner of his eye.

Wow, she thought, *even tears this time*.

"I truly believe with all my heart that you and I are meant to be, and I'm crawling out of my skin with ways to make you smile." He nodded. "I've seen how determination and persistence can pay off, and I believe that if I want something bad enough, no matter what it is I can make it happen." He smiled wide. "Lindsey, the day may come that I become determined to make you my wife, and it may come sooner than you think."

She gagged slightly; she couldn't help it.

He studied her face, clearly surprised that he hadn't made more ground. "Okay, so I made a mistake. And now I'm not entitled to happiness?"

"Of course you are, Joe," she said, "but not at the sake of mine."

He paused for air. "Maybe we could just be friends then?" His dimpled grin and raised eyebrow was like a spider's web, awaiting its prey in the morning sun.

The temptation was stronger than Lindsey would have liked. She was standing at a dangerous crossroad, and they both knew it.

Joe stepped forward again and held out his hand. "Come on, Linds," he whispered. "It would be a real shame to throw away the connection we share."

He's unbelievably sexy, she thought, but was already shaking her head. *But it's best to eliminate any opportunities before I'm the one making the mistake.* "I can't," she said. "I met this guy."

"You're saying *no* because you just met a guy? You don't even know him, Linds."

"I'm not sure about that," she said.

He was shocked. "You're not going to give me another chance because you like some new guy?"

"No, Joe. It's because I like myself." She shrugged. "Besides, you've had enough chances." She shook her head. "You are what you are, and that's never going to change." She nodded confidently. "It's never going to happen, Joe. We're done."

"Well, it's your loss then!" he said.

"I know," she said, trying to be kind and afford him at least one shred of dignity.

"But you don't," he said, growing more angry. "You have no idea." He walked away, pouting like a little boy who'd just heard the word *no* for the first time.

He's so damn beautiful, Lindsey thought, and sighed heavily, *but there are a million Joe's out there*. She then pictured David's baby face and smiled. *And I want much more.*

◻ ◻ ◻ ◻

David lay on his cot, staring up at the billet's corrugated ceiling. *So much has happened*, he thought. *When we first landed here, it didn't look like there was anything worth fighting for. If it weren't for the constant reminders that we were fighting terrorism, the entire thing would have seemed ludicrous.* In the grander scheme of things, though, David believed it was a just cause. He nodded to himself thinking, *Either way, when the fighting kicks off, politics, big band anthems and waving flags play no role in combat. Men fight for their brothers who stand beside them; it's that simple.* He placed both hands behind his head and sighed. *And when the bullets start flying, there's much less fear than I'd ever imagined there would be. The fighting's instinctive*, he thought. He and the boys merely reverted back to their rudimentary training, which had been taught at a third-grade level through relentless repetition.

Most days, thoughts and emotions are put on hold, where they can be dealt with afterward—regardless of how long that might take. And when visions of the enemy's family—to include small, dependent children—danced in David's head, causing him to stay up at night, he offset it with other grotesque pictures of the Taliban's cruelty. When it was quiet at night, this internal war raged on inside of him. He sometimes wondered, *What will my mother think of me now that I've made the transition from fighter to killer?* He wondered even more—*what will Lindsey think of me?*

After eleven months in Afghanistan, David needed to confess, to tell the truth—anything to lighten his soul. But the last thing he wanted was to burden his family or friends with the sins he'd been ordered to commit. He immediately thought about Captain Eli, his mentor and confidant. *Captain Eli won't judge me*, he thought. *He just won't.* He grabbed a pen and paper and wrote:

Dear Captain Eli,

I hope this letter finds you well. It's been a while since I've written. Forgive me, as there hasn't been anything I've been anxious to share. This is a tough place to describe, and I think it's even tougher to explain how I feel being here. But I'd like to try.

As rangers, we're constantly on the move. And after eleven months, it's become very cold and lonely. When we first got here, it was pretty exciting being in a far-off, mysterious land, but the place lost its novelty long ago.

Captain Eli, although I've never backed down from a fight in my life, I never knew what a fight was until I got here. We've engaged the enemy several times. Just two days ago, a small band of Taliban fired on us and we returned their fire. The entire thing lasted no more than a minute, but it was such a devastating sight—so wasteful and permanent. When it was over, one of my bullets killed a man.

Most people have no idea about the price that's paid for freedom. It's so confusing here. We love that all of America is behind us, but we also know that the government's sold the words "patriotism" and "democracy" to justify everything that we do. And trust me, Captain Eli, not everything should be justified.

Well, I need to write Mom and let her know I'm okay. Since Dad passed, she writes me almost every day, bless her soul. Most days, mail call is the only ray of sunshine in this pit. Thanks for listening. See you soon.

David

◻ ◻ ◻ ◻

There was no fanfare. No long goodbyes. One afternoon, the ranger team was kicking in doors and screaming life-or-death instructions in a language that the Afghan people could never understand. The following afternoon, they were boarding a C-130, heading for home.

On the last ride out of camp, David glanced back. *Camp Phoenix*, he thought, *rising from the ashes*. He shook his head. *Bullshit.*

◻ ◻ ◻ ◻

Inside the rumbling belly of the C-130, David located the most comfortable-looking canvas sling and took a seat. After checking his gear, he looked up and took a different inventory: *Four rangers from a different team are gone forever; three from multiple AK47 rounds, and the other by the blast of a successful improvised explosive device, from which he'd bled out. Another poor bastard was maimed from shrapnel and he'll probably be unrecognizable to his own parents.* And then he thought about Big Al Correiro from his own team—who'd been sent home months earlier—scratching two perfectly healthy legs off the plane's original manifest. *Freedom isn't free at all,* he thought and closed his tired eyes.

Throughout the lengthy flight, David wore a set of bulky headphones, as the whine of the motors made him feel like his head was going to pop off. As the hours ticked off, he felt confused. He was excited to be going home alive after his first combat tour, but he also realized that so much had happened—terrible, life-changing experiences that needed to be processed. *How will people understand?* he wondered. *Can they?*

After finally dozing off, he awoke panting for air, his heart racing out of control. *What the hell? It's over,* he thought and, using the sniper techniques he'd been taught, began to calm his breathing. Within minutes, he slowed his breathing and heart rate but not before coming to the stinging realization that there were some very dark emotions boiling and bubbling just beneath the surface—evidently seeping out in short panic attacks—building and waiting to erupt. *Maybe it's not over,* he thought.

The crew chief came through, handing out MRE rations. David took off his headphones. "Enjoy your dinner," the crew chief said, with a smirk.

David looked down. He'd drawn the dehydrated pork patty. "Are you kidding me?" he yelled over the motors. "This is what we're getting fed?"

The man nodded. "It's an MRE or nothing."

David threw the nasty plastic-looking meal onto the deck. "*Nothing* sounds better," he said, and jammed the headphones back onto his ears.

With his stomach churning, David nodded off again. Not an hour later, he awoke shivering. There was nothing but a canvas flap separating his back from the steel fuselage. He put on his parka, zipped it up and thought about Lindsey. A rush of joy and excitement washed over him, but he quickly pushed it aside, afraid to bring something so pure and good into this nightmare he was fighting to emerge from. *I can't ruin things with her,* he decided. *I have to get my head on straight, or I'll destroy any chance we have at being together.*

He'd never told Lindsey when he was flying back to Georgia—exactly—so there wouldn't be anyone waiting for him when they landed. This also brought mixed feelings that he felt too exhausted to analyze. Instead, he picked up the MRE and tore it open. *Dinnertime*, he thought, and felt his stomach convulse over the disgusting sustenance he was about to ingest.

While he gagged down his supper, David took a serious accounting of his time in Afghanistan. *For the older soldiers, those who already know who they are, the fighting and killing is just something they were tasked to do. For the younger soldiers, though, there's definitely the danger that it'll become who they are, and not just something they were ordered to carry out.* David was still young enough to feel it in his soul.

He took a drink of water, trying to push down another bite. *Words like* freedom, honor, nobility *and* courage *aren't just words anymore*, he thought. *They're ideals; a creed to live by.* He felt so torn over the entire experience.

He looked at the men who shared the ride home; Max, Kevin, Billy and Nathan. Among hundreds of other brave soldiers, they'd served side-by-side. And their perspective of the war was very different from the sanitized version CNN opted to show at home. Besides the terrible fighting, they'd witnessed multiple children slaughtered by roadside bombs. *More evidence of the hefty costs of freedom*, David thought.

David's ranger team shared every trying experience one could imagine during the twelve months of fighting. There were friends made and lost and battles waged on an internal front. Though most soldiers were returning home visibly whole, what they were bringing with them as a result of inhumane fears and pent-up rage was going to be hell to pay. *But it was a just cause,* David told himself again, and closed his eyes for the rest of the flight.

◻ ◻ ◻ ◻

It was a Thursday afternoon when the C-130 flew its final leg into Fort Benning, Georgia. David tried to stretch out his cramped back. As he yawned, he took a look down the line at his combat-hardened comrades. For U.S. Army Rangers—men who normally wore masks of strength and callousness—pure excitement was seeping from their pores. He smiled.

The crew chief made his announcement, "Wheels down in twenty, boys. Welcome home." From his indifferent tone, he'd made the announcement a hundred times before. Still, David felt a charge of excitement rip through his body. It was a pure thrill, like a boy riding a roller coaster for the first time. He calmed his breathing, while his mind continued to race. *Maybe I should've told Lindsey I'd be flying home today,* he scolded himself.

The wheels hit the tarmac and screeched, making the plane bounce once. David was rocked in his canvas sling, while the engines roared in an attempt to halt the heavy beast. "Home," he said aloud, and felt his eyes start to fill. Although he successfully fought back the tears, he could have never contained his smile, even if he'd wanted to.

Once the plane came to a complete stop, David stood, finished stretching out his back and began to gather his things. He looked left and locked eyes with Max. "We made it," he said.

Max nodded solemnly. "Some of us anyway."

David's joy was instantly challenged by the hard truth of Max's words. David's heart sank, and his mind lined up one face after the next—men who would never descend stairs to greet their families. Instead, they'd be received in flag-draped caskets.

David looked back at his friend, realizing, *Max was unusually quiet during the flight.* He watched him. *And he's definitely not as excited as everyone else to be home...which is strange, considering all he ever talked about over there was Max Jr.* David wondered about this. *Then again, Max took two confirmed kills and tried like hell to save a child who'd tripped a roadside bomb.* He shook his head. *And he's had a tough time living with all of it.* For the moment, David decided not to question it.

The pilot and co-pilot met them at the door as they juggled their gear and prepared to descend the stairs onto American soil. "Thank you for your service and welcome home," they said.

With Max walking in front of him, David took his first step outside the plane and sucked in a lung full of domestic air. A pang of joy arose again, immediately challenged by a wave of grief. *Not everyone made it home,* echoed in his head. He searched for the feeling of excitement again, but it was no longer there.

David descended the stairs, while the cheering crowd swayed within the hangar, people dressed in red, white and blue, celebrating like they were at a rock concert. David took another deep breath and descended the steel staircase.

David watched as these modern-day gladiators ran into the opened arms of their loved ones. If only for a moment, there was no threat of death or pain or a future paved with suffering. People swayed in each other's arms and cried. As though all the months of worry and fear and the real possibilities of facing death were suddenly melting away, a terrible weight lifted from hundreds.

Like the professional observer he was, David scanned the hangar and watched all of the subtle details that were taking place. There were men who struggled to hold back and remain strong in the face of their weeping families. David also found the stronger of them allowing their emotions to show, to take its natural course, without care of anyone else's opinion. *They'll probably readjust a lot quicker than the rest of us*, David thought, and envied them for their courage.

People wailed and cried, mourning the time they'd lost together and grieving the absence of innocence in the faces of those who'd returned. Many of them had left as boys but come home as aged men. As David watched everything around him, he shook his head. *I should've told Lindsey I was coming home today.*

He looked at Max, who was blanketed by his loving and supportive family. Like a spider monkey, young Max Jr. had his arms wrapped around his father's neck. David felt torn to witness it; he was happy for his friend but sad for himself.

And then the caskets, square aluminum boxes draped in American flags, were unloaded from the belly of the steel gray beast. The roar of the crowd was immediately silenced. Among the hushed sobs and whispers, soldiers in full dressed uniforms carried the silver caskets to a different area of the hangar, away from the celebration where the less fortunate families were waiting to receive their fallen sons and daughters.

Although the hugs and kisses continued in the main hangar, the silence remained.

¤ ¤ ¤ ¤

Lindsey was just getting dropped off from her girl's night out. She'd lost seven dollars at the mini Texas Hold'em tournament but made it up in the wine she'd enjoyed. Courtney, the designated driver, shared one last laugh with her before saying good night.

"David should be home soon," Courtney said, getting back in her car. "You must be counting down the days, right?"

Lindsey shook her head and then grinned. "More like the hours."

They both laughed before Courtney backed out of the driveway.

Lindsey stepped into the house to find her father standing two feet away from the television; he was just standing there, looking straight ahead. "Did you finish that Three Stooges marathon?" she asked, chuckling.

He turned and looked at her, his eyes devoid of true consciousness.

He's sleepwalking, she realized, and froze—fear locking her knees in place.

"You think I'm afraid of you?" he hissed, his nostrils flaring like a mad bull.

"Dad, go to bed. You're..."

"Well, I'm not!" he screamed. Rage couldn't begin to describe his demeanor.

Oh no, she thought, but having experienced his awful temper many times before, she knew it was already too late to react.

He lunged at her and threw a right cross that landed squarely on her nose. For a suspended moment, the world flickered like a television on its last leg. Flashes of light pulsed in her peripheral vision, dragging the darkness toward the center until she nearly blacked out. That's when the nerve endings started firing, the intense pain shocking her back into consciousness to where her father stood over her, his fists clenched and his chest heaving. Between the excruciating drum beats in Lindsey's head, a small voice—her childhood voice—screamed, *No more!* The pain was blinding.

Then, as if an invisible switch was thrown, reality registered in his eyes and the rage was instantly replaced by horror. "Oh no! Oh Lindsey..." His eyes were wide and filled with terror. He dropped to his knees and held out his hand. "Oh God, what have I done?"

Even if Lindsey had wanted to take his hand, she was too busy catching the puddle of blood in her cupped hands, while trying to get her head back on straight from the vicious assault. She stood, spraying blood everywhere as she did. "Not now, Dad. Just leave me alone. I'll be fine." She hurried into the bathroom to get cleaned up.

As the door closed behind her, she heard him let out a war cry. Moments later, the front door slammed closed and the car started in the driveway.

She looked down at the white facecloth, now completely stained red, and began to cry. "Oh Dad..."

Ashamed and riddled with guilt, Denis Wood was off to check himself into the VA hospital and cut himself off from the rest of the world.

¤ ¤ ¤ ¤

David stepped into Fort Benning's Retention Office and stood at parade rest. The smiling recruiter gestured that David take a seat and relax. He remained standing. The recruiter sighed. "Another four, Sergeant?" he asked, giving it a shot.

David shook his head, hardly surprising the man.

The recruiter flipped open a brown folder. "But your record indicates that you went above and beyond the call of duty during your deployment in Afghanistan," he said, intent on delivering his best sales pitch. "Why wouldn't you..."

"I'm done," David said, staring straight ahead.

"But what if we offered you..."

"I'm out," David said again, this time his tone was less professional.

The man snapped the folder closed and threw it on his desk in surrender. "All right then, but I'll be here if you happen to change..."

David had already executed an about-face and was halfway out the door.

¤ ¤ ¤ ¤

Three days later, David flew home under the radar. Taking a cab from the airport to his house, he found his mother exactly where he'd left her—seated at the kitchen table.

"Oh my God, David, you're home," she yelped and hurried to him.

David dropped his duffel bag on the worn linoleum floor and hugged her tightly. Trying to conceal his broken heart, he joined her at the table.

His mom studied his face, his eyes, and began to cry. "Oh David," she repeated, reaching for his hand. "Your dad's service was very beautiful," she said, confusing his terrible sorrow for grief over his dad's death.

He scoffed at the idea of such a foolish notion but still nodded kindly.

She stood and hugged him from behind. David remained unmoved. "Do you want to talk about it?" she asked gently.

He shrugged. "I wouldn't have the words, Mom." he said, and thought for a long moment. "I wouldn't even know where to start."

After a half hour of sitting in relative silence together, David looked up to find his brother standing in the kitchen's threshold.

"You're home!" Craig called out and ran to his brother. David stood and they hugged.

"Why didn't you call me? I would have given you a ride home from the airport."

"I didn't want to bother you," David said, making both his brother and mother gawk at him, concerned.

Craig pulled on David's arm. "Come with me. I have something to show you." He was smiling from ear-to-ear.

David looked at his mother, who was wearing the same mischievous smile.

The three of them stepped outside. David gasped. His old, beat-up Mustang convertible looked brand new. The fender had been fixed and the entire car painted. Even the vinyl top was new—*which isn't cheap,*

David thought. The new tires shined, and as David stepped closer, he could see that the entire interior had been detailed as well. "How did you..."

Filled with pride, Craig threw his arm around his big brother's shoulder. "One piece at a time."

David's eyes filled. *Craig must have spent three month's wages to pull this off*, he thought. "You shouldn't have, Craig," he said, his voice quivering.

Craig looked at him like he was on fire. "Are you crazy, bro?" He tightened his grip. "You're a war hero."

David glared at his brother. "I'm no war hero," he said firmly.

"Well, no one deserves it more," Craig said quietly.

David nodded once and tried to speak but couldn't. He hugged his brother. "Thank you," he finally managed.

As both brothers discreetly wiped their eyes, Craig asked, "Have you seen Lindsey yet?"

"Nah," David said, shaking his head. "She doesn't even know I'm home."

"So you're gonna surprise her, huh?" Craig asked, grinning.

"When the time's right," David said, heading back toward the house.

There was such sorrow in David's voice that Craig blurted, "Won't that be something?"

David nodded once, never looking back.

Chapter 7

□ □ □ □

David was walking with his friend Al on the beach. They were joking and laughing. "I think I'm pregnant," Al said, rubbing his belly. "The blood tests should be in soon though." He shook his head. "There were so many guys at the party I'm not even sure who the father is."

Suddenly, there was a loud explosion. While a cloud of dust was still settling, David screamed, "I'm sorry, Big Al. It should have been me."

Al shook his head again, but this time there was a strange look in his eyes. *Sympathy, I think.*

Al pointed to David's left leg, which was now a bloodied stump. "Your turn, McClain," he said and started laughing.

□ □ □ □

David awakened, clutching his chest and trying to breathe. He jumped out of bed on two healthy legs and fought desperately to fill his lungs with air and hang onto life. His head wasn't pounding. Rather, it was growing numb with a thousand confusing thoughts—a tornado of doom and gloom creating fragments of hideous pictures with just enough reality to be absolutely and completely terrifying. His palpitating heart was racing so fast that his extremities—hands, feet, fingers, toes, and even the tip of his nose—began tingling. Pure and relentless panic was rushing from his core, filling his entire body with a fight or flight response from something that existed only in the darkest recesses of his mind. It was self-preservation in the face of peace.

¤ ¤ ¤ ¤

An hour later, David was sitting on a gurney. The balding emergency room doctor entered, holding a chart and smiling. "I have great news. We can't find any evidence of a heart attack. It was probably just a panic attack."

"Can't be..." David said.

"These attacks are sometimes caused by the building tensions of everyday life," the doctor explained. "Anything could have triggered the attack." He studied David's face. "Anything new going on—something that might be causing lots of stress?"

David shook his head, playing the dunce.

"I think you should go talk to someone," the doctor advised.

"I'll go see my primary care physician tomorrow," David said.

"That's great, but I was thinking more along the lines of a therapist."

David looked at the man in disbelief. As the doctor left the room, David collapsed back onto the gurney, placed his hands over his eyes and let out a wounded grunt.

David pulled the shiny Mustang into his driveway. He stepped out of the car and watched as the *Welcome* flag waved in the wind. From the greeting sign and lawn ornaments in the front of the house to the pristine patio out back, it was the perfect picture of happy, middle class America. Looking at the manicured lawn and his mother's flawless flowerbeds, David reached his front stairs and snickered. *What bullshit!* He slammed the door behind him.

◻ ◻ ◻ ◻

A full week had passed. David sat quietly, staring out the kitchen window and way beyond whatever lay in the yard. Not so much a dreamer anymore, he was reliving the same nightmares over and over and over.

It only took a second to change the outcome of an entire lifetime. He thought about the Afghan boy who'd been beaten to death. *Or several lifetimes.*

David continued to stare out his kitchen window. *My life is in complete chaos, but maybe if I tried talking to Lindsey?* He shook his head. *No,* he thought, *it wouldn't be fair.*

Though distinct, the front door softly closed. Uninterested, he continued to stare into nothingness. He smelled Lindsey's perfume wafting through the stale air before he ever saw her. He looked up to find her standing in the middle of his kitchen. Her eyes were filled with tears, the left one purple and black. *She's been hurt,* he thought, and took a deeper look into her eyes. *But I've hurt her more.* There was a piece of him, a very subdued piece that was beyond excited to see her again. And then reality hit. *I wish she didn't see me like this.*

"I thought you were supposed to meet me at our bench?" she said sadly.

A dream from a long-forgotten time, he thought, shrugging. "Sorry," he whispered.

His baby face had been replaced with a man's chiseled features. And his hazel eyes no longer sparkled, his love for life extinguished somewhere in Afghanistan.

"So you made it home," she said, breaking the terrible silence.

He nodded. "I did."

"I hope you don't mind," Lindsey said, "but when I heard that you'd come home I asked Craig to let me see you. Please don't be mad at him."

He shook his head, the tears building fast behind his eyes. "Of course not." He stood and took a step toward her. "I'm sorry, Lindsey," he said, "but..."

She threw up her hand, stopping him from getting any closer. "No need to be sorry, David. If you didn't want to see me, all you had to do was be honest."

"It's not that at all," he swore, the first few tears breaking free. "I've never lied to you. It's just that... You don't understand." He was already struggling to take in oxygen.

"Of course I don't understand, David," she said, her voice changing from sorrow to anger. "And how could I unless you explained it to me?"

David considered this and shook his head. Life had dropped him to his knees, and the view was very different now. *A full night spent on a park bench is much different from that same night on a rooftop,* he thought. His innocence had been replaced by a harsh maturity. *Things are different now. I'm different.*

"Just because I didn't experience what you experienced doesn't mean I'm not here for you," she said and began to cry.

"I'm sorry," he repeated, unable to say anything more. He was just trying to breathe.

"Oh David," she squealed and hurried out of the kitchen, shutting the front door behind her.

I'm sorry, Lindsey, he thought, and began to weep mournfully—while gasping for air.

⊡ ⊡ ⊡ ⊡

The following night, David sat for supper with his mom and Craig.

"I have a job interview this week," Betty told her boys proudly.

"Good for you, Ma," Craig said, reaching for the large bowl of pasta.

"Your dad never wanted me to work, so I've never been on an interview. I'm a little nervous."

"You'll do great, Ma," David said. "It's about time you got out there and lived for yourself."

The woman smiled gratefully.

"When are you going to tell me what it was like over there?" Craig blurted to David, changing the subject. "I've been asking for a week and you..."

Betty slapped Craig's arm, stopping him.

"It's okay, Ma," David said and took a deep breath. "It sucked pretty bad I guess."

Craig slid to the edge of his seat. "Yeah, I know that. But what happened when you first..."

David's mind began to drift. He couldn't help it. His breathing quickened and beads of sweat formed on his brow. Aware of his lack of concentration and the fact that he couldn't stop squirming, he eventually stood and cleared his throat. "I need to use the bathroom," he said and hurried out of the kitchen.

David rushed to the bathroom and closed the door behind him. He splashed cold water on his face and then stared deeply into the mirror. "What is wrong with me?" he asked his frightened reflection. "Dear God, what in the hell is wrong with me?"

Avoiding any further conversation, David left the bathroom and sat in the living room recliner. He threw on the TV and, while Craig and his mom gave him his space, worked on calming his breathing. In desperate need of peace, he decided, *Sleep, and lots of it, is probably best*. It took nearly an hour, but he finally nodded off in the recliner.

Suddenly, David flew from the chair and opened his mouth to yell for help. He didn't. Instead, he fell into a heap and began to cry. While his sweaty, trembling hands covered his face, he tried to catch his breath. He thought about telling Craig or his mother to call for an ambulance. *No*, he thought, *no hospital*. He climbed back into the chair. *Am I going crazy, or is it some disease spreading through my body?*

Minutes later, when the cruel wave had completely washed over him, he sat up to face another long bout with insomnia. It was becoming a nightly routine for him. He felt so alone.

¤ ¤ ¤ ¤

Halfway across Gooseberry Island, Lindsey lay in bed staring out her window into the star-filled sky. *How could I have felt so much closer to you when you were half-way around the world?* she asked David in her mind. *And now you're only a few miles away, but you might as well be on Mars.* She shook her head, breaking the first tears free. *I miss you like crazy, and I have to believe that you miss me too.* On the verge of sobbing, she watched as the North Star flickered brightly. *Don't you still see what I see, David?* she asked in her mind. *Don't you still want us?* She wept like a child.

◻ ◻ ◻ ◻

The following afternoon, David found himself in his own trusted physician's office. Dr. Lauermann was a tanned, well-conditioned medicine man who was easy to talk to. "There's no evidence of heart trauma," Dr. Lauermann reported. "It's probably just anxiety."

"Just?" David asked, surprised. David was falling apart and felt ready for tears. He thought about his old friend, Coley. *I need to go see him.*

◻ ◻ ◻ ◻

A half hour later, David and Coley sat in the gleaming rag top. "Are you sure you're not going to march in the parade?" Coley asked. "The whole island wants to give you and Max a hero's welcome home."

David shook his head. "Not a chance in hell." He looked at Coley. "Did they already ask Max?"

Coley nodded and then grinned. "He said the same exact thing."

David nodded.

"So what's eating at you?" Coley asked.

David opened his mouth to answer but couldn't. He realized, *Coley will never understand.* He looked at his friend. "I have to go," he said.

Coley shook his head. "I'm here for you, you know," he said.

"I know," David said, "and I appreciate it." *And if I ever need pointers on picking up girls, you'll be the first one I come see*, he thought, smiling.

Coley nodded and jumped out of the Mustang.

It's Captain Eli who I need to see, David thought.

◻ ◻ ◻ ◻

A half hour later, David was standing on the bow of *Serendipity* with Captain Eli.

"I don't know what it is, Captain Eli. I feel so different now. There's nothing really wrong, nothing going on, but I'm down. I'm always down and"—he shook his head—"when I'm not, I feel like I'm having a heart attack."

"You need counseling, David. I mean, my God, from the letter you sent me, there's some pretty heavy stuff you need to process before you can get beyond Afghanistan." He looked into his friend's eyes. "You can only carry so much weight, David, before you break your back."

David inhaled deeply. "But I was trained for everything that happened over there."

Captain Eli reached into his wallet and pulled out a business card. He handed the card to David. "His name's Brad Perry. I've been seeing him for years." Captain Eli shrugged. "What can it hurt?" he asked.

David looked at the card. Without thinking, he pulled out his wallet and slid it in. *For years?* he thought. *What can it help?*

A few golden nuggets of wisdom later, David headed back for the Mustang—feeling as lost as ever.

◻ ◻ ◻ ◻

Surrendering to grief and despair, it was as if Denis Wood was forfeiting the rest of his God-given days on earth. Lindsey wished she could help him, but she'd tried everything she could think of. His scars were deep and the wounds beneath them dark and festering.

Weeks had already turned into months, and he was still at the VA Hospital, still cut off from her and the rest of the world.

The bloody nose and black eye were long gone when Lindsey finally went to see him. "Are you ever going to get out of here, or are you planning to stay forever?" she asked him.

He could barely look at her. "Seems it might be best for everyone if I stay locked up."

"I disagree," she said, and her hard tone forced him to look up.

"I...I..." He couldn't articulate his feelings into words.

She took a seat at the edge of his bed and peered into his eyes. "Dad, I understand. It's okay."

"How is it okay, Lindsey?" he asked, almost at a scream. "What kind of father hits his daughter...the person he loves most in this world?" He shook his sorrowful head. "You've been there for me every step of the way, and it hasn't been a fun trip...for either of us." He pointed to her eye. "And how do I repay you? I..."

"You didn't mean it," she interrupted.

"What difference does that make?"

"All the difference in the world, Dad. You have PTSD, and I understand that. If you had diabetes, would I get angry at you when your sugar got low?"

"So it's okay for me to slap you around when I don't have my wits about me?"

"Not at all!" she answered defiantly. She looked at him and softened her tone. "We obviously need to come up with a better strategy, but you need to let go of your guilt for this. You need to forgive yourself." She grabbed his hands and kissed his forehead. "Because I've already forgiven you."

He opened his mouth to reply but couldn't. Instead, he started to cry. At first, it was a few tears that he tried to conceal. And then he began to sob, harder than Lindsey had ever seen him. The pain was so intense, it was just oozing out of him.

She held onto his hands and cried hard right along with him. "We'll be okay, Dad," she whimpered. "Everything's going to be okay."

In truth, she knew that their relationship had been reduced to small talk, Boston Red Sox statistics and an occasional visit to a safely selected memory. *But it's something*, she thought. *And he needs to know that he's not alone.*

¤ ¤ ¤ ¤

David had been home for six weeks when he pulled into the market, preparing to locate everything on his mother's grocery list. As he approached the store, he spotted a young teenage boy walking out; he was holding a brown bag. An older man approached the boy and reached out his hand. David gasped and his dizzy mind immediately raced back to Afghanistan and the horrific beating of the young Afghan boy:

> There was movement three hundred yards out on the street below. *Unusual*, David thought. It was a teenage boy, maybe fourteen, carrying a burlap bag and hurrying home before dark. *Never seen him before*, David thought.

> In a flash, a man—a Taliban fighter— jumped out of the shadows and grabbed the boy's arm, pulling him to the street and spilling the contents of his sack. As the teenager yelled for help, another Taliban soldier emerged from the darkness. The boy screamed louder, but not a single soul came to his aid...

It only took a few seconds, but the whole scene played out in sequence in David's mind—both men yelling and slapping the boy as he screamed for help, the slaps turning to a vicious beating until finally the boy was dead. He could almost hear Command say "Negative" again after he asked if he could intervene. He felt the anguish in his soul threatening to overwhelm him, but it was quickly replaced by a burning rage.

His eyes filled with tears, David returned to the present and started for the man in a mad rush. He was three steps from the shocked stranger when reality clicked in. *It's the boy's father*, he realized. *He's...he's okay.*

David's body convulsed. He'd forgotten he was home, and the reality of it slapped him hard in the face.

The man pulled the teenage boy close to him; both of them were frightened by David's sudden charge toward them.

"Sorry," David said, though it sounded more like "Sigh." Trying unsuccessfully to smile at them, he turned on his heels and hurried back to the Mustang.

¤ ¤ ¤ ¤

For the next hour, David sat alone in his car, trying to calm the physical effects of his anxiety. Once he'd reined that in, he spent another two hours beating back the depression that always followed in anxiety's wake.

He wasn't sure whether the abyss existed within his heart or mind, but he knew that he was now filled with a great void—nothingness. There was no light there, only darkness. There was no hope, only despair. In time, he'd learned to embrace the silence, as the screams and whimpers of faceless victims became echoes that returned again and again, pushing the line of madness. Yet, the solitude was relentless, enveloping, merciless. *It would have been better had I never existed*, he thought, fearing another moment more than cashing in and leaving it all behind. *No love*, he thought, *no peace.* His memories were slanted in such thick negativity that his entire past would have been better off erased. *And no one knows I'm dying inside*, he thought, inviting another wave of panic attacks to crash onto the shore of his weary mind.

He closed his eyes tightly and tried to calm the short labored gasps. *Just ride the wave*, he told himself. *Just ride the wave.*

But in another room in his mind, he knew that even if he rode that wave—and didn't crack his skull on all the rocks beneath him—he'd have to take the ride again and again. It didn't take long before the jagged rocks seemed like the more merciful option.

□ □ □ □

Enough time had passed for Lindsey to realize David was not coming after her. *He's obviously in a lot of pain*, she thought, *and doesn't want to burden anyone with it.* She shook her head. *But I care way too much about him to let him go through this alone.*

With Craig's permission, she slammed David's front door behind her and marched through the living room into the kitchen. "Don't you dare play the coward with me, David McClain," she shouted before even reaching the room.

As she expected, David had been staring out the kitchen window into nothingness. With tear-filled eyes, his head snapped up. "Don't you ever call me that word...ever!"

She stared at him for a few long moments before her heart softened. "Then go ahead, tell me that you don't want to see me anymore and I'll leave you alone forever."

He looked at her with tormented eyes but didn't say a word.

"But you can't, can you?" she said, her entire insides starting to tremble.

"It's not you," he vowed. "It's me. I'm just not..."

"Don't you dare feed me that tired line! I spent a year praying for you...writing letters and wishing for us to..." She stopped, trying in vain to contain her emotions.

His face looked panicked, as his mind obviously spiraled out of control to gather the right words. "I don't have the words," he said in less than a whisper.

"After the first time I came here, I thought for sure you'd chase after me," she said. "I'm not stupid, David. I realize something happened over there that has you all twisted up. But I also thought that once you saw my face, you'd..." She stopped again and began to cry.

David placed his hand on hers. She started to pull away, but he stopped her, intertwining their fingers. "Lindsey, please...please don't say anything until I finish. Just hear me out. Okay?"

"Okay," she said, her tears threatening to flood her face.

He took a few deep breaths. "I've given this a lot of thought, and I want you to know that I've never lied to you...and I don't plan to now." He shook his head. "I'm so messed up right now, Lindsey, I can't even explain it." He could barely hold eye contact with her. "I really hope we can be together someday...more than you can ever imagine. But I'm just not ready yet. I...I need to heal," he stuttered.

She took a deep breath and held it.

"Torn isn't even the word for what I'm feeling over this," he babbled on. "The last thing I want to do is hurt either of us."

"I don't think we have to say goodbye, though," she said, feeling the panic of desperation creep into her soul. "Don't you remember the night we shared on that bench?"

His eyes grew even more distant. "I really wish things were different," he said, "that life didn't have to be so difficult." He shrugged. "Time will tell, I guess."

"You guess?" She returned his shrug to him, perturbed.

"Lindsey, I don't know what the future holds, but I do know that I don't want to destroy any chance we might have at it...just because I might not be ready for it yet." He grimaced. "I need time to find myself, okay?"

Lindsey, the child of a PTSD victim, shook her head. "You don't have to find yourself, David. You just have to remember who you are...who you've always been."

He nodded, tears streaming down his face.

Lindsey took a deep breath and surrendered. "David, I've told you the way that I feel for you and what I want for us. That's all I can do. The rest is in your hands." She peered into his dull eyes. "I can only hope that you'll think of me every day, as I will you. I hope a lot of things, David." She paused to collect herself. "Most of all, I hope the day will come when Afghanistan is behind you and we can fall in love all over again and catch up on all the things we've missed." Mimicking him, she shrugged. "Maybe you're right. I guess time will tell." She pulled her hand away from his and felt her heart rip clean out of her chest. "Until then, you'll be in my thoughts," she whispered.

"I'm so sorry, Lindsey." He sobbed, his shoulders rocking.

"I love you, David," she said and, with one final attempt, grabbed his chin and forced eye contact between them. "Now tell me you don't want to see me and I'll leave you alone," she whispered.

As he looked at her, Lindsey could clearly see the anguish in his eyes.

"You can't, can you?" she said, hopefully.

His tears continued to leak down his cheeks. "I don't want to see you...for now," he said, and turned his eyes away from hers.

It felt as though someone had just slugged her in the gut. "Okay." She gasped and ran out of the house crying harder than she'd ever cried before.

Long after Lindsey had run out of the kitchen, David remained catatonic—until he grabbed a drinking glass off the counter and threw it onto the floor where it broke into a hundred pieces. Enraged, he began smashing everything he could get his hands on in the kitchen. At the end of the violent outburst, he collapsed to the floor and began to weep. With his head in both hands, he screamed, "I love you, too, Lindsey."

Day turned into dusk and, like most nights, just beyond the sobs and sniffles the world turned quiet and black.

¤ ¤ ¤ ¤

After four or five weeks of self-imposed solitary confinement—a punishment filled with death-defying panic attacks and long, treacherous tunnels of depression—David decided to reach out to the men he had served with. *They're the only ones who can relate*, he thought. *And I wonder how they're doing...really doing?*

David's first quest was to find Max and talk to him. Since he also lived on Gooseberry Island, David figured, *It should be easy enough*. But visits to his home and multiple telephone messages went unanswered. Max proved to be more elusive than the Taliban.

He's obviously avoiding me, David thought, and it pissed him off—making him feel strangely abandoned by his friend.

"From what I've heard, Max has been drinking pretty hard," Coley reported.

"What about his son, Max Jr.?" David asked.

"I'm sure he sees him," Coley said, "but a few guys I know say that Max has been closing the bars every night."

"If you see him, tell him I've been trying to get in touch with him," David said, disgustedly.

"Sure thing, *if* I see him."

David nodded, thinking, *I get it. It's probably too hard for Max to see me and kick up a bunch of bad memories that he's trying to drink away.*

¤ ¤ ¤ ¤

After tracking Nathan Michaels down on Facebook and getting his cell number, David picked up the telephone and dialed.

"Hey brother, what's going on?" Nate asked, excited for the call.

"Nothin' much," David lied. "I was calling to ask you the same thing."

"I'm still in," he said.

"Really? I thought you'd get out with the rest of us when we got back."

"Where else can I go? Have you tried finding work yet?"

David shook his head. "Not yet. I'm still on break, trying to get my head on straight."

"Well, good luck with the job search once you get started. There's nothing out there, and here's a news flash for you...nobody gives a damn that we can navigate mountainous terrain or stop the bleeding on an open abdomen wound."

"That bad, huh?"

"Everybody I've talked to is out of work. And it doesn't matter how many medals they won over there." He paused. "You okay, Davey?"

"I've been better. You?"

"Same. I still haven't been able to see my boys." By their senior year of high school, Nate had gotten his girlfriend, Lois, pregnant and decided to do the right thing by making her his wife. In a valiant effort to save what was already lost, they had another baby boy. Things quickly went south down misery lane. Nate tried to stick it out, but in the end everyone was suffering. It was a painful exit.

Dillon was now five. Bryan was three. He adored them both, but being powerless with the courts, his visitation had been sporadic at best. Nate suffered terribly from having failed them as a father.

Poor Nate, David thought. *He actually cares more about his kids than he does himself.* In Afghanistan, he'd watched Nate walk through mental hell for his boys.

"I'd rather spend the rest of my life fighting in Afghanistan than not see my boys on a regular basis," Nate added, his voice choked with emotion. For him, the separation from his children wasn't a choice.

"What does your lawyer say?" David asked, forgetting his own hell for the moment.

"He says I shouldn't push things right now with my boys; instead, I should look at the big picture." Nate sighed heavily. "The whole thing's been a nightmare."

"That sucks," David said, shaking his head.

"Oh, but it gets better," Nate said. "Last week, I was walking through Home Depot when I heard a young boy call out for his father. I never even bothered to look up. The boy's voice called out again. And that's when I turned to find Dillon standing in front of me, alongside some strange man. The wrongness of it actually took my breath away and nearly dropped me to my knees. The guy caught it and quickly extended his hand, introducing himself as Jack. He told me that he was a friend of my ex-wife's." Nate paused. "I don't remember shaking the guy's hand, but I guess I did. Talk about feeling lost..." Nate stopped again to take in the air he needed to finish the story. "There was my son, standing beside a stranger instead of me. After I gave Dillon a kiss, I told him to be a good boy and to listen to Jack." Nate tried to clear his throat. "My five-year-old smiled at me and then walked out of the store with a guy I've never even seen before." He took in another deep breath. "Now tell me that's not screwed up."

"It is, Nate," David agreed, quietly. "It's definitely screwed up."

There was another long pause. "But enough about my troubles," Nate said. "What's going on with you?"

"Like I said...same, same," David said, deciding not to burden his brother with more weight.

"You sure?" Nate said, lowering his volume. "Because I can't tell you how many sleepless nights I've already spent listening to a teenage boy screaming for help in my head."

David immediately covered the telephone receiver and began to cry.

"Davey?" Nate asked. "You still there?"

¤ ¤ ¤ ¤

Lindsey pulled her car into McDonald's drive-thru and placed her order. A minute later, one bagged lunch was received through the window and paid for. She pulled the car up a few feet, stopping to check that the order was right. When she looked up, Tonia was standing right in front of the car. *Oh crap*, Lindsey thought, and instinctively attempted to avoid her old friend. But it was too late. The woman waved and started toward the car. Lindsey cursed under her breath and tried to fix her unruly hair in the rearview. *Damn*, she thought, shaking her head at the lack of makeup. Tonia's face suddenly appeared in the window. Lindsey took a big breath and put on her best smile. She rolled down the driver's side window.

"Hey stranger," Tonia said, "there've been rumors that you actually fell off the face of the earth. And to tell you the truth, I was starting to believe them."

"Oh no, not at all," Lindsey said, forcing a smile. She was at a loss for words.

Tonia smiled, too kindly. "We haven't seen you at the Thursday Night Club for more than a month. Is there any particular reason you've been avoiding us?"

Lindsey shook her head and blushed, embarrassed.

"Good, then we'll see you this Thursday?"

"Sure," Lindsey said. "I'll be there."

"I hope so, Lindsey. We've really missed you." As Tonia turned to leave, she offered a knowing wink.

Lindsey returned the gesture along with another fake smile and then sat for a while parked. *I just don't want all the questions about David*, she thought, eating a handful of hot fries, *or the man bashing that'll definitely follow.*

◻ ◻ ◻ ◻

On Thursday night, two hours and a half case of wine were already gone before anyone dared to mention David.

"Any word from him?" Sandi finally asked for all of them.

Lindsey shook her head, trying to conceal her pain over it.

"Probably for the best," Ana commented, eliciting sour looks from everyone.

Tonia placed her hand on Lindsey's arm. "If David comes around, then great..."

"...but you need to come out of hiding, Linds," Courtney blurted.

"Yeah, and get back in the game," Christine added.

They all nodded, doing their best to be supportive.

"You're right," Lindsey said. "You're all right." With the phoniest smile she'd ever worn, she downed another glass of wine.

◻ ◻ ◻ ◻

A few long weeks passed when David decided to take the ferry to the mainland and see the ranger he respected most: Lieutenant Kevin Menker. Kevin had joined the Army, became a ranger and served for six years with pride and honor. Decorated during the war, he'd returned to Fall River to start a new life. As a first step, he'd recently graduated from the local police academy. They met at a bar to swap stories from overseas.

"I haven't told anyone about what we experienced," David told him, sipping his draft beer.

"And why would you?" Kevin asked, guzzling his own draft. "No one would understand anyway." He looked at David. "You having a tough time getting past it?"

David nodded.

"Me, too," Kevin admitted, shocking David. "There are nights I can't sleep at all. And I've had my fair share of nightmares...so real that I wake up ready to kill someone." He shook his head. "And I feel really depressed sometimes."

"Me, too," David said, thrilled that he wasn't alone.

"But even if it got worse," Kevin said, "I'd never admit to it."

"What?" David blurted, surprised again.

"That's right. They'd have me bounced off the force in a heartbeat if they knew." He nodded. "And if I'm to have a shot at a normal life—a wife, kids, a house—then I need to keep it together or at least pretend I have it together." He shrugged. "I'd rather suffer than lose my job."

David's heart rate increased and his breathing became shallow. His reunion with Kevin was awakening some really bad memories, playing out in feelings rather than thoughts. A strong adrenaline rush was followed by a brutal panic attack. David sat quietly at the bar and concealed it. "How's police work after going through what we went through?" David managed to ask with an even voice.

Kevin shook his head. "Actually, it's strange, but I feel normal when the adrenaline's pumping hard. It's when I'm sitting quietly on the couch that I feel like I'm going to lose my mind or crawl out of my skin." He looked at David. "How 'bout you come with me some night on a ride along and see for yourself?"

"You serious?"

Kevin nodded. "Let's shoot for tomorrow night."

◻ ◻ ◻ ◻

David arrived at the police station much earlier than he should have and waited in the deserted lobby. *Where are the police when you need them?* he thought, and chuckled to himself.

As the next shift began to arrive, the captain granted David entrance. He was waiting in the corner of the roll call room when Kevin approached. "You ready to ride, brother?"

David nodded, ignoring the mumblings from the other cops. One signed waiver later, David was ready to patrol the mean streets of Fall River, riding shotgun.

After roll call, David and Kevin stepped outside. It was a warm, clear night, with nearly a full moon in the sky. Assigned to Sector Three, four to midnight shift, David jumped in the cruiser, while Kevin conducted a brief equipment check. Once he got into the car, he turned to David. "When it's warm out, the calls are nonstop," he said. "Be prepared for a busy night." He grinned. "Let's get to work."

David buckled up. The radio squelched once before Kevin spoke into it. "Two-zero-three to three-six-four," he said. "Clear for calls." As they pulled out of the station lot, he turned to David. "I'm starving. You?"

"No," David said, "my stomach's been giving me trouble lately." He then sat back, as Kevin proceeded to their first stop of the night—a fast food drive-thru. *This is going to be an easy ride*, David thought.

Not three minutes into the shift, the radio began to call out and never stopped—each time beckoning for people in trouble, or others who just thought they were. "Three-six-four to two-zero-five—an elderly woman having difficulty breathing..." David expected that they'd be off in a flash.

Kevin smiled. "That's not our sector," he said, while one of his brother officers responded to administer the medical assistance needed.

After placing his fast food order, Kevin looked at David for an extended moment. "How you feeling right now?" he asked.

Not good at all, David thought, but said, "Looking forward to this ride."

"Cool," Kevin said and swallowed down his dinner within minutes.

Driving past a few of the infamous bars in the city, Kevin looked at David and grinned. "Ever been in a bar fight?" he joked.

David chuckled. "Yeah, against a bunch of navy guys. And as I remember it, you and Billy Brodeur started the whole thing."

Kevin laughed.

"Hey, have you heard anything from Billy?" David asked.

Kevin's eyes lit up. "Billy Brodeur? Man, that kid's so tough it isn't even funny." He shook his head. "One night, after we got back from overseas, I watched him beat the hell out of a night club bouncer twice his size. When I finally jumped in to..."

The radio called out, "Three-six-four to two-zero-three, see a female party at Border City Mills Apartments on Weaver, car break." Kevin turned the cruiser around and they were en-route to their first call.

Upon arrival, a young girl stood beside her compact car, trembling from nerves. The car's rear window had been smashed in. "Anything missing?" Kevin asked. She shook her head. Kevin surveyed the damage and then began the paperwork on malicious damage to a motor vehicle. While he wrote, David monitored the heavy radio traffic. The calls were coming in one after the next. *I can only imagine what a heat wave might bring*, David thought. As adrenaline rushed through his bloodstream filling him with anxiety, he also thought, *This ride along might have been a bad idea.*

David was still trying to calm his breathing when Kevin finished his paperwork. "Now, where were we?" Before David could answer, his face lit up again. "Oh, yeah, good fights. Anyway, Billy beat that poor bouncer senseless, and it took me and a few other guys to make him stop." Kevin looked at David for a reaction.

David shrugged. "We're wired the way we're wired, I guess?"

Kevin nodded. "True, and some of us are wired wrong."

The radio called out again. "Twelve-year-old female, no pants, standing outside of Castle Court on

North Main. Her father threw her out..." David waited for Kevin to punch the gas.

He shook his head. "Not our sector."

"Fogland Bar, the corner of Columbia and South Main Streets. Two males fighting..." and several cruisers were dispatched to quell the violence.

The radio squelched again and a brother officer called for backup from the Sunset Hill housing project. David looked to Kevin. He nodded. "That's a domestic dispute," and nonchalantly returned to finish his paperwork.

David was amazed. *To Kevin, this is just another night at the office.* It was obvious that he cared, but David honestly couldn't fathom what it might take to rattle him. And then David realized that he also felt some strange comfort in the adrenaline. *Kevin's right. At least the anxiety makes sense when there's something causing it.*

While they drove up one street and down the next, their conversation thankfully covered subjects other than fighting. It was 2000 hours, or 8:00 p.m., when they were dispatched to a motor vehicle accident, negative injuries. The rotary blue lights illuminated the night when they arrived to find two females engaged in a heated argument. Kevin jumped out and, although he possessed both the presence and ability to force his will on most people he encountered, he chose a different tactic. He quickly de-escalated the situation, while treating both parties with respect.

Once Kevin had calmed everyone down, he surveyed the scene and quickly determined the party at fault. Evidently, the pizza delivery girl was checking house addresses when she drove head-on into another vehicle. Kevin cited the responsible party: a person who now became a harsh critic of Kevin's chosen profession.

While Kevin did his job, David continued to monitor the radio. It was more exciting than he'd expected. As sirens wailed over the radio, an officer reported, "Three-six-four, be advised, coming in with a lockup."

Another, "Eastern Avenue, out-of-control child, parents requesting that he be removed from the premises..."

Then, as they awaited the arrival of a tow truck, a police officer on the other side of the city was involved in a foot pursuit. From the fragments of information David could make out, two females had stolen a brown Honda Accord in Corky Row and while trying to maneuver through the narrow streets, had hit a pole and fled on foot. As David slid to the edge of his seat, a panting officer offered a description of the suspects. Seconds later, his backup arrived, and both parties were successfully apprehended.

While Kevin chuckled at David's enthusiasm, David realized that his ex-patrol leader had chosen to submerge himself in a world of organized chaos.

At the end of the shift, without even slowing down near a donut shop, they reported back to the police station to type up all the reports—enough paper to alarm any Green Peace fundamentalist.

"Too bad for you it was a quiet night," Kevin concluded, and David waited for his friend's laughter. It never came.

Kevin's serious, David thought. *For him, this was a quiet night. No one got stabbed or shot to death. There were no rapes to investigate. Life didn't get much better.*

On the ferry ride home, David's head was spinning from the *quiet* night. And then the same question arose in his mind: *Where are the police when you need them?*

He now knew the answer: *In some dark alley, or any place you don't want to be. And that's why you called for one of them in the first place.* David shook his head. *Kevin can keep it.*

And then it started—shallow, labored breathing; a pounding heart and light head—another dreaded panic attack. *It's the price I have to pay for tonight,* he told himself, and began to ride the sadistic roller coaster once again.

Chapter 8

□ □ □ □

"Chivalry is dead," Lindsey complained.

Courtney chuckled. "Tough commute this morning, or is the dating life starting to get to you?"

Hunched behind the office partition, Walter Brady, the summer recreation director, eavesdropped on the latest man-bashing session and smiled.

"Dating life? What dating life?" Lindsey asked. "Most guys only want one thing today, and they think that a trip through the drive-thru should be more than enough to get it."

Courtney laughed again. "So the commute wasn't bad, huh?" She shook her head. "I'm so glad I don't have to deal with being single anymore."

With a sigh, Lindsey fired up her computer and collapsed into another depressing Monday. "I'm all set with men," she mumbled, still feeling cheated over not being with David. "I can't wait for this summer to be over."

It wasn't ten o'clock when Lindsey returned from the fax machine to find a white envelope covering her keyboard. She picked it up. It was sealed, and there was no writing on it. She looked around. *No one's watching*, she thought, and tore it open.

Juliet,

I dreamed about you last night. We were together, locked in each other's eyes. You smiled at me, and I couldn't help but pull you close and kiss you. You moaned once and the rest of the world disappeared. And then we made love, without ever removing a stitch of clothing. The glances, kisses and touching were so intense. I'd never felt that close to anyone. It was as if I experienced your soul, your very essence far beyond the physical world, and I finally discovered what it means to make true love. And then we undressed...

I dreamed about you last night, without ever closing my eyes.

Romeo

The note had been typed and wasn't signed.

Lindsey took in the oxygen she'd forgotten to breathe. The words had touched her soul. *David?* she wondered, but quickly dismissed the thought. She looked around again. The sounds of cogs busy at work filled the large room. She peered over the partition. "Walter, did you see anyone drop off an envelope at my desk?"

He shook his head. "I haven't seen anyone come by here. Why?"

She half-shrugged. "Oh, nothing. I think someone might have delivered it to my desk by accident." With a smile, she disappeared back behind the portable wall.

◻ ◻ ◻ ◻

The day grew wings and flew by. Lindsey asked everyone in the office about the mysterious envelope. No one knew anything. Even Courtney, the woman who knew everything that went on at work, was at a loss.

Lindsey wasn't two feet from her car when she spotted another white envelope tucked under her windshield wipers. Her heart raced as she plucked it free. There was no denying it this time. The name *Lindsey* had been typed on the front. Her trembling fingers hurried to open the prize.

> My Juliet,
>
> I've pictured you and I walking down a wet cobblestone street in Europe (who cares where). It's just past dusk. The streetlights have come on. We walk past several cafes, past other couples talking and laughing. With a quick look at each other, though, we smile and silently decide not to join them. Instead, we hurry into a shop for a stick of bread, a wedge of cheese, some assorted fruit and a bottle of wine. Hand-in-hand, we hurry back to our little bungalow located just above the busy street and strip each other of our clothes. Dinner takes place while we make love, the windows to our

refuge left open to allow in the breezes
and the happy conversations of foreign tongues.

Will you meet me there?

Romeo

Lindsey gasped and held the invitation to her chest.
David? she thought again, but scolded herself for even
allowing the thought.

Walter approached the car parked alongside hers.
"Hey, did you end up finding out who that envelope
belonged to?" he asked.

Lindsey's eyes swung up to meet him. "I think so,"
she whispered. "I'm pretty sure it was meant for me."
An excited squeak accompanied the word *me*.

Walter nodded and smiled. "See you in the morning," he said and jumped into his Chevy Camaro.

"Oh, I'll be here," she whispered. "I'll definitely be
here."

¤ ¤ ¤ ¤

Lindsey arrived at work earlier than ever, only to find
an unaddressed envelope sitting on her keyboard. She
looked around. There was no one there and no evidence
that anyone had been there earlier than she. *Strange*,
she thought.

Juliet,

You light a few candles. I pour us each
a glass of wine. No TV, just music—
dreamy music that puts a tantric

rhythm in our heads. I play with the
straps on your camisole as we move
together, standing, swaying. Our lips
meet, my hands are now in your hair.
We pass our wine glasses to the table,
barely. I press myself against you and
you breathe hard into my ear. We look
at each other, but there is no need for
words. Minds whirling, hands sweep-
ing, lips touching everywhere, time
eludes us as we feel the softness of the
carpet on our knees, our backs...

And then we make love without ever
losing eye contact.

Romeo

She felt faint. "That's it," she said to no one. "I have
to know who this is."

¤ ¤ ¤ ¤

Courtney and Lindsey spent the entire morning sifting
through ambiguous clues and listing possible suspects.

Walter spent the same time watching them and
sharpening his next arrow.

Lindsey hadn't been away from her desk for five
minutes before another letter appeared. With Courtney
over her shoulder, she tore into it.

Juliet,

The most important thing to me is
to enter into a union with a woman
who will become the second half of a

whole, someone who will allow me to
love her without restraint and love me
with the same effortless passion—you.

Romeo

Even Courtney broke out into a sweat. As the two
shared a moment of breathless silence, Walter walked
up behind them and handed Lindsey a single rose.
"You," he whispered.

Lindsey's knees wobbled once, and she nearly went
down.

Walter Brady was a mysterious man with looks that
were extremely kind on the optic nerve. Tall, with mas-
culine features, he had green eyes and perfect teeth. He
was well built, bold and charming—the perfect catch.
Lindsey swallowed hard.

◻ ◻ ◻ ◻

They began flirting, hard. Every secret email made
Lindsey feel like she was alive again.

What if I don't live up to your expectations? she replied.

*There's no way you can't live up to them because they
don't exist,* he countered.

If we could have one date, what would you want to do?
she asked.

Turn it into fifty-five years, he responded, and then
turned up the heat:

Juliet,

I constantly fantasize about being with you.

Romeo

This guy's too good to be true, Lindsey thought and
sent him another note. *When can we go out?*

◻ ◻ ◻ ◻

It was a Monday night. They were halfway through dinner when Lindsey reached across the table and grabbed Walter's hand. "I've been walking around smiling a lot more lately. Thank you for that."

He nodded.

"Where do you think this will lead?" she asked, surprising them both.

He squeezed her hand. "The clock started the moment I saw you," he said.

Lindsey studied him and shook her head. "Why do you seem so perfect?" she asked.

He chuckled. "Not quite," he said, shrugging. "I'm married."

"You're what?" It took a few moments for the first layer of shock to allow the truth in. "But you emailed me all those things," she muttered. "How could...?"

Walter stared her straight in the eye. "And I meant every word, Lindsey."

And it hit her. Walter Brady was deceitful and selfish, traits revealed only when the sun went in behind the clouds. Lindsey was heartbroken, though it wasn't Walter who caused it. *I'm with the wrong Romeo*, she realized, and rage quickly replaced sorrow. "You piece of garbage," she hissed and stood up from the table. "You think you can just play with people and..."

Walter rose to meet her. As he tried to quiet her tone with his growing pupils, he reached for her hand. "Lindsey, please. We don't have to..."

"No!" she yelled, slapping his hand away. "You mark my words. You'll get yours!" She tossed her linen napkin in his face and stormed away.

On the way out, David's face appeared in her mind. *I was with the wrong Romeo*, she told herself again.

◻ ◻ ◻ ◻

It was midday. David was perched on a barstool at Bobby's Lounge. The place was dimly lit. Bobby LePage, a husky, unshaven barkeep, was wiping down glasses behind his bar. A talk show, dancing in and out of static, was on the tube above the bar's long mirror. The clock read 12:45 p.m. The place was empty. David was slouched over, inebriated but free from anxiety attacks.

"Want to tell me about it?" Bobby finally asked David.

David slammed his glass on the bar, making Bobby's eyes go wide. "Everybody's a therapist," David hissed. "Why don't we just talk about another drink, okay?"

Bobby shook his head and poured another one, leaving the bottle and swiping David's twenty-dollar bill off the bar. "Knock yourself out, partner."

David gulped the whiskey, while Bobby returned to his glasses. "Have you seen a guy by the name of Max Essington in here?" he asked.

Bobby shook his head. "Sure, I know him. But he's not allowed back in my joint," he said, angrily.

"Why not?"

"Because he's a troublemaker and a deadbeat who won't pay his tab." He shook his head. "And stupid me, I let him run it up because he was just back from the war."

"Deadbeat?" David asked at nearly a roar. "Max Essington is a war hero, and I was there to witness it!"

Bobby stopped wiping down glasses and leaned his chest against the bar. "Really? Then maybe you'd like to pay that *war hero's* bar tab?"

David shook his head. "When I see him, I'll tell him to square up with you."

"Yeah, you do that."

David poured himself another shot and downed it.

¤ ¤ ¤ ¤

An hour later, David slid into the Mustang's driver's seat and started the ignition. There was a pile of mail sitting on the passenger seat. He picked it up and, through hazy eyes, sifted through it. There was an envelope sent from the Disabled American Veterans. He ripped it open and began to read. "They're looking for donations," he said aloud and tore up the letter angrily, throwing the pieces onto the floor.

"I've given enough!" he screamed and threw the shifter into drive. While the first drops of rain hit the windshield, he pulled out of the parking lot and swerved into traffic.

¤ ¤ ¤ ¤

Lindsey sat on the park bench and looked around. Gooseberry Island had always been a magical place where tourists flocked to in the summer. The community was still small enough to be quaint. Lacking any industry or technology, the stars always seemed to shine brighter here. As a result, many dreams were cast from the water's edge, where Earth met heaven.

Lindsey tried hard to remember the details of that magical night with David, to relive those same feelings that made her feel like she was walking on air.

But I can't feel anything anymore, she thought.

Gray, swollen clouds were stacked high and wide, threatening the world below. *So much for dreams coming true*, she told herself.

Just then, a hurricane of wailing winds launched their attack, pounding the shore with one combination after the next. Tiny tornadoes, whirlpools of ocean water, were hovering across the sea. With warning signs of danger all around her, Lindsey remained seated and watched. And then the downpour came, hard and fast.

With sheets of rain draped over her face, Lindsey fought back a hurricane of dark emotions. *I guess I can feel something*, she thought, and began to cry for all that could have been.

◻ ◻ ◻ ◻

David was enduring an agonizing struggle back to normality. Along the way, he'd learned, *Not all war wounds are visible, nor are they all suffered on the battlefield. War's a state of mind, and there's no way a man can live in two worlds at one time. Eventually, there has to be a truce.*

Tragically, his brother, Max Essington, was never able to find that truce.

No one questioned that Max was having a tough time trying to heal. While in Afghanistan, he'd tried to patch up one of the many local kids who'd come across a roadside bomb and never survived the meeting. David knew that the gory memory had haunted Max terribly.

Upon their return, the rangers parted ways. The best explanation was that it actually became less painful to avoid faces that only served as reminders of a difficult time—no matter how much the people were loved behind those faces. Max was never alone in his struggle, perhaps the greatest tragedy to come out of the war. Not one of them had to suffer alone. Yet, that's all any of them did.

David's comrade eventually switched from alcohol to heavy drugs, surrendering to any means that might dim the nightmare and bring relief from his demons. Max fought desperately to beat them back. His son was only five when those demons finally won. When the police responded to Max's home, they found him cold, fresh track marks peppered up and down his thirsty arm. Although Max had escaped, he left a child behind—a son—Max Jr.

A coward's escape, David thought, when he first got the news. When the truth settled in, though, David wept like a child who'd just abandoned all hope. To him, family wasn't only a birth rite, contingent upon a name or blood type. Family was chosen. *And I just lost a brother*, he thought, grieving hard for it.

◻ ◻ ◻ ◻

David stepped into Rosini and Rosini Funeral Home. Family, friends and brothers at arms filled the place. The air was cool, with a nauseating scent of carnations, mixed with cheap perfume and cologne. Soft music played from hidden speakers. Rows of folding chairs were set up to face the casket, creating an audience for Max's final show. *He would have really hated this*, David thought, keeping his pain locked tightly behind a thick door—for the time being.

Overstuffed chairs lined the left wall, creating a receiving line for immediate family. Although old ash-tray stands—relics of the past—were spread throughout the home, smoking was only permitted downstairs. Evidently, it was one practice that was still good for business. Gold wallpaper offset the paisley print carpeting with extra padding. It felt like you were walking with a bounce. Anthony Rosini, a third-generation undertaker and second-rate greeter, wore a smile that attempted empathy. *Poor attempt*, David thought.

Family and friends signed their names in a book that no one would ever read. At the podium, there was a stack of prayer cards with Max's picture on the front and the Lord's Prayer on the back. Everyone took one while waiting in line to pay their respects at the casket. David took a deep breath and marched off to the polished mahogany boat in which his friend was preparing to sail off to eternity.

David kneeled at the casket and offered his heartfelt prayers for a brother he was going to miss for the rest of his life. "Thank you for having my back over there, Max," he whispered. "I'll be seeing you soon." He stood and took a seat in the second row.

He watched as some people stood and others kneeled, weeping for a man they admired for his bravery and selfless service. Boxes of tissues were strategically placed throughout the home and were used aplenty. But after the initial shock of seeing their deceased hero and offering their prayers, the gathering became a family reunion. It was a real social event and one that Max wouldn't have minded at all. Knowing Max, he would have never cared for such a morbid ceremony—dressing up a corpse and putting it on public display for a few days.

The casket looked like a square boat in a sea of flowers. The bottom half of the box was covered in an American flag.

David watched as a young boy and his grandmother, a peculiar site, approached the box to pay their respects. The young boy clasped his hands together and closed his eyes, just as he'd clearly been taught. He waited a few moments before slowly opening one eye. His grandmother's thin lips were moving at the speed of light, a ramble of whispered secrets escaping them. The boy closed his eyes again and quietly waited for her to finish.

The priest arrived and spoke of "tragedy and faith and eternal life."

David spent the time remembering his fallen friend and a few of the laughs they'd shared back in Afghanistan.

> As always, David's team was dropped, via deuce and a half, six miles out from camp into "the projects" of South Kabul.
>
> Max was walking point, leading the squad along the safest possible route. As the morning sun hit its zenith, the boys were following up on some local intelligence, sweeping through three locations—two houses and a dilapidated community building. With the help of a translator, three tips produced two different tips but no

suspected Taliban.

After another late and nearly inedible lunch, the team worked its way through the city back toward camp.

"Keep your eyes and ears opened wide boys," Lieutenant Menker said. "The bad guys are just waiting for us to drop our guard and become careless."

David nodded.

"Maybe they're just waiting for us to drop our lunches, so they can enjoy some fine American cuisine," Max joked.

Big Al laughed. "Good point, Maximillian," he called out. "A few dozen dehydrated pork patties might do just as much damage as any firepower we can unleash on them."

Everyone laughed.

"And that's coming from a guy who eats anything that's put in front of him," Billy commented.

"To include the dreaded dehydrated pork patty," Max added.

Everyone laughed more.

As the patrol started back toward camp, David pulled his father's note out of his pants cargo pocket and read it a few times.

When they returned to camp, they showered and grabbed some hot chow. Max asked David, "Want to play cards?"

David shrugged. "Sure, but I'm keeping my clothes on this time," he joked.

"We'll see about that," Max said, laughing.

David heard names being called to visit Max's casket for the final time. He stood and made a beeline for his car. *Max isn't in that wooden box*, he thought. *He could never lay still for that long.* He nodded. *Max is in a better place.*

As the family headed out to the black limo, six pall bearers filled the flower car, and the long convoy headed off to the mausoleum.

◻ ◻ ◻ ◻

While the priest's words echoed off the white marble walls, he offered a brief sermon, blessed the casket with holy water and incense, and then turned the show over to the military contingent. David stood and walked out again. *I'm all set with this dog-and-pony show*, he thought.

David reached his car and looked back toward the cemetery. *I guess that's the funny thing about life*, he thought. *None of us is getting out alive.*

¤ ¤ ¤ ¤

Lindsey checked her Thursday horoscope after dinner to see how close it had come. *Not even close*, she thought. It was a silly game, anyway—allowing herself to believe the good stuff and ignore the bad. She'd learned that thoughts were a powerful thing, and she was still looking for any sign that David would come around.

The Thursday Night Club had just convened when Ana approached Lindsey; her face was troubled. "Did you hear that David's friend, Max, committed suicide?" Ana said.

"Max Essington?" Lindsey asked, holding her breath.

"Yeah, that's David's friend, right?" Christine asked.

"His best friend," Lindsey said, her face bleached white. "How?"

"Drug overdose," Ana reported.

"Oh God, I didn't know," Lindsey squealed, panic filling every cell of her body. "I need to go see David!"

"I thought he didn't want to see you?" Sandi said.

Lindsey shook it off. "David's so messed up right now he doesn't know what he wants." She thought about it. "He's going to need as much support as he can get."

¤ ¤ ¤ ¤

Feeling like his life was folding in on itself, David sat in his Mustang, tipping the half-empty bottle of Vodka to the new vinyl top. He'd wept so hard his chest ached.

Damn you, Max, he thought. *Why didn't you reach out for help? I would have been there for you. I would have...* He sobbed like a child, his shoulders rocking back and forth. He shook his head and put the bottle back to his lips. *Damn you, Max*, he thought again, and took another long gulp.

A half hour later, David staggered into Bobby's Lounge. The other patrons quickly scattered, steering clear of him.

Bobby took one look at him and shook his head. "You're shut off," he said.

"Shut off? Are you nuts?" David argued.

"Look buddy, you've already had enough for the both of us, so why don't you just call a friend and..."

"Because I don't have a friend," David screamed, "that's why!" He shook his head. "And I don't have a girl-friend anymore," he slurred. "I don't have anything..."

Bobby rounded the bar and approached him.

David stood. "Looks like Max's tab will have to go unpaid," he slurred and threw a round-house punch—missing the bartender by a mile and landing on his butt.

"Any other day and you'd be wearing my boot in your backside," Bobby said, "but it's clear to me that no one's gonna do anything to you that you haven't already done to yourself." Bobby extended his hand. "Now get up."

David eventually took the man's hand, sliding onto a nearby chair. "I've lost everything," he whimpered, "...my whole world."

"I'll call you a cab," Bobby said and headed for the telephone behind the bar.

Once he spotted his opening, David sneaked out the door, slid into the driver seat of the Mustang and fired up the ignition. With one eye open, he pulled out of the crowded parking lot.

Halfway through another sappy love ballad, the road's yellow lines began to blur and then disappear. *What the hell?* David thought. There was a loud bang, followed by the sounds of breaking glass and twisting steel. The world outside the windshield appeared to tumble end-over-end. *Whoa...* Everything became hazy and confusing. There was one long hiss, almost as if the motor was breathing a sigh of relief. And then there was silence. A flash of light closed in on itself until there was only a pinpoint leading to complete darkness. David closed his eyes, preparing to greet the afterlife.

¤ ¤ ¤ ¤

David wasn't three miles from his house when instead of being in bed, sleeping—where he should have been—he was soaked in his own blood. The police discovered him at the gruesome scene, hanging onto the bare thread of life. "This is a bad one," someone screamed out, as others frantically worked on sustaining his life. The medical chopper finally touched down, lifted him into the air and carried his fate into the hands of whatever surgeon was on duty.

In short, official reports indicated that David's Mustang was traveling southbound on Route 103 at 1:15 a.m. when it careened out of control and flipped several times. The Mustang, now totaled, rested upon a guardrail with most of its driver's body folded in half on the passenger side floor. While David was suffocating on his teeth and jawbones, nearly ten minutes had elapsed before the accident was reported. Not a soul stopped to help. Finally, at approximately 1:30 a.m., medical personnel arrived on scene. "Too bad people don't stop today and help," the exhausted paramedics complained over the whine of the helicopter's cutting blades.

A preliminary investigation was brief. From the empty vodka bottle, with blood splashed all over it, there was no need to search any deeper for the cause of the accident. Given that it was a convertible, it was a miracle that he hadn't been crushed to death.

◻ ◻ ◻ ◻

Lindsey was surprised to get the call. As she listened in shock, Craig said, "I know you and David haven't seen each other in a while, but he's been in a bad car accident, and he's in critical condition." There was a long pause. "He just got out of surgery, and he's in intensive care." It sounded like a cruel joke. "The nurse says he's not doing well at all," Craig finished. "You need to get here as soon as possible."

Goose bumps covered Lindsey's body, and she burst into tears. It took a few minutes for the shock to wear off before she grabbed her car keys and headed for the door.

Time switched speeds, as a veil of fog was pulled down over everything. Before she knew it, she was speeding down the highway, alternating her thoughts between David and her father. En-route, she picked up the cell phone to ensure that Coley, David's best friend, had been notified. He confirmed he was on his way. The panic in Coley's voice made her drive faster. Before

Lindsey knew it, she was sitting in the hospital parking lot panting like an exhausted dog. As she jumped out of the car, a bolt of fear struck the core of her soul. *David's in trouble and needs help*, she thought and started for the hospital at a sprint.

¤ ¤ ¤ ¤

Craig was the first person Lindsey spotted. He was standing in the hallway, talking with the head nurse. His eyes were red and swollen from crying. Lindsey hurried to him. Craig grabbed for her and wept hard. "David's dying," he sobbed.

Lindsey took his face in both hands. "Well, we'll just see about that," she forced past the lump in her throat.

Craig nodded, and Lindsey let go of his hand to follow a young nurse, a woman who obviously had a difficult time concealing her feelings. As they stopped at a curtained-off room, she whispered, "He's in here." She sighed. "I'm sorry."

Lindsey looked back curiously, but the nurse was gone. She snapped back the curtain and immediately understood why the young lady had apologized. Betty, David's mom, was lying beside a poor soul who might have been vaguely mistaken for a human being. David's body was broken almost beyond repair, his mind already beginning the sequence of shutting down his organs.

As if NASA had decided to create a hideous cyborg, there was a tangled maze of hoses and wires protruding from David's deformed head and swollen face. Black patches of skin were now located where hazel eyes had once been. White gauze covered a nose ten times its normal size. A red, ribbed flex-pipe—inserted into his throat—spewed a steady flow of steam from his taped mouth. Lindsey gasped, realizing, *Without it, David could never breathe*. A white sheet was wrapped tightly around a body that sporadically spasmed. David's left arm hung over the edge of the elevated bed. His hand was bloated and discolored. *He's a terrible mess*, she thought.

Betty looked up, leapt from the bed and rushed toward Lindsey. Lindsey tried to coax her spaghetti legs to meet the heartbroken woman halfway, but they wouldn't move. Lindsey just couldn't help it. For that one moment, she completely lost it. Her shoulders bounced to her heartbreaking sobs. She felt as if she were six again. "No, David," she cried. "Please God..."

Betty wrapped her arms around Lindsey. After a long embrace, she grabbed Lindsey's hand and escorted her to David's side. Lindsey scanned David's damaged body, her pupils dancing between horror and grief. At last, she fell to her knees and simply wept. Between sniffles, she whispered messages to both David and God. As Betty rubbed her back, Lindsey mourned so deeply she felt like she was going to have a heart attack. She couldn't even speak. The only clear words she offered David was "I'm sorry," though the reasons for that would remain in her heart alone. She looked over to find that Betty had also dropped to her knees and was now praying for her dying son.

The grief was indescribable, except to say it was consuming and changing reality by the second. Lindsey kissed whatever skin remained exposed, then stroked the patches of David's matted hair. In response, he gurgled and convulsed. The beep of the life-sustaining monitor marked off each precious moment that he lived. Between the uncontrollable bouts of crying, Lindsey and Betty prayed. Strangely, in the midst of Lindsey's desperate pleas, her thoughts began floating to other areas in her mind. She questioned, *Why?* But to her growing rage, no answer came. She vividly recalled the night she'd spent with David, as well as everything they'd shared over email and Skype, and hugged him for each memory. She worried about Coley, wondering, *Why hasn't he arrived yet?* She then thought positively, believing, *David will come out of this alive. He has to.* The next moment, her thoughts turned negative, and she screamed out in agony. *It doesn't make sense,* she thought, *any of it. David's dying.* Her body, the parts that loved him so deeply, ached with a sharp, indescribable pain. In her heart, she was already mourning the loss of her greatest hope for an amazing life.

Breaking Lindsey's cruel trance of grief, Betty whispered, "The doctor says they've done all they can for him. The rest is up to him and God." A dramatic attack of grief ended the explanation. She couldn't mutter another word.

As Lindsey wept with Betty, she squeezed her tightly, trying as best she could to offer the hurting woman any strength she could.

In the same broken whisper, Betty concluded, "They say it's a miracle he's still holding on. None of them can figure it." For a second, they grinned proudly at each other. They knew.

Lindsey wept again.

Before long, Coley burst into the room. The shock of David's apparently hopeless condition nearly bowled him over, and the sight of it clearly took his breath away. Falling into Betty's arms, he looked like a small boy. Lindsey wanted to run to him but didn't. *He's in good hands*, she figured.

Completing the family circle, David's Aunt Jeanne arrived. She never stopped to acknowledge anyone, but went straight to David. The room turned silent when she bent and kissed the blue flesh of her nephew's cheek. "What did you get yourself into now?" she asked and then lay beside David and began to cry, "Oh, David. Oh, David..." Again, the wave that had subsided took a turn of the tide, and the tears started breaking. The entire room was immersed in both grief and love.

David is so loved, Lindsey thought, *and I really love him too.*

Emotions ran in vicious cycles, and to experience them all was overwhelming, leaving both the body and mind exhausted. Of course, grief was the most predominant. When it came to one of them, it acted as a contagion, spreading wildly through the room. Screams for mercy were followed by the soft whimpers of victims. Anger then took its strong hold. With no fingers to point, God took the brunt of it until that phase was replaced with a series of promises and negotiations with that same God. In time, perhaps from the merciful numbing of shock, laughter also filled the room. Family and friends held each other and shared stories of David that helped define their unbearable pain.

Amazing, Lindsey thought and watched as the once-darkened room gradually became filled with a light that could only be described as love. There were apologies for differences long forgotten and amends made for neglecting to share in each other's busy lives.

The realization of life being taken for granted was brutally clear. And through it all, David hung on.

Nurses came in and out, avoiding any real eye contact with the family. At one point, just after Aunt Jeanne had barged in, Father Baker arrived to administer the last rites. Grief reared its razor sharp head again, and the room rocked to the wails of the permanence they now faced. Father Baker praised God and prayed, "It is quite apparent, Father, that this man wisely used the time you gave him. I have seen very few loved more." Lindsey witnessed these words bringing everyone in the room even closer, until they actually swayed in each other's arms.

Moments later, the whole room stood for another bout with misery.

As the sobs gradually subsided, a loving debate took place. Although it was David's wish, the family felt torn about donating his organs, so they discussed the possibility of offering up the final gifts. Lindsey was horrified. Craig put everyone's objections to rest with one simple question. "Can you imagine this world without David's heart in it?" There was a moment of silence followed by the beginning of another cycle of tears.

When they'd first arrived, the doctors had sworn David was minutes away from death. Now, seven hours later, he showed a part of himself that had only been revealed to those who knew him well. He showed his will. As he used to say, "The good Lord never put the heart of a lion into an elephant." All of the machines and monitors in the world could have never measured the strength of his spirit.

◻ ◻ ◻ ◻

Somewhere deep in the thick fog, David heard a sound. It was a low hum, like the drone of a secret conversation. He tried to concentrate, but the heavy exhaustion would not permit it. In the darkness, he noticed two horizontal slits of light. But no matter how hard he tried, he couldn't get anywhere near the shiny cracks. He shivered as he felt a blast of cold air running the length of his body. He looked down, only to discover that his body was no longer there. A moment later, as the exhaustion pressed its entire weight upon him, the light completely disappeared.

A moment later—or maybe it was hours or even days—David felt suspended in air when he heard another sound. He listened harder this time, concentrating on what it might be. *It's crying*, he realized and felt bad for the people who were weeping. "Oh David," he heard. It was a woman's voice; it was Lindsey's voice. *What is it?* he tried to ask her, but his words remained silenced prisoners within his frustrated mind. *I'm here, Lindsey*, he thought and began to frantically search for those slits of light. *It's my only way out.*

Another moment later—or maybe it was hours or even weeks—David witnessed a flash of light burst before him. Somehow, he knew it was only happening in his brain and not in front of his eyes. It didn't matter. It had gotten his attention. He searched the darkness with his thoughts until he spotted the two thin cracks of light off in the distance. Concentrating hard, he slowly traveled to that place. Once he reached it, he watched as Lindsey turned and smiled at him. *Oh Lindsey*, he thought, trying desperately to share his true feelings with her. *I've missed you so much.*

She never responded but continued to smile.

I love you with all my heart, he thought. *What have I done?*

With the innocent giggle of a child, Lindsey waved him toward her. "Come on," she whispered, her words dripping with the hopes of a life worth living.

◻ ◻ ◻ ◻

It might have been the very next moment or another week but, as if stuck in a delusional dream, a sledge-hammer inside David's skull slammed the cranium from within. Struggling to return all the way to the surface, he slowly opened his eyes. The light was now overwhelming and painful; it took a few brutal moments for him to adjust. When his eyes were finally able to focus, he saw Lindsey sitting by his bedside.

I'm not dead, he realized, but didn't feel any physical relief from the truth of it.

Lindsey grabbed his throbbing hand. Her eyes were red and swollen from crying. "We thought we were going to lose you," she whispered.

He stared at her and tried to smile, but his entire face felt like it was going to shatter.

"If you're going to kill yourself, David..." she started, but emotion stopped her from finishing the thought.

"I didn't try to kill myself," he mumbled, barely able to form human words from the extensive damage in his mouth. He tried to wipe away the cobwebs and remember. "I just went drinking and..."

"Don't lie to me, David," she said firmly. "Don't you ever lie to me!"

He opened his mouth again but decided against digging his hole any deeper.

"You *were* trying to kill yourself," she continued, stating it as a matter of fact, "and if you decide to do it again, please don't put anyone else at risk because it's not fair." She was crying mournfully now. "And... and until you get your act together, I refuse to be part of your life and watch you destroy yourself." Without another word, she got up and walked out of the room, never looking back at him.

David laid there in terrible pain—physical, emotional, even spiritual. *It's not fair*, he repeated in his throbbing head. He couldn't decide whether Lindsey was referring to the other drivers on the road or herself. His head hurt too much to give it any more thought at the moment.

◻ ◻ ◻ ◻

The following day, David stood before the hospital room's bathroom mirror. *It was war*, he told himself, looking deeply into his own eyes. *And you're going to let your whole life just slip away because of a war you served in?* He shook his angry head. *No, I don't think so!*

He peered hard at his reflection. His eyes might have grown old in Afghanistan, *but my heart's still in there somewhere*, he thought. *Get knocked down and live with it for a time*, he told himself, *but remain seated and live with it forever.* He shook his mangled head. *Nobody can punish us more than ourselves.*

David thought about Max. *And I'm not going out like that*, he vowed. Remembering fragments of his recent dreams, he thought, *I still want a shot at creating my own life and living it, not just drift by each day in a state of oblivion.* He rummaged through his wallet and slid out a business card. He picked up the phone and dialed the number.

A machine answered. "Hi, you've reached Brad Perry at Psychology Associates. Please leave a brief message, and I promise to get right back to you. If this is an emergency, beep me at five-five-five-one-three-five-five. Have a great day."

David cleared his throat at the beep. "Hello, Mr. Perry, my name is David McClain," he said, speaking as slowly and as clearly as his broken mouth would allow. "I need your help. When you get a chance, can you please call me at five-five-five-four-five-eight-seven? I'd appreciate it."

Chapter 9

¤ ¤ ¤ ¤

It was a gray morning consisting of a light, miserable drizzle one degree away from a snow flurry. With his heart in his throat—more from embarrassment than fear—David climbed the stairs to the massive courthouse.

After passing through the metal detector, he waited in the marble-encased hallway on a small metal chair. It was a cold environment. David observed that it was like a reunion for many who sat around him. *Frequent fliers*, he presumed. One kid was draped in gold chains, with tattoos on his neck and hands. He was wearing baggy clothes and new sneakers. *He must have a good job*, David thought sarcastically, and became angry with himself for having to be there.

A half hour later, his attorney arrived. The man talked like an auctioneer, obviously trying to juggle his dozens of clients while keeping their problems separate. He wore a suit, but it was wrinkled. His hair might have seen a comb earlier in the week, and the bags under his eyes betrayed the heavy weight—and loss of sleep—that he carried. "Are you ready for this?" he asked.

"Let's just get it done and over with," David said and stepped into the courtroom.

The room was wrapped in rich mahogany, from the half walls to the judge's bench that loomed four feet off the marble-tiled floor. The wall's chipped plaster was painted off-white, and there were hanging lights, frosted globes indicative of the turn of the century.

If these walls could talk, David thought, and looked around. *I can't even imagine the things that have taken place in this room.* It was a foreign environment, not much different from entering a war zone. And no matter what was about to transpire, David knew, *This isn't going to be good.* His heart rate became elevated, and his mind buzzed from taking in too much oxygen.

An older stranger wearing a black robe entered the room. "All rise," the court officer bellowed, and everyone did—with those who looked like real criminals getting to their feet a little slower than the rest.

Right from the start, the experience was surreal. David watched as the justice machine turned out one continuance after the next. There were sidebars, or whispered conversations followed by a laugh or two. *This place isn't about justice*, David decided. *It's about making deals.* Even the court officers appeared indifferent to everything that was going on. David continued to regulate his breathing.

David's attorney stood and announced, "It was an accident, Your Honor," grabbing David's undivided attention. Although it was now his turn, he felt like he was watching it happen to someone else.

The judge looked past his glasses and down his nose at the lawyer. "A drunk driving accident, correct?"

While the lawyer nervously shuffled his paperwork and offered an explanation that added up to, *He did it, but it'll never happen again*, he said, "Your Honor, my client has already enrolled in counseling. He's a veteran of the war in Afghanistan, and he's displayed signs of PTSD."

Signs of PTSD? David thought and struggled for air.

No one else batted an eye over the claim.

In the end, the judge found David guilty of the DUI charge and sentenced him to three years of probation. "You'll also be required to perform twenty-five hours of community service and pay for the damage you caused to that guard rail. Understood?"

David nodded. "Yes, Your Honor," he said, thinking, *This is the first time my service isn't voluntary.*

¤ ¤ ¤ ¤

It was the morning before Thanksgiving when David parked his mother's car in front of The Rocking Horse Pub.

Fourteen years earlier, Jack Oliver, the compassionate owner of the local eatery, decided to do something good. He and a handful of patrons jumped into their cars and proceeded to Jerry's Lodging, a homeless shelter, returning to the pub with fifty of the needy to share both food and companionship.

As David stepped out of the car, he realized that although court-ordered, he was looking forward to giving the compassionate man a hand.

Walking into the quaint, dimly lit restaurant, David could sense an atmosphere of intimacy and kind-heartedness. It was also obvious that preparations were already underway for the Thanksgiving holiday. Dozens of donated blankets were piled high in one corner, while the telephone rang off the hook.

In between calls, Jack spotted David and waved him over. "Just give me a minute," he said, covering the phone with his hand.

Beaming with the smile of a saint, Jack told the person on the other end, "Chad's Chowder House has pitched in with some food, and the folks at the Swansea Grange have been very generous, but it's the children in this community who've made the real difference." He nodded. "The kids at the high school donated hundreds of dollars through a penny drive, and the elementary school kids have collected personal hygiene items to be handed out. And others have even offered their time." He winked at David. "We're expecting two hundred and fifty of the needy to eat in the pub this year, but we'll need at least a hundred volunteers to transport a thousand meals to shut-ins, the sick and the elderly." Jack's smile brightened even more, as if it were possible. "That's great news," he said. "God bless you."

When Jack got off the phone, David handed him the court paperwork. He read it and looked up. "Be honest with me. Are you here as a prisoner or do you want to help?"

David grinned. "I'm happy to be here," he said, feeling more relaxed than he'd expected.

Jack nodded. "Good," he said and pointed to the pile of colorful comforters. "People have been great this year, but we had to purchase almost five hundred more blankets." He shook his head. "For some, it'll make all the difference in the world on the cold winter nights."

As Jack gave David his ten-cent tour, he explained how his cause got started and where it now stood. "We feed more than twelve hundred at Thanksgiving and the same amount at Christmas. The final cost is around ten thousand dollars."

David whistled.

"Exactly," Jack said. "I had some real tough times back in the day, and I'm still trying to give back what I received from this community." He sized David up. "Trust me, son, the greatest act you can ever commit is to help someone who can never pay you back." He winked again. "You can never be too generous, but you'll have regrets for the times you could have reached out and didn't."

David nodded and went straight to work in the kitchen, never once looking up until Jack called for his attention.

"No one sleeps here," Jack teased. "We'll have plenty more to do tomorrow."

As they walked out, David asked, "Have you ever considered spending the holiday with your family?"

Jack smiled. "My two children and I have learned to have our dinner a little later." He winked. "You'll meet both of them tomorrow on the serving line."

◻ ◻ ◻ ◻

Long before the sun arose again, David met Jack in front of The Rocking Horse Pub.

"Couldn't sleep?" Jack asked.

David shook his head. "It's an old Army habit I haven't broken yet," he fibbed. The truth was, thanks to the anxiety attacks David couldn't remember the last time he'd slept through the night.

Before the front door closed, Jack was already cooking for a family that grew by the year. *And from the smell of things*, David thought, *Jack can really cook.*

While they slaved away, a bus traveled throughout the city, picking up those who needed a lift as well as a sense of true brotherhood.

Volunteer after volunteer arrived: attorneys, bankers and many who had once gone to eat but had since improved their lives and now offered a hand and rolled up their sleeves. "When you give," Jack sang, "there's no better feeling."

After working the serving line for two hours, Jack told David, "You've done enough. Go eat."

David filled his plate and took a seat beside a young man who was unkempt and clearly hung over. "Name's Mark," the blue-eyed stranger said, extending his hand. "I served in Afghanistan," he said, as though he felt compelled to explain his appearance, "and I'm still trying to get my shit together."

David's hair stood on end, while he shook his comrade's hand. "Where in Afghanistan?" David asked, swallowing hard and deciding not to divulge that he'd done the same.

"Camp Eggers just outside of Kabul," the man said, "for eleven God-awful months." He shook his head again. "I don't like talking about it."

David nodded. Camp Eggers was only a few clicks from where he'd served—another hot spot filled with mayhem and death. "What about the VA?" David asked. "Have you gotten any help there?"

The man looked at David like he was insane. "Have you ever been to the VA?" His eyes turned even bluer. "They're too busy rejecting my claims, saying that my problems aren't service-connected. This way, the bastards don't have to send me a check."

David nodded. *I'm definitely hurting*, he thought, *but there are people far worse off than me*. David spent the next hour talking to Mark and watching in awe as his own troubles seemed to melt away. *Finally, a piece to the puzzle*, he thought.

At the end of the day, David stayed longer than mandated to help Jack clean up. He handed Jack a paper with his phone number on it. "Give me a call when you start setting up for your next shindig. I want to help."

"I appreciate that, but I'll still sign off on the community service if..."

"And I appreciate that, Jack, but I'm not talking about the court order. I'm talking about really lending you a hand." David then explained his situation and how he ended up at The Rocking Horse Pub; it was like offering his confession to a priest.

"We'll all make our mistakes while we're here, David," Jack said, "but in the end, there's only one question you need to ask yourself: is the world a better place for you having walked through it?"

David nodded. "Thanks for everything, Jack," he said and walked away thinking, *Looks like I'm not done serving after all.*

◻ ◻ ◻ ◻

Lindsey opted out of the Thursday Night Club to spend the time considering David's recent madness. As she sat at her kitchen table, she realized it was the kind of dilemma she would have loved to share with her mother. *This isn't a conversation I can have with my dad,* she thought. *But a heart-to-heart with Mom would require an all-out global search, with an FBI kind of effort.* She shook her head. *Thanks for nothing, Mom.* For the first time since she could remember, she felt alone.

She pictured David's face again. It wouldn't leave her mind or her heart.

But I've already gone through this insanity with my father, she thought, *and I'm not sure I have it in me to do it all again.*

She thought for a long while and shook her head angrily. *I don't need it. And I don't deserve it. I just don't think I can walk down that path again.*

She sighed. *But I can't help it. I love him. I really love him, and I don't think it's even possible to go back to the life I knew before I met him.* She nodded. *Or to go forward without him.*

□ □ □ □

David took a seat in Brad Perry's office, feeling like he was going to sneak out of his skin. *I shouldn't be here,* he thought.

"So tell me what's going on," Brad said and sat back.

To David's surprise, he said, "I've been having some real trouble with anxiety and depression since I got back from Afghanistan." He then rattled on for a full hour about his war wounds that no one could see.

Dr. Perry took a peek at the wall clock. "Is this the first time you've talked about any of this?" he asked.

David nodded. "Pretty much."

"And how did it feel?"

"Better than I thought, but..."

"But?"

"What if my wounds are just too deep to heal?" David asked, revealing his greatest fear.

The doctor shook his head. "I've been at this game for a few years now, and I've never come across scar tissue that was too thick to penetrate." He leaned forward. "David, what you're searching for is redemption and forgiveness."

"Forgiveness?"

He nodded. "That's where you'll find peace again." He took a deep breath. "Imagine living within the skin of someone who can't forgive? Even themselves? Nightmares should be so horrifying." He stood, indicating that their session was over. "Listen, I can certainly treat you, but you're much better off going to the VA Hospital, where they specialize in service-connected issues."

"Okay," David said, "but I haven't heard too many good things about the VA."

Dr. Perry extended his hand for a shake. "Give them a call. Trust me, they're the best in the business."

David pulled into the giant VA Hospital compound. His breathing lost rhythm and picked up speed. His chest felt tight. *Relax*, he told himself. *You have to do this*.

He breathed past each colorful wooden sign until he found Building 8—*Mental Health*. He cringed when he read it.

An older man dressed in pajama bottoms and a tweed sports coat was walking slowly, scanning the ground in front of him. David shut off the ignition, sat back and watched. The man bent several times, picking up something. *He's picking up litter*, David surmised and watched a few moments more. The man passed several wrappers and bent to pick up something smaller. David focused in, more curious now. Then it hit him. *Cigarette butts*, he realized, *he's gathering butts for enough tobacco to roll his own cigarette.* David looked back at the building and could feel his panic build.

David willed himself out of the car and marched toward an unknown future. As he reached the heavy door, he looked back at the bum. *At one time, he was probably an Army officer with his whole life ahead of him.* He shuddered at the sobering thought, took another deep breath and stepped into the red bricked asylum.

Dr. Ken Weiss was David's assigned therapist. "I've been in the business for four decades now, plus I've had some experience on the job." He grinned.

David was confused and didn't conceal it.

"I served two tours in 'Nam," Dr. Weiss explained, "and one too many."

"So you know what I'm going through?"

"Nope. Only you know the hell you're going through," he said, shrugging. "But I found my way out of hell, and I'd like to show you the way back too."

David's eyes filled with tears of hope. "Do you think you can?" he asked, trying to keep his tears restrained.

Dr. Weiss nodded. "I do."

"I just wish I could put all this behind me and move on. I'm so afraid"—David stopped and collected himself—"that my mind will stay stuck on some damn rooftop in Afghanistan."

Dr. Weiss stood. "There are two things you need to know right off the bat: The first is that it takes great courage to admit fear or that you need help. Just by being here, you've proven that you have the courage. And the second is that we never get what we wish for—ever." He shrugged. "We get what we work for." He looked into David's eyes. "Are you prepared to put in the work, David McClain?"

"I am, Doctor Weiss."

"Good," he said, shaking David's hand. "Then I'll see you again on Thursday."

◻ ◻ ◻ ◻

Though it took nearly three weeks to be able to share it, David finally told Dr. Weiss about Max's drug overdose. "They say it was a suicide, but I'm not sure," David said, still trying to defend his deceased brother.

Dr. Weiss raised an eyebrow but never debated it. "David, do you realize that suicide has already claimed more veteran's lives than all combat operations in both Iraq and Afghanistan combined? From what I understand, the average right now is twenty two veteran suicides a day."

"What? Twenty-two suicides a day?"

"That's right. Just because soldiers make it home doesn't mean the war is over for them. In fact, for many, the fighting's just begun."

"I hear that," David said.

"But the real killer is silence. Those who don't reach out and ask for help are the ones in real trouble."

David stared at him.

The man smiled. "But you're one of the smart ones, David."

"I'd hardly say that," David said.

"I would," the doctor said, nodding. "You're here, aren't you?"

¤ ¤ ¤ ¤

Preferring to avoid in-patient treatment at all costs, David began seeing Dr. Weiss three times a week. And each session was more difficult than the one before it. Dr. Weiss challenged David's negative thinking at every turn.

"So, you're a victim then?" Dr. Weiss asked, in his usual tough-love approach. "Someone not in control of his own life?"

"I never said that," David said.

"Then what is it? What are you trying to tell me, David?"

"An Afghan boy got beaten to death over there... and I was..."

"Are you trying to tell me that you beat a boy to death in Afghanistan?" Dr. Weiss asked. He was taken aback and unable to mask his feelings toward it.

"Not exactly," David explained, allowing the ten-ton monster out of the closet for the first time. "But I am responsible for the death of that boy," he said and began to cry.

Dr. Weiss prodded David to detail the traumatic event—"No matter how hard it is for you to share it," he told him.

David explained every grisly detail, concluding, "And wouldn't you know, our target never even showed. The mission was aborted..." He began to wail. "I could have stopped it. I could have saved him." His breathing was so shallow, he felt like he was suffocating.

Dr. Weiss sat back and let David mourn. Ironically, unlike most combat soldiers, David wasn't tortured over taking a human life; he was tormented from not taking lives in order to save a teenage boy.

The session went way over, and Dr. Weiss kept his next patient waiting. When David was composed enough to walk out of the room, Dr. Weiss said, "Two animals were responsible for the death of that boy, not you." He placed his hand on David's shoulder. "Your greatest crime was being a good soldier."

David shook his head.

"Get here early next week," Dr. Weiss said.

¤ ¤ ¤ ¤

Weeks passed. David was hurrying across the VA grounds when he nearly ran right into Billy Brodeur. David thought about the Brodeur fight story Kevin Menker had shared and figured, *Billy must have been court-ordered to get help.*

They shook hands. It was as if they'd just met at the local bait-and-tackle shop, without acknowledging where they actually were.

"Hey, I heard about that bouncer you beat down in Brockton," David said.

Billy laughed. "Yeah, that's why I'm here," he said, confirming David's suspicions. "Imagine that? Back in Afghanistan, I would have won a medal for a beatdown like that."

David shook his head. "Good luck, brother."

"You too," Billy said, still laughing.

¤ ¤ ¤ ¤

David wasn't three minutes into his weekly therapy session when he said, "Ken, do you mind if I ask you something?" They were now on a first-name basis.

"Of course. Anything."

"How is it that I've been sitting in this chair for weeks, spilling out my guts, while you just sit there and listen and tell me nothing?"

"What do you mean, tell you nothing?" Ken asked.

"You've never told me what's wrong with me," David explained.

Ken looked shocked, as if he'd explained this to his patient before. He leaned forward, folded his hands on his desk and spoke softly. "David, I'm sorry. I thought it was evident. You've been diagnosed with depression and post traumatic stress disorder or PTSD."

David's body locked up.

"As a result of your service in Afghanistan, your anxiety level became so severe that it was nearly impossible for you to function normally. But with the medication..."

"I'm screwed," David blurted.

"No, David. You're not screwed. You're just sick."

David began to cry. Ken walked around the desk and comforted his patient. "David, listen to me. Many of the problems you've suffered in recent months are not your fault. They're really not. You have to start to believe that."

David looked up but didn't believe a word of it. His mind was riddled with guilt.

"It's not your fault, David," Ken continued, "even the attempted suicide."

"Attempted suicide?"

"The car accident," Ken said.

David didn't argue the point.

"I'm telling you, we have to get rid of the guilt before you can heal," Ken said.

By now, David was too busy crying to respond.

"Although millions of Americans suffer this same plight, many don't even know they have it. For reasons too many to count, many more refuse to investigate why they feel the way they do." He shook his head. "Some try to alleviate the symptoms of panic with alcohol or sheer force of will. But as you've learned, either attempt only carries them deeper into their own hell."

David nodded.

"David, the real question has never been whether or not you're sick. It's really about what you're planning to do with your illness."

"But what can I do?"

"You need to take your medication, no questions asked. And we can monitor the dosages for effectiveness."

David nodded. "No matter what it takes, I have to move forward. I have to move past that rooftop a half a world away." He took a few deep breaths. "How long?"

"How long what?"

"How long 'til I get better?" David asked.

Ken smiled. "You're already better, David. But your progress will be a lifelong quest."

"Oh..."

◻ ◻ ◻ ◻

Months went by, hard months filled with work so painstaking it made Ranger School look like kindergarten. Hours upon hours were spent in therapy, adjusting medications, religious worship, transcendental meditation—anything David could do to bring a greater sense of peace and well-being to his world. It had taken time, but he'd finally gotten a handle on his anxiety and depression. He still suffered with his bouts, but now he'd armed himself with knowledge and an arsenal of coping strategies. Every time he felt panicked or down in the dumps, he no longer laid down and surrendered to it. *I'm not going crazy*, he told himself again and again. *I'm not going to die*, he repeated. And it worked.

Life's too damn short to begin with, he thought, no longer wanting to wish the days away. *Instead, I want to make the most of each one of them.*

◻ ◻ ◻ ◻

One morning, David climbed up on his mother's roof and laid flat. *I'm so sorry*, he told the young Afghan boy in his mind. *If I could have taken that from you, I would have.* He cried shamelessly, feeling more burdensome weight float from his soul. *Please forgive me. Please forgive me*, he kept saying over and over, until he realized he was now talking to himself.

◻ ◻ ◻ ◻

David's next stop was the local cemetery, his father's gravesite. As he approached the short marble headstone, he realized that this was the first time he'd even seen it. He went to his knees and prayed. *Sorry, Pop*, he thought, *for a lot of things. I just hope you're at peace now.*

He sat quietly with his father for an hour before clearing his throat. "I'm all done keeping my head down, Pop," he said aloud. "It's time I looked up to see what's in front of me."

Like the tip of an angel's wing, a slight breeze blew across David's neck. Alas, he was brought to tears before his father. "Thanks, Pop," he said, and felt his heart lighten even more.

◻ ◻ ◻ ◻

David sat in the car, knowing exactly where his final stop would be.

It was dusk when he pulled up to the beach and walked to the park bench. Taking a seat, he looked out onto the bay. *Even the ocean's at peace tonight*, he thought.

He concentrated on Lindsey and the magical night they'd shared all those months ago. For the first time since Afghanistan, he could see it...

> Sitting with Lindsey on the bench, he pointed at the lighthouse. "Look right over there," he told her.
>
> She did.
>
> "Whenever you feel lost or alone," he said, "all you have to do is come here. No matter how dark or stormy, that light will always guide you home... back to where you need to be."
>
> While her eyes filled, she wrapped her arms around him and kissed his cheek.

I am stupid, he thought, remembering his own advice. *How could I have been so stupid?*

He looked to the heavens and cast a silent prayer, *Please God, just one more chance with Lindsey. I'll never ask you for anything again.* And this time, his fingers weren't crossed behind his back.

¤ ¤ ¤ ¤

Lindsey walked out of work to find David standing by her driver's side door. *Oh my God*, she thought and her jaw dropped. *It's really him.*

"Hi beautiful," he said, looking down at her left hand. "Please tell me you haven't gotten married." He smiled.

His baby face was still gone, but the sparkle in his eyes—his love of life—had returned. She wanted to run to him but forced herself to remain calm. "What are you doing here, David?" she asked.

"I came to see you."

She was taken aback but did her best to conceal it. "After all these months?" she asked.

He nodded. "Please have dinner with me, Lindsey."

She shook her head. "I...I'm not sure I can do this with you, David. I've walked through hell with my father and..."

"I've spent months healing from my demons, Lindsey, or I wouldn't be here jeopardizing the second chance that I've prayed so hard for." He gazed into her eyes. "I don't just *want* to see you again, Lindsey. I need to."

For a moment, his honesty stole her breath away, and she gasped. As she composed herself, she gazed back into his eyes. There were times when the strongest statement she could make was to remain silent. This was one of those times.

"Please don't end this before it gets started, Lindsey. It would be unfair to both of us."

She shook her head, this time less convincingly. She was coming around to his irresistible charms quicker than she wanted to.

"I'm not sure of the last time you've heard this, but you really are an incredible woman. You're beautiful and intelligent and kind." He went down on one knee and grinned.

She shook her head and laughed. "Get up," she said. "You don't have to beg."

"So you want to see me again?" he asked, springing to his feet.

She nodded slightly. "I do, but..."

"But?"

"I found my father's Army trunk in the cellar, David. There were love letters that my mother had sent to my father during the war, sharing the same hopes and dreams that you and I have shared. And look how..."

David grabbed her hand, stopping her. "If I've learned anything over the last year," he said, "it's that we don't get what we wish for; we get what we work for." He kissed her hand. "Love isn't only a feeling, Lindsey. It's a choice." He pulled her close. "It won't always be easy, but I can guarantee that I'll never quit on you, or us...ever!"

Her eyes filled, and she hugged him. *He's right*, she thought. *He won't quit, and neither will I.*

"Have you missed me?" he whispered, while they hugged.

"Not one bit," she answered, picking up right where they'd left off.

"Good," he whispered and pulled back to look into her eyes. "I've also learned that home isn't a place at all.

It's a person. It's you." His eyes filled with tears. "And I want to be the man that you've always seen in me."

She quickly moved in toward his mouth and kissed him gently. It was their first kiss since he'd returned home all those months ago.

Her knees buckled slightly, and she fell back into his arms where she stayed for as long as she could. As she pulled away, she said, "So where are you taking me to dinner?"

He smiled. "What do you think about Capriccio's, then maybe a movie at the Footlights Theater?"

"Ummm, that sounds good, but I was thinking we could get a dozen clam cakes from the Bayside, then take a long walk on the beach."

"Even better," he said. "Tomorrow night at eight o'clock?"

She shook her head. "I can't. I have to help my dad with something. If I said Friday night, would you still be interested?"

"I'd be interested no matter what you said."

"Friday then, and seven would work better," she said, smiling.

"Then seven it is. Where should I pick you up?"

"One Twenty-Three Reed Road. Just beep and I'll..."

"I'll see you at your door tomorrow at seven," he graciously interrupted.

"Great," she whispered. "I'm looking forward to it."

"Me too," David said. "You have no idea."

They kissed one last time; this time, it was much less gentle. It was hungry. It took them forever to say good night.

Chapter 10

◻ ◻ ◻ ◻

It was nearly dusk when David pulled up to Lindsey's house in his mother's car. With flowers in hand, he approached her door.

"Hi beautiful," he said, his eyes locked onto her. "You ready to go?"

She smiled brilliantly. "I've been ready for months."

He'd forgotten she had the voice of an angel and his chest felt warm.

◻ ◻ ◻ ◻

At Bayside Seafood Shack, a nineteen-pound lobster called "Big Boy" peered out of his massive tank. No matter how much money folks offered to buy him, and the bids went well into the hundreds, the owners never sold.

David scanned the menu, which offered scrod. He laughed. *There's no such fish.*

While Lindsey ordered clam cakes and chowder, he ordered a fisherman's platter with fried clams, shrimp, scallops, and fish. "And give us one boiled lobster on the side," he told the girl behind the counter.

Lindsey laughed. "I remember someone telling me that he'd live a happy life if he never ate seafood again."

David laughed. "During the war, I actually dreamed about boiled lobster in drawn butter."

"I wish I'd known that," she said. "I would have..."

"This isn't our last meal together, is it?" he asked.

"It better not be," she said and reached for her wallet to pay for their meal.

David pushed her money back into her wallet and paid for the food, as well as two cold sodas. "I just got a job working at The Rocking Horse Pub," he said. "After I pay off my court fees, I'm going to get the Mustang fixed up."

"Good for you," Lindsey said, "That car must mean a lot to you."

He shook his head. "Just as soon as it's repaired I'm giving it to Craig." He smiled. "Doing what he did for me is what means a lot."

She smiled. "There may be hope for you yet, David McClain," she teased.

Juggling all the food, they clasped hands and started their walk down to the beach, where they ended up on their park bench.

He turned to her and shrugged. "I told you I'd meet you back on this bench," he said.

She smiled. "Yes, you did."

"I'm sorry I'm late, Lindsey," he whispered.

She wrapped her arms around him. "The only thing that matters is that you finally made it."

They hugged for a long while.

As they ate, a young boy and his dad were flying a kite in the distance. David was hypnotized by this, a smile plastered across his face. Lindsey shared the smile.

"I once promised myself I'd never buy you jewelry made of shells..." he started to say after they'd finished eating.

"Why?" she asked, grinning. "I love seashell jewelry."

"Good," he said and reached into his pocket. He pulled out a shell bracelet and handed it to her. "I've started to reassess a lot of things I once said."

She put the bracelet on and admired it for a moment before falling into his arms. "It's so beautiful, David. Thank you."

"No," he said. "*You're* beautiful."

The night covered them like a warm blanket while they picked periwinkles in the moonlight. She kicked water at him. He took chase. At one point, they even lay on a patch of beach grass, staring up at the stars. "I cast many wishes up there while you were gone," she said.

He smiled. "I hope they all come true."

"Things are definitely looking up," she whispered and blushed when she said it.

He smiled, placed his hand in hers and looked back toward the sky. "There you are," he said excitedly, pointing toward the North Star.

"Did you think of me when you saw it over there?" she asked.

He turned to her, his face turning serious. "It kept me alive, Lindsey," he whispered.

He couldn't hold back any longer and kissed her—getting lost in the kiss.

When their lips finally parted she whispered, "It's about time."

He chuckled and kissed her again.

And again, she returned the passion. This time she whispered, "Welcome home, handsome." It was the first time she'd said it.

They sat together in silence for a very long time, his arm wrapped around her soft shoulder. There was no need for words; they only needed to share the same space.

Finally, she pointed at the lighthouse's searching eye and told him, "Whenever you feel lost, David, and there will still be times when you do, just come back here. It'll guide you home, back to me."

His eyes filled, and he tightened his grip on her shoulder. "I still wouldn't mind living there," he said, referring to the lighthouse.

"All by yourself?" she asked surprised.

He shook his head. "Absolutely not! I'd only live there if you were right there with me."

They kissed again before nodding off to the rhythm of the surf and each other's relaxed breathing.

¤ ¤ ¤ ¤

The sun was just breaking the horizon when they awoke and realized they'd spent the entire night together—again.

"What time did you say your curfew was?" David teased, stifling a yawn.

"I didn't," she replied with a mischievous grin. "I pretty much have forever."

¤ ¤ ¤ ¤

That morning, Lindsey still went to work, a glow illuminating her face.

Courtney sauntered over. "That smile is going to make me sick," she joked.

Lindsey giggled. "I'm sorry. I can't help it."

"Does David really make you that happy?"

Lindsey was spellbound. "I've dreamed about falling in love my whole life and I knew it would be wonderful, but..." She sighed.

"Oh, please," Courtney said and walked away.

An hour later, the phone rang. "Community Art Center," Lindsey answered.

"Lindsey Wood, please?"

"David?" Lindsey asked excitedly and then switched to a whisper. "I was hoping you'd call."

"Miss me yet?" he asked in a similar tone.

"Not at all," she said.

"Good. Me neither," he said. "When can I see you again?"

"Tomorrow night. And I pick the place this time."

"I thought you picked it last night."

She giggled.

"Okay. But should I be scared?"

"No," she whispered. "I'm going to take you to my favorite place in the whole world."

"Can't wait to see it. I'll be at your house at seven."

"See you then," she said and hung up. As she placed the telephone in its cradle, she buried her giant smile into her shoulder, wondering whether its glow might give away her overwhelming joy to her co-workers.

¤ ¤ ¤ ¤

The following afternoon, Lindsey approached her car after work and discovered a folded paper stuck between her windshield and wiper blades. *This better not be from Walter,* she thought. She plucked the paper free, unfolded it and read:

> *Beauty*
> *for Lindsey*
>
> *She radiates with the light of a thousand candles, while her movements have the energy of a lightning storm.*
> *The sweetest aroma lures even the strong, though it is the scent of confidence that takes the kill.*
> *With the giggle of an innocent child, her tone is soft and gentle—almost heavenly.*
> *She expects nothing, but her silence demands the best.*
> *Her forgiving heart beats in the ears of all men, yet it is her untamed spirit that screams out loudest.*
> *Like a beacon in the darkest night, her comfort is safety.*
> *Rarely revealing her deepest thoughts, her words remain simple, for she is a mystery.*
> *Her tender touch can be soothing or sensual, as she is unconditional love—both maternal and passionate.*
> *In a word, she is beauty—*
> *and you should see her on the outside.*
>
> *David*

◻ ◻ ◻ ◻

That night, Lindsey drove while David pretended to be a frightened passenger. They laughed and held hands. Music played softly in the background. The sun was just going down for the night when she pulled into the marina near North Beach. It was the same place they'd met, the same place they'd had their first date. Captain Eli was aboard *Serendipity*, and he was smiling.

Though David was confused about the location of their date, he waved to Captain Eli and gestured for Lindsey to meet his old friend. "Captain," David announced. "I'd like you to meet my friend, Lindsey Wood."

Lindsey smiled. "Friend?" she teased under her breath.

Captain Eli climbed down from his boat and extended his hand. "Well, hello Lindsey Wood. Nice to meet you."

"It's nice to meet you, too, Captain. I hope you don't mind me saying..." She waited until he nodded. "I love your accent. It sounds familiar, but I can't seem to place it. You're not from around here, are you?"

Captain Eli smiled. "I suppose we all came from somewhere." He searched her eyes. "But home for me isn't so far from here." He looked out onto the water. "Gooseberry Island is as good a place as any, though."

"I agree. I absolutely love it here."

Captain Eli nodded again. "I hope you're staying close to our friend, David. We wouldn't want him to get lost again."

David's face turned bright red.

The old sea captain laughed. "Don't be so serious, David," he said, "it's only life."

David's skin prickled.

Lindsey nodded. "And life is better than good," she added grinning.

David nodded, realizing that he wasn't being judged. They were obviously both thrilled that he was finding his way back.

Captain Eli winked at them both and gestured toward the horizon. "I don't suppose you two want to spend such a beautiful sunset talking to an old seadog, now, do ya?"

David and Lindsey looked at each other and smiled. Lindsey turned back to Captain Eli and offered the same smile. "Again, it was nice meeting you. I hope we'll see each other soon."

"I'm always here."

Lindsey nodded, looked at David, and then started running for the beach. "Come on slowpoke," she called over her shoulder.

David waved to Captain Eli and took chase.

A few hundred yards up the beach, Lindsey stopped short and turned to meet David in the sand. He nearly ran into her. She opened her arms for a hug. "Well, here it is," she said, gesturing around with her hand, "my favorite place in the whole world."

It's the exact location where we met, David thought, and then it hit him. He grabbed her face with both hands. After staring into each other's eyes, they kissed for a long while.

She broke away first, anxious to speak. "At the risk of scaring you away," she said, "I...I need to tell you something."

He nodded nervously.

"I feel safe and comfortable and excited..." she babbled. "I feel everything when I'm with you, and I never stop thinking about you." She quieted her tone. "I know this is going to sound strange since we've only just reunited, but you're everything I've ever dreamed of, David. And you're going to think I'm crazy, but..."

He gently placed his finger over her lips and grabbed her hand.

Lindsey collapsed onto the sand and pulled him to her. Passionate kisses were shared throughout the night.

While a choir of crickets sang and the elephant grass danced in the sea wind to the rhythm of a gentle tide, David announced, "I have big plans for you next weekend. In fact, I'm told I need a suit for this place, so you'll have to wear a nice dress..."

"Where are you taking me?" she asked excitedly.

"You'll see next weekend," he said, and kissed her into silence again.

◻ ◻ ◻ ◻

During the week, even though David was trying to stay positive, he found himself slipping into the darkness again.

Lindsey sat on the phone with him, doing all she could to make him feel the sunshine. "Listen to me, David, you're doing great and getting better all the time now. But like Dr. Weiss told you, it's going to be a life-long effort."

"Sure," he said, "but there are no guarantees that I'll ever completely stop feeling depressed."

"Wow, you've really become a glass half-empty kind of guy, huh?" she said, teasing him.

"I'm just a realist."

"Mmmm, I've always thought that reality is what we believe it to be."

He grinned slightly at her positive attitude. "I just need to find peace again," he said.

"I know and I have an idea," Lindsey said. "How 'bout we go on a whale watch?"

"You're kidding me, right?" he said.

"Nope. I'm not. We're going."

□ □ □ □

As the boat left the dock, David took note of the bustling traffic in the harbor. Besides the commercial fishing vessels, a large number of private sail and power-boats navigated the water.

"Look!" Lindsey said and pointed out their lighthouse.

As they made their way out of the mouth of the harbor, David asked the boat's naturalist, Jenna, "What happens if we don't see a whale?"

"In all our trips, there've only been a handful of times we haven't seen whales. If we don't see a whale today, we'll give you a pass to come again for free. Okay?"

David nodded. "You have a chow hall where we can get food?" he asked.

Jenna nodded. "It's called a galley and yes, we serve hot dogs, hamburgers, pizza, and other goodies on board."

"What if it rains?" David fired at her, trying to make Lindsey laugh with his relentless questioning.

"The boat has an enclosed cabin out of the weather, but even if it starts to rain I like to throw on a jacket and still look at the whales outside."

David was impressed with the woman's patience. "What kind of whales will we see?" he asked.

Lindsey laughed. "Stop, David," she said under her breath. "Leave the poor girl alone."

"Every trip is different," Jenna said, remaining professional, "but we could see humpbacks, finbacks, minke whales, and maybe even a northern right whale. There's also a chance we'll spot dolphins, harbor porpoises, seals, ocean sunfish, tuna, and sharks."

"Sharks?" Lindsey squeaked.

"Sharks," Jenna repeated and smiled right along with David, who wrapped his arms around Lindsey's waist.

Chugging out into open water, Jenna settled everyone down and began describing the things they might see. "We're going to see many seabirds throughout the trip. Some are native and others are just stopping by for a rest while they migrate."

Suddenly, an osprey appeared in the distance. The giant bird hovered over the water, watching the surface below. "She's looking for her breakfast," Jenna said in an excited voice. The "sea eagle" dove steeply, its talons outspread, and went right into the water. Within seconds, it resurfaced and flew off with its catch, adjusting the fish in its sharp claws.

David looked at Lindsey to find her staring at him and smiling.

Jenna then pointed out a few more common birds. "The herring gull is known as the seagull along the coast. Since the 1960s, they've become very abundant due to readily available food at landfills and garbage dumps. Although it's a scavenger, it also eats large numbers of fish and marine animals."

David looked up at Lindsey and whispered, "I like to feed them in the parking lot at McDonald's."

Lindsey shook her head and laughed.

Jenna pointed out the seagull's big brother. "The great black-backed gull is the largest of its kind and can be seen year-round hanging out with the herring gull. In fact, the two species nest together in mixed colonies, even though this big guy likes to bully his smaller cousins. It preys on almost anything smaller than itself, eating ducks, fish, and shellfish."

As they got farther out, Jenna began to explain what they should be looking for when whale watching. "The whales are usually feeding at this time of the day, which can be very exciting because they normally feed in groups. The whales will surface together in pursuit of their favorite food, small shrimp-like creatures called krill. Watch to see if any of the whales have calves with them. The best place to look is right alongside the larger whales because the calves stay close to their mothers."

Lindsey clasped her hands together and sighed happily. David smiled at her reaction.

They'd covered a few hours of open water before Jenna called out again. "What a treat!" she said, her voice more excited than it had been all day. "If everyone will look on the left side of the boat, you'll see a humpback and her calf." Sure enough, big momma and the little one were swimming side by side. "The humpbacks are easily recognized by their long flippers and lumpy dorsal fins." Jenna shook her head. "Unfortunately, the humpback is a rare breed in the world today and few people will ever have this wonderful opportunity to see one. These whales were once numerous, but they're slow swimmers and were easily hunted by whalers. It's now believed that there are only around fifteen thousand humpbacks left in the entire world."

Sensing the importance in Jenna's voice, David looked up at Lindsey. There was worry in her pretty face.

"The humpback is called the 'singing whale,'" Jenna said. "Although we don't know why they sing or how they make their haunting sounds, their songs have been recorded many times. Today, they're studied in warm-water breeding grounds like Bermuda and Hawaii."

The mother humpback and her baby stayed with them for a few minutes before taking a left and swimming out of sight.

David turned to Lindsey. "I'm hungry."

As the captain turned the boat back to port, they ate their lunch and listened while Jenna detailed the northern right whales and longfin pilot whales, neither of which were seen during the trip. She also talked about blue whales, beluga whales and sperm whales like Moby Dick. She directed their attention to a band of common terns flying gracefully over the water, searching for small fish and shrimp. She also pointed out a sand-colored piping plover and the loud wailing call of the common loon.

It was nothing exciting and David realized, *That was Lindsey's intention all along.*

At the first sight of land, Jenna told everyone to cast their eyes toward a cluster of rocks. David and Lindsey couldn't make out anything but small black dots until they got closer. And then they saw them.

"Those are harbor seals basking in the sun," Jenna explained. "They like to lie around ledges and sandbars during low tide and forage for food during high tide. In the water, harbor seals can be bold and curious about humans. I've even seen some of the young ones surface next to the boat and stare at me."

Lindsey laughed.

The entire trip took nearly five hours. Before they knew it, they were safely back at the dock, full of stories to share about their latest adventure together.

Not one bad memory or a hint of anxiety all day, David thought, smiling.

They thanked Jenna more than once and bid her farewell.

Exhausted and sore, David and Lindsey dragged themselves into the small souvenir shop at the end of the dock. The place carried everything one would expect: T-shirts, hats and mugs—each with one whale or another printed on the front. There were dolphin sculptures, pewter seagulls, ceramic sandcastles, scrimshaw jewelry, Christmas ornaments and wooden calendars. On the back wall, books, videos and posters of whales were offered at a discount. Lindsey picked out two matching hats to commemorate their voyage together. A vote was taken, and the humpback whale won hands down.

At the register, David and Lindsey waited behind a little boy holding his father's hand.

David gestured toward the boy and teased, "I have to get one of those someday too."

She smiled. "Let's start with the hat and see where things go."

He laughed and, as they left the store hand-in-hand, he thought, *After all this time, who knew peace could be found off the shore of Gooseberry Island?*

Just outside the shop's door, he stopped and pulled Lindsey in for a hug. "Thank you," he told her.

"You're welcome," she said, already wearing her humpback hat.

He looked into her eyes. "No, I mean it. I didn't realize how much I needed to get outside of my head for a few hours, but you did." He kissed her. "You knew exactly what I needed."

She hugged him tightly. "You don't have to go through any of this alone, David," she whispered. "I'm right here with you."

▫ ▫ ▫ ▫

On the ride home, rather than picture the gory details of Afghanistan, David remembered his childhood. It was the first time he'd gone back in his mind and visited it in a very long time. He could see it all as if it were yesterday.

> As the lazy days ticked by on Gooseberry Island, the wonderful smell of freshly mowed grass lingered. There was plenty of swimming and talk of skinny-dipping lasted all summer, though nobody ever went through with it. As if chased by bees, he and his friends ran through open fields

past the dark, scary wood line all the way to their fishing hole. Games of Marco Polo turned their hair from dirty blonde to platinum, their skin from pale to desert tan. "Good health's found in the rays of sunlight," his mother would say. They'd drip dry in their hidden tree fort and return home from their adventures to find a sweating pitcher of fresh-squeezed lemonade waiting. *Ma was good*, he thought.

The carefree and lazy days of youth afforded the time to dream; to guess which shapes the crawling clouds created. There were no clocks or calendars. Time was marked by the rising and setting of the sun. *And not a moment of it was wasted*, David thought. *Rather, it was the most well-spent time—ever.*

David returned to the present and looked at Lindsey. *She was right*, he thought. *I only need to remember who I am...who I've always been.*

As if reading his mind, she smiled. "And there's plenty more where that came from," she said.

¤ ¤ ¤ ¤

The weekend finally arrived, revealing David's big surprise; he took Lindsey to dinner at Avenue One, a four-star restaurant located in the Hyatt Regency. The atmosphere was intoxicating with its dim lighting and festive jazz band. Lindsey dipped wedges of bread into a flaming pan of cheese fondue, while David enjoyed his boiled lobster. And they talked.

"More lobster?" she teased.

He laughed. "It's the strangest thing, but I can't get enough of it," he confessed.

"Are you still talking about the lobster?" she joked.

"Nope," he said, never cracking a smile.

They spent the entire meal talking about the things they'd each dreamed of sharing together. "Long, romantic walks along the beach, skinny-dipping at night, fancy dinners on the mainland, and nights at the theater where we can sit side-by-side and hold hands," Lindsey said.

"Skinny dipping?" David repeated, grinning.

She slapped his hand. "The whole time you were away," she said, "I imagined us spending rainy nights together and watching movies under a thick blanket." Her eyes grew distant. "And getaway weekends at a bed and breakfast up north, making out in darkened movie theaters, and playing with each other's feet beneath restaurant tables."

He laughed. "That sounds awesome. All of it!" He took a sip of water. "How about hiking and camping and sleeping beneath the stars out in the middle of nowhere, where no one can hear your passionate screams?"

It was her turn to laugh.

"Preparing dinner together and lying in each other's arms—sharing our secrets and dreams, everything." He nodded, his eyes glassing over in a dreamlike state. "Skiing in the winter and horseback riding in the fall..."

"And getaways out on the town, dancing the night away," she added. "Picking apples and pumpkins.

Snowball fights in December, water balloon fights in July, and lots of laughter..."

"Everything," he whispered, grabbing her hand. The list was endless and both understood that it would take a lifetime to fulfill, the best of it costing more imagination than money.

After David and Lindsey shared a decadent dessert, the waiter moped back to the table with the check. David quickly snatched it out of Lindsey's reach and opened the black, faux-leather fold. "I should have ordered two lobsters," he joked.

◻ ◻ ◻ ◻

As they reached the parking garage, Lindsey slid into the passenger seat. David stood at her door. "I need you to do me a favor and close your eyes for a second," he said.

"What?" Lindsey asked, her face already beaming in anticipation.

"Trust me."

Lindsey's eyes slammed shut. As she squirmed in her seat, David kissed her. She returned the kiss, keeping her eyes closed tight.

David popped open the trunk and retrieved a wicker basket filled with neatly wrapped presents— each gift holding its own little greeting card. After sliding into the driver's seat, he whispered, "Okay. You can open them now."

Lindsey did. "What is this?" she asked excitedly.

David placed the basket onto her lap. "Go ahead. Open them."

The first was a small, silver picture frame with a birthday card attached.

Lindsey's forehead wrinkled with curiosity.

David said nothing. He could only smile.

Lindsey unwrapped the next. It was a wind-up snow globe with two angels dancing. There was a Valentine's Day card attached. Tears welled in her eyes, and she looked at him for an explanation.

"It's for your birthday and Christmas and Valentine's Day—" David explained, "for all the days I should have celebrated with you but missed because I was overseas, or trying to find my way back home to you." He paused to fight back the growing lump in his throat. "It's for all the nights we should have been holding hands instead of searching for each other."

Lindsey wrapped her arms around David and began to cry. "I love you so much," she whimpered.

"I know. Me too," he said. "I love you so much that it actually hurts to be near you sometimes."

She sighed. "I know. I feel the exact same way." She smiled, mischievously. "And I'm really looking forward to working on that list with you."

David kissed her. "I hope it takes us forever," he whispered.

□ □ □ □

Lindsey returned home to find her father sitting in his recliner, half-asleep. She studied his face. *No sign of flashbacks*, she thought, and took a seat on the arm of the recliner.

He opened his eyes wide and looked at her. "Oh, hey kid," he said yawning.

"Dad, I've been seeing this guy who I want you to meet."

Denis sat up straighter, fully awake now. "Who is he?" he asked.

"His name's David McClain," she said. "I've been seeing him long enough that I think it's time you meet him."

"That serious, huh?"

She grinned.

"What does he do for work?"

She paused. "He's working at The Rocking Horse Pub for now because he just..." She stopped.

"Just what?" Denis grunted, betraying a hint of disapproval in two words.

"Because he just got out of the service," she blurted, coming to David's defense.

"Service? What branch?"

"Army," she said, unsure whether she should have disclosed it.

"Did he serve overseas?" Denis asked tentatively.

It took a few moments, but she finally nodded. "He was a ranger in Afghanistan. He..."

Denis actually gasped. "Oh Linds, no."

"But he's a good man, Pop," she countered.

"So am I," he muttered, shaking his head, "Or was anyway."

She hugged him. "You still are, Pop. You just have things that..."

"If he was a ranger, then he's seen action," he interrupted, "which means he'll have *things* to deal with too." His eyes filled. "The price is heavy, sweetheart. You know that."

"I know."

"I know you do. And you can't imagine how sorry I am about that."

"There's nothing to be sorry for," she said.

"Is he worth the risk, this David McClain?" he interrupted again.

Lindsey smiled wide. "Oh yeah."

Denis stared at her and finally nodded. "Well, if I've learned anything, there's nothing that can sway the heart when it knows what it wants," he said. "Just keep your wits about you, Lindsey...please."

She hugged him again. "I will, Dad. Don't you worry."

◻ ◻ ◻ ◻

David and Lindsey never wasted a minute. Late Saturday morning, they took a leisurely walk in the park and talked. In the afternoon, they took a long ride and talked. That night, after David had cooked and served Lindsey dinner, they headed to an outdoor café that played live acoustic music—and they talked. Before the band's last set, David grabbed Lindsey's hand. "Let's go for a walk."

As they strolled along, they sneaked swigs of wine from a paper bag like love-drunk adolescents and continued their amazing descent into love.

"I am so drawn to you when I look into your eyes," Lindsey told him, reaching for his hand. "And I feel such an uncontrollable passion for you."

He kissed both her hands.

"When I'm near you, it's my heart that controls me, not my mind," she said. "I've seen more than everything in your eyes, and it kind of freaks me out. In case

you haven't noticed, I don't spend too much time looking into your eyes when we talk. I just can't."

He peered hard into her eyes and smiled. They
walked in silence for a long while. That was the thing—
conversation wasn't necessary between them. Even in
the silence, Lindsey reminded David of who he was
before Afghanistan. *Everything I learned as a child is
everything I've ever needed to know: don't fight, use your
manners, share, be kind to others.*

At the end of the night, David pointed up at the
North Star. "There you are," he said. "Whether I was
on patrol or on a rooftop, you were always there with
me, Linds."

"I'm still here," she said, hugging his arm, "and I'm
never going anywhere."

"Me either," he said.

"I know."

He stopped and faced her. "Do you?" he asked.

"I do."

¤ ¤ ¤ ¤

In the weeks that followed, David met Lindsey's family over a casual dinner party. They spent all the time
they could at North Beach. They shared picnics, flew
kites, and played in the water like children. At the summer carnival, they visited a fortune-teller together and
teased each other about the woman's vague predictions.

"The gypsy woman said I was on the right path to
finding my soul mate," he said, and grinned. "I hope I
find her soon."

Lindsey slapped his arm. "Well, she told me that
I've already found what I was looking for."

David's healing was a slow-moving process and, even with all the positive progress, Lindsey sensed that he was still screaming inside but wouldn't let it out—a need to confess that clawed at his soul. She grabbed his hand. "Please, David, never second-guess how I might take something you say or do. I know where your heart is, and that's all I need to know." She smiled brilliantly. "Once you know someone's heart, really know it, the rest is an easy read. And you and I already have that part covered." She peered into his eyes. "I don't want you to worry about saying anything to me, and I want you to feel free with me." She tilted her head sideways and squeezed her grip. "I won't break, you know."

He nodded.

"You can even tell me what happened over there," she said. "In fact, I think you should."

He smiled at her but shook his head.

"There's no need to keep any of it from me or bottle it up. Let's get it out now and deal with it, so we can put it behind us, together."

His eyes filled, and he shook his head again.

"One night, and I'll never forget it," she said, "my dad took me to George's Hot Dogs for a late dinner. As usual, he was drunk and the place was packed. No sooner did we sit down to eat when a guy got thrown through the screen door, his enemy right behind him to finish the pummeling. Plastered, my dad looked across the table at me and screamed, 'Girl, don't tell me you're afraid?'

"I didn't say a word, but my eyes begged him to be quiet.

"My father then stood up and pointed around. 'Don't you ever be afraid of people like these,' he screeched, and all eyes were on him. 'They're all drunks,' he yelled.

"I begged him to stop, but he didn't listen."

David held her tight.

"And then I watched my father get the worst beating you could ever imagine," she said and began to release old unshed tears.

"I'm sorry, babe," David whispered.

"But I wasn't," Lindsey said, "and that's the point." Tears cascaded down her face, while the rest played out in sniffles. "I was happy it happened. I was happy that someone bigger and stronger than my father could punish him like that." As her eyes filled, she shook her head in shame. In David's lap, her body trembled over the terrible memory.

After a while, he whispered, "It's funny how the invisible scars run the deepest, isn't it?" He shook his head. "Trust me, I understand." He hugged her tight.

"You can share with me, too, you know," she said, composing herself. "You can tell me anything and I'll never judge you."

"I know," he said, and looked at her. After a long moment, he cleared his throat. "It was a calm night," he said, "and we were on another ordinary patrol..." His eyes grew distant and immediately filled with tears.

"Go on," she whispered.

"When Max screamed, 'Davey!' I turned and saw three Afghan men, a small band of Taliban, raising their AK47s in our direction. I hit the deck, while the first few rounds whistled over me, where my head had been just two seconds before. We returned their fire. It felt like I was looking through a window, watching the whole thing go down." He shook his head. "When it started, there wasn't any fear, really, just a morbid curiosity about how it would play out. Bullets began flying, and men were collapsing onto the dirt in front of us. To tell you the truth, I'm not sure any of my bullets hit..." He began to cry. "But I'd be lying to claim that they didn't." He looked into her eyes, all the world's sorrow filling him. "If it wasn't for Max, I would have been a goner that day. He saved my life."

While he grieved, Lindsey hugged him tight.

Through the sobs, he said, "It hasn't been easy living with the fact that I've taken a life. For all I know, that Afghan soldier had a wife and children, or a girl just like you waiting for him at home. My heart's been sick because of it ever since." He wiped his face. "It's hard to explain, but I have this real sense that I'm going to spend the rest of my life trying to get past that firefight."

She leaned back and peered deeply into his eyes. "Be honest, David. If you hadn't shot that man would he have killed you?"

He nodded. "Yes."

She sighed heavily. "Then thank God you pulled the trigger," she said and fell back into his arms.

David eventually emerged from his painful past, his face awash in tears. He looked at Lindsey. She was crying right along with him, sharing in the pain. He hugged her tightly. "I've never felt so close to another human being in my life," he whispered.

"Me either," she said, wiping her eyes.

"And then Max died," David said, shaking his head. "And it kills me that I never got a chance to really thank him for saving my life or to say a proper goodbye."

"Then go and do it now," she said.

He looked at her like she had just stepped out of her mind. "What?"

"Go see him now and tell him," Lindsey said. "Gather your brothers and go say a proper goodbye to Max."

Chapter 11

◻ ◻ ◻ ◻

It was Veterans Day when ten brothers rallied at David's house. Handshakes and hugs were exchanged all around. *Each one of them looks so much older*, David thought. The fine lines in their faces revealed the harsh weather endured along the paths they'd each traveled, with some of the more difficult and dangerous miles shared together in Afghanistan. They were brothers, representing a third of their rowdy platoon. From the moment they reunited, the smiles never left their faces. Enough time had passed that it was now good to see each other. Reminiscent stories started off the day, and the laughter quickly followed. From the first chuckle, it never stopped. Each one had a shot at, "Remember when..."

Big Al showed up late. David was taken aback. "Wow, I'm surprised you made it," David said, looking down at his friend's prosthetic legs.

"They were legs, Davey. Not my soul," Al said, smiling.

"How's life?" David asked, still feeling guilty about the incident.

"Better than good," Al replied.

David was taken aback again. "That's what my girl-friend always says."

"Smart lady."

David chuckled. "A lot smarter than me, that's for sure."

Al looked around. "So are we gonna drink beer or make out?" he asked. "And I'm hoping for the beer..." He slapped his plastic legs. "'Cause I don't have the legs to run from you anymore."

David laughed hard, feeling an odd sense of relief. It was obvious that Big Al held no resentment toward him or the IED that claimed his natural mobility. David had held more guilt than he'd realized and could feel the weight lift clean off his slumping shoulders.

As if he was making sure that David understood, Al added, "My boy likes riding on the back of my wheel-chair. He thinks it's a chariot, so we pretend to be glad-iators." He smiled. "It's very cool stuff."

The old team stuffed themselves into three vehi-cles and ventured off to the Cavalry Cemetery halfway across the island.

As they arrived at the sacred burial grounds, they found that two more brothers were already there, wait-ing with Max. Nate Michaels was still in the Army and was appropriately dressed in his camouflage uniform and black beret, and Billy Brodeur, who looked consid-erably older than his twenty-three years. Handshakes were exchanged again, and then there was silence.

The stone read: *ESSINGTON MAXIMILLIAN*, his date of birth, premature date of death, and the inscrip-tion, *I believe I can fly* toward the bottom. The granite stone was black and buffed to a shine. Private prayers were offered, while comments about Max's quiet neighbors broke the thick tension. Other mutterings about Max's "view" took care of the rest. All twelve brothers joined in the morbid laughter.

It didn't take long before beers were cracked and the first sips were poured into the ground for their fallen comrade. After an informal toast to their guest of honor, gifts of love were presented. There was a wreath made of red, white and blue flowers, and a banner reading *4ᵀᴴ RANGERS* placed at the tomb of their *well-known* soldier. Several old ranger team photos wrapped in plastic were pierced through the ground by a small American flag.

To top it off, two unit patches, a U.S. Army nametag, and Max's rank of sergeant had been framed by another brother and carefully set down by his stone. A full can of beer finished the offerings.

As if erecting a base camp, a picnic table was set up with its umbrella opened wide. They were careful to ensure that Max's headstone was located at the head of the table. Full coolers were carried over, and everyone gathered around the circle of love.

For the next two hours, they visited with each other, reveling in their brash stories of the past and catching up on their tamed stories of the present. To someone unaware of what was going on, this entire display would have appeared disrespectful—as if they ignored the friend who now lay six feet beneath them. It was the complete opposite. As they smoked, drank, remembered and laughed, Max was sitting right there beside them. He couldn't have been more included in the festivities. He was the very reason they reunited and they were grateful. There were many reasons why Max was the guest of honor.

There were passersby, but nothing disrupted the celebration until a man escorting his two young sons stepped up to the gravestone beside them. David approached the stranger and explained, "My comrades and I intend no disrespect to you or your deceased loved one. We're actually honoring our fallen brother by carrying on a tradition." He shot a smile at the young boys.

The man grinned. "The name's Eric Holloway," he said and extended his hand, "and I understand. If I'd served with you guys, I'd be drinking with you today too." The rangers nodded. The man then asked, "What did he die from?"

David hurried to answer. "He got sick from his time in Afghanistan and..."

"He died of a broken heart," Kevin Menker interrupted.

Eric nodded solemnly.

David did the same, thinking, *It couldn't have been said any better*.

While Eric and his sons concluded their prayers and sauntered away, the rangers followed suit. They finished their beers, closed up the umbrella and placed the table back in the rear of Kevin's truck. Several kisses on the stone and a few more silent prayers later, David placed a sealed letter at the base of the stone. Though none of the others would ever know what it contained, it read:

> Dear Max,
>
> It seems like forever since we served together in Afghanistan. Since we've been home, I thought about it and I don't think I ever really thanked you

for saving my life that day. Thank you, Max. I wouldn't be here if it wasn't for you.

Your mom told me that besides the nightmares and flashbacks, you suffered from severe headaches, respiratory problems and digestive problems. But the VA denied each one of your claims, refusing to offer you the treatment you needed. It's criminal, I know!

But the physical pain was only a fraction of it, wasn't it? Men like you and me were forced to learn that the hard way. More than anything, I wish I could have helped you find the peace you needed, brother.

I learned, far too late, that you turned to drugs and got hooked. It brought relief from your demons, I'm sure. I'm also sure that you fought to beat it back. I heard that you died at home with your mom right by your side. When I heard this, I wept like a kid. But I was also relieved that you didn't die alone. I am so grateful that you passed over with someone who really loved you by your side. Now, I can only pray that this incredible tragedy has finally brought you peace.

I'm writing you now to let you know that I haven't forgotten—you saved my life in Afghanistan. And although I may not be able to clear my debt until Max Jr. gets older, you have my word that I'll be there for him on the day he really needs someone.

I promise that Max Jr. will know that his dad was a great man. Brother, you were loved very much and still are! And, you are still respected by people who don't show respect unless it's earned. I miss you terribly, Max, but have also experienced enough to know in my heart that it's only a brief matter of time before we reunite and laugh over old times.

I love you, brother. I'll be seeing you soon.

Your eternal comrade,
David

The group assembled back at their convoy on the road. Looking back, they offered a final salute, confident that Max would have loved the bizarre remembrance. In fact, had it been one of the others resting in their eternal bed—*Max would have been right there with us doing the same*, David thought.

A dozen men drove off back to their lives. Thanks to an old friend, they were firmly reminded of their obligation toward honor—especially for their departed brother's kid. If young Max Jr. knew that decent men loved his dad, then the boy could never question the decency of his father. And this would certainly not be the rangers last example of love.

In return, for David, life was placed back into perspective even more. A shared pride was renewed, reminding him that he'd once served a purpose higher than himself with people who also chose service over self—people who equally valued the crazy notions of patriotism, loyalty, courage and honor. Perhaps Max's greatest reminder to them, though, was that they'd each helped pay the price for freedom. They'd paid by losing the embrace of a cherished brother, who was sure to serve as the guest of honor for many Veterans Days to come.

Thank you, Lindsey, David thought as he drove home. *It's exactly what we needed to do.*

◻ ◻ ◻ ◻

Within a few days, David received an email from Max's mom:

Dear David,

When I went to the cemetery on Veteran's Day, I was overwhelmed that you guys took the time to go to Max's grave and leave what you did there, as well as to visit with him for a while. I saw the wreath and pictures, and I was touched at the thoughtfulness of you and your friends. Even though you experienced incredible horror in Afghanistan, it's comforting to know you had each other and in the end, you are still brothers...that Max is loved and honored by his friends. He spoke of your ranger team with great fondness.

A Grateful Mother,
My love,
Joan Essington

He immediately replied:

Dear Mrs. Essington,

You are very kind, and I thank you
from the bottom of my heart. Trust
that your son was loved very much
and still is.

David

◻ ◻ ◻ ◻

Over the winter, David finally met Lindsey's dad. They
weren't quite done shaking hands when Denis bluntly
asked him, "Have you quieted your demons from the
war?"

"Dad..." Lindsey blurted, embarrassed.

David waved her off and gave the man's concern
some considerable thought—until it bordered on an
awkward moment. "I'm taking them head-on," he
finally answered.

"Are you winning?"

David shrugged. "Some days are hell, but it's getting easier."

Denis nodded. "You keep fighting, you hear me?"

"Yes sir." David looked at Lindsey. "Until every one of them is silenced."

They settled down at the kitchen table with a bucket of fried chicken and all the fixings.

As David and Lindsey started to leave, Denis pulled David off to the side. "Listen, David, you seem like a great guy. But my daughter..."

"Is the best thing that's ever happened to me," he quickly answered, "and I won't mess it up."

"And if you can't silence those demons?" Denis asked.

"Then I'll walk away," David said firmly. "There's no way I'll drag Lindsey down. You have my word on it." His eyes filled. "She belongs in the light, not the darkness."

The old man shook David's hand again, and this time he meant it. "My daughter was right about you," he said.

David's eyebrow stood at attention.

"You *are* a good man."

"Thank you, sir."

Once they were alone in the freezing car, Lindsey turned to David. "I can't imagine not sharing my life with you, David McClain."

He looked into her eyes and whispered, "You're reading my mind now too?"

□ □ □ □

Gooseberry Island in the spring was magical. Ancient oak and maple trees—sprouting new buds—lined the sidewalks, causing the concrete to buckle and ripple at each base and proving that Mother Nature's roots were stronger than any man-made materials. White crushed-seashell driveways created aesthetic boundaries, while gas-lit lanterns illuminated the walks in front of each home.

Early mornings were truly the most beautiful and serene. In the solitude of dawn, Lindsey thought, *Even God feels close.*

While she sipped her morning coffee, she took it all in. Steam rose from a ground fresh with dew. Birds chirped, the wind sang in the trees and, for a moment, there was silence; it was a new day filled with hope.

The sun peeked over the brim of the world to chase away a dark, shadowy horizon. Flowers turned their faces toward its welcomed warmth. Slight breezes played ping pong with the distinct smells of decaying leaves and wet earth—a reminder that the world was waking up again amid the sweet aromas of pancakes and coffee.

Animals stretched out and began another day of fending for their young. Cars were started and pulled out of their respective driveways, dads and moms off to work to put food on tables and shoes on feet.

The sky—a vast patch of baby blue—squeezed out the last of any gray clouds that remained. Gooseberry Island was a place where faith became reality every day—or could.

Lindsey thought about David and how he'd also made it through some harsh winter storms. Although his body was nearly healed, more importantly his soul was on the mend and his spirit had finally returned to its true essence. *He's been knocked down about as hard as a human being could be, but he's gotten back up, and that's what defines the man I love,* she thought, proudly.

◻ ◻ ◻ ◻

Life got busy and in the way, with David working more—as a draftsman apprentice at Luna Bella Architecture—and seeing Lindsey less.

Deciding to resurrect an important piece of their past, where it all began, Lindsey emailed him at work.

> My Love,
>
> My heart is totally yours. As long as we give ourselves completely to each other, every moment we share will be magical.
>
> Just so you know, the man I marry will be the one I share the rest of my life with, all of me, in every way—until my last breath. And you are the man I will become one with.
>
> Lindsey

He responded:

> Babe,
>
> I've missed you, too, but I'm always with you—never any farther from you than your mind. Close your eyes for a moment and there I am—wherever

you want me to be.

Sometimes we have to work in the present in order to enjoy the future.

I love you completely and look forward to every moment we'll spend together.

David

While Lindsey was at work, David headed over to her house to speak to her dad alone.

Denis opened the door. "Oh hi, David. Lindsey's still at work," he said.

David nodded. "I know, Mr. Wood, but I'd like to..."

"Call me Denis, please."

David nodded and took a deep breath. "Denis, I love your daughter very much and would like to spend the rest of my life with her." He took another deep breath. "And I'd like to ask your permission..."

"I appreciate the gesture, David," Denis interrupted, "I do. But I'm afraid I might have forfeited that right with some of the bonehead moves I've made. I wish..."

David placed his hand on the man's shoulder, stopping him. "Lindsey loves you very much, and she respects you a lot more than you realize." He nodded. "And I also respect you and would never ask for Lindsey's hand without your blessing."

While his eyes filled, Denis placed his hand on top of David's—and simply nodded.

"Yes?" David asked.

"Yes," the man said, fighting hard to keep his emotions behind the wall he'd spent years building.

¤ ¤ ¤ ¤

The doorbell rang. As she rushed to answer it, Lindsey nearly bowled her father over. *It just has to be David*, she thought.

She tipped the young messenger and rushed the package into the house. *For such a large box, it's surprisingly light*, she thought. Under the watchful eye of her curious father, she tore through the brown wrapping. The most beautiful dress she'd ever laid eyes on was hidden among the tissue paper. As she lifted the white lace into the air, a folded piece of stationary floated to the floor. She picked it up and read:

Baby Cakes,

Sometimes I say things I don't mean—things I wish I could take back as soon as they leave my lips. There are times when I get frustrated and angry, unable to understand where you are. But then I wish I was right there with you. Sometimes I'm stubborn and defensive, feeling as if I've lost control, but I must also remember to let go and trust. There are times I want to go to you, but for fear of rejection I hold my ground and do nothing. And that has always been the wrong decision. Sometimes I don't listen as well as I should, failing to hear what you're really saying, and I respond in ignorance.

Lindsey, I love you, and because I love you I'll try harder to understand, to have more patience and to always admit when I'm wrong.

I saw this dress and thought of how beautiful you'd look in it. Please wear it tonight and meet me at Capriccio's. I can be out of work by 6:00 and I'll shoot right over. I can't wait to see you.

David

P.S. I really do love you, Lindsey.

Lindsey wiped her eyes and caught her father's grin. She smirked.

◻ ◻ ◻ ◻

It was almost 6:30 when Lindsey screeched into Capriccio's lot. She intended to be a few minutes late, but never expected it would take her so long to get ready. As much as she wanted David to wait, she also wanted him to gasp when he saw her. The valet attendant opened the car door, took one look at her and swallowed hard. She smiled. *The extra time paid off,* she thought.

She expected the maître d' to escort her right to David's table. The older man smiled and handed over a dozen long-stem roses. "Mr. McClain called and said he was running late. He said that the card would explain." Her father's daffy smile covered the distinguished man's face.

Blowing a wisp of hair from her eyes, Lindsey reached into the baby's breath and retrieved the card. It read:

> Babe,
>
> I would say that I'm sorry, but those would just be words you've heard before. This time, I'll say I love you, a truth that lives within my heart. I do love you, and I want things to always be good between us—with no need for excuses or apologies, only room for laughter and the whispers we secretly share. Let's always remember our love and return to it every day.
>
> Meet me at the Eagle for drinks. I can definitely be there by 7:00.
>
> I love you,
> David

Lindsey looked at the maître d', who continued to grin. "Did he say anything else on the phone?" she asked.

"Not exactly," the kind man muttered. "Just that he can't wait to see you."

"It certainly doesn't seem that way," she said.

As Lindsey reached the parking lot, she was surprised to find that her car hadn't been moved an inch. The valet attendant opened the door and smiled sweetly. "Best of luck," he said.

"Same to you," she replied, confused by the curious comment. Within ten minutes, she was at the Eagle.

¤ ¤ ¤ ¤

The Eagle was much less posh and sophisticated than Capriccio's, but they served one heck of a margarita. Lindsey made a beeline to the lounge, grabbed a table in the shadows and checked her watch. *I'll give David ten more minutes,* she decided. *If he doesn't show, I'm going home.*

The bartender sauntered over. "What'll you have, miss?"

"Margarita, no salt and a cup of ice on the side."

"Cup of ice on the side?" the man repeated, a silly grin dancing across his tanned face.

"Yeah," she confirmed, her sarcastic tone reaching toward anger. *If I didn't know any better, I'd swear that I'm playing the butt of some stupid joke,* she thought. The man nodded once and turned on his heels. Lindsey checked her watch again and thought, *David has seven more minutes.* Looking down at the beautiful white dress, she shook her head. *What a waste,* she thought, and could feel herself getting upset.

Within seconds, the bartender returned with a bottle of champagne. The smile never left his face.

"I ordered a margarita," she snapped and felt sorry for the outburst before the attack left her lips. "I'm sorry," she added, quietly. "It's just that my boyfriend was supposed to..."

"Meet you here at 7:00, I know. He called a few minutes ago and asked that I pour you a glass of champagne. He also asked me to give you this card." The man poured out the bubbly and handed her another of David's cards. With a wink, he was gone. Lindsey reluctantly opened it.

Sweetie,

Please bear with me. There are going to be times when other things might seem more important to me than you, but you have to trust that they're not. I love you more than anything in the world.

I guess the rest is up to faith. I'll be at the Dockside by 7:30. I'm hoping more than anything that you meet me. Please be there, and bring the champagne.

David

Lindsey stood and noticed that every patron in the bar was gawking. *I was right*, she thought, *there is a conspiracy.* Her first thought was to go home and put an end to David's foolish game. Then it hit her. *There's no way he would have had the time to drop off both cards. This is something he's planned.* Looking back at the crowd, she smiled. *This is something he's planned very carefully.* Her excitement made her legs start moving. Within minutes, she was in her car and speeding off to the Dockside.

As expected, David was nowhere to be found. Instead, a white stretch limousine sat idling in the front of the dilapidated shack. The chauffer held a sign reading, *LINDSEY WOOD*. Her eyes watered when she saw it.

With her dozen red roses and bottle of champagne, she climbed into the back of the car. The driver offered a familiar smile and handed her a tiny card. It read simply:

> Lindsey,
>
> I knew you'd come. I knew you'd do what it took to find me, again. Enjoy the ride. I'm waiting for you!
>
> All My Love,
>
> David

Even though it only lasted minutes, Lindsey enjoyed the ride. As the car slowed to a stop, for the first time she stole a peek out the window. They were at the beach. *David's waiting somewhere in the dunes*, she thought.

The driver parked the car, opened the door and helped her out. "Have a great time," he said. "I'll be here when you get done."

Lindsey felt like hugging him for his smile. She'd seen it in the faces of many different people all day. *Something big is up*, she thought, *and my quest is not yet complete*. Grabbing her roses and champagne, she picked up her shoes and started for the ocean.

A path of small seashells glimmered under a full moon of light. It was obvious. *Each one's been carefully placed*. They were the last clue on David's peculiar map. The row of shells looped and meandered through the shifting dunes until reaching several enormous conch shells, arranged in the shape of an arrow. Lindsey took a deep breath before stepping over the last dune.

The sight nearly pulled her to her knees. David was seated at a small round table right smack in the middle of the beach. He was dressed in a black tuxedo, and he stood when he saw her. Their eyes locked and, even with the distance between them, Lindsey could see that his eyes were filled with tears. She hurried to him.

On the table, with the help of a magical moon, a hurricane lamp illuminated two place settings, an empty vase and an empty ice bucket. Beyond the table, the lighthouse stood guard in the distance, keeping a bright eye on everything. Soft musical notes drifted on the gentle breezes, beckoning Lindsey to her thoughtful prince. Allowing herself permission to cry freely, she finally picked up the pace and sprinted.

As she reached him, she expected him to embrace her. He didn't. He dropped to both knees, grabbed her hands and blurted, "Be my wife, Lindsey, and spend the rest of your life with me."

Instinctively, she dropped to meet him in the sand. "Yes," she answered through the sniffles. "I thought you were never going to ask!"

David laughed and pulled her to him. "I love you," he whispered.

"And I love you," she countered before gesturing toward the table. "And I love all of this. But why the treasure hunt?"

"I wanted to let you know that this is the last time you'll ever have to find me."

"So you're mine now, all of you?"

"I am," he whispered.

"Good," she said with a giggle, "because this is the last time I chase you."

Between the laughter and tears, they kissed passionately. When they came up for air, he said, "I went to your dad to ask his permission for your hand."

Her body tensed in his arms. "And what did he say?"

David smiled. "He said that he's never seen you so happy, which is exactly what you deserve." He kissed her forehead. "He said I could have both your hands."

After a long hug, he grabbed her hands, pulled her to her feet and led her down the beach. They stopped at the very spot of their first date, in the sand just in front of their park bench. David pointed and Lindsey looked down at a huge sandcastle sitting near the dunes.

"Oh David," she whimpered, and buried her face into his shoulder.

"Every princess deserves a castle," he said and grabbed her face to stare into her eyes. "I want to spend the rest of my life, every moment of it, with you on Gooseberry Island," he told her and became completely choked up. "Falling asleep to the rhythm of the surf. And if either of us ever feels lost again"—he pointed back toward the lighthouse in the east—"there's the light that will guide us home to each other. Neither one of us will ever have to feel alone again."

She began babbling but couldn't speak past the emotion.

"The sandcastle is only temporary," he whispered. "We'll work hard and save and build a house someday where we can raise our children and spoil our grandchildren."

She nodded. "Count me in," she said and kissed him again. "David McClain, I fall deeper in love with you every day, and I'm so looking forward to spending the rest of my life trying to figure out why your eyes shine when you smile at me."

◻ ◻ ◻ ◻

Minutes before David and Lindsey were going to exchange vows, she stood with her father—both of them taking a few deep breaths.

"You look beautiful," he said. "Just like your..." He stopped.

"Thank you, Dad."

"What is it?" Denis asked, sensing there was something wrong.

"I'm excited to be getting married, but..."

"But what?" Denis said. "David's a very good man."

"I know, Dad, but..." Her eyes filled. "But I'll be leaving you and..."

"Oh Linds, please," he said, his own eyes filling. "You've been my crutch for way too long, and you've paid a heavy price to help me. I'm so sorry for that... more than I can say. But I'd be even sorrier if you hesitated to live happily ever after on my account." He hugged her. "You're my guardian angel, and I thank God for you every day. That's never going to change." He pushed her away enough to peer into her eyes. In that moment, it seemed impossible that his face could ever be contorted in fear or fury. His eyes were filled with overflowing love. "I'll be fine. I promise. But you need to start thinking about yourself and go live the life you're meant to live." He kissed her cheek. "You need to follow your heart, sweetheart."

"Thank you, Dad. I will."

He bent his elbow and extended it to her. "You ready?" he asked.

"Oh yeah," she said and grabbed his arm.

"Good," he said, and kissed her cheek. "Now let's go get you that happily ever after."

◻ ◻ ◻ ◻

David and Lindsey were married on North Beach at dusk, family and close friends in attendance to celebrate. Under the shelter of a white tent, the two exchanged their heartfelt vows, while the sun bid farewell on the horizon and Denis struggled to keep his feelings at bay. Betty, on the other hand, cried like a baby—shamelessly. David and Lindsey wore matching tattooed wedding bands, not rings that could be slipped on and off like tattered raincoats.

Hurricane lamps and candles lit the tent. David and Lindsey had their own table—identical to the one they shared on the night of their engagement. It was private and romantic and the perfect spot to watch Coley chase the girls all night.

The dinner ended with a toast. With glasses raised, Craig announced, "To David and Lindsey: whether your path leads through sun or freezing rain, may you always travel it together. And may all the love in this tent go with you."

Glasses clinked. The young couple kissed.

At the end of the reception dinner, David called for everyone's attention by proposing a toast to his new wife. All glasses were raised. "To Lindsey," he said, "the love of my life. When you were born, the angels danced, and I feel like you were sent just for me...that we were born for each other." He peered hard into her tearing eyes. "I will love you forever."

The girls of the Thursday Night Club swooned and, after soft applause and sniffles, the music began. David and Lindsey's first song—the entire song—lasted one kiss.

Denis and Lindsey danced next, both crying into each other's shoulders. "I want the best for you," he whispered.

"I know, Dad," she said, and looked at her new husband. "And that's exactly what I've been blessed with."

¤ ¤ ¤ ¤

Had David and Lindsey waited a decade, that first night together would have been worth the wait.

It didn't take long to learn each other's pleasure spots. They began touching and teasing each other with their fingers, their tongues. They gently caressed one another. The heat between them was intense. Kissing passionately, they shamelessly shed the rest of their clothes. David teased Lindsey until she was on the edge and surrendered to him. They then moved together in ripples of ecstasy. Sweaty and panting, they held each other until they could begin again—all night—anything they desired.

David stared at her. "I knew that once I had your heart, the rest would be absolutely amazing."

She purred. "I thought it would be incredible, too, but I could have never imagined this," she said and then initiated another round of lovemaking.

Chapter 12

¤ ¤ ¤ ¤

For David and Lindsey, married life was a blur of wonder and ecstasy. At night, they enjoyed the warmth and security of lying quietly in each other's arms. Many nights, soft music played in the background, while the dim light of flickering candles offered just enough light to reveal the contours of their naked bodies. While David stroked Lindsey's hair and offered the sweetest, most gentle kisses on her forehead, she stroked his broad chest and said aloud, "Thank you, God, for bringing such a beautiful man into my life."

Hand-in-hand, they took long walks—usually at the beach. Sometimes, they stopped along the way to sit on their park bench and steal a kiss from each other. On the ride home, they stopped off at the local ice cream shop to treat themselves to giant cones of double chocolate. While they ate, both counted off the minutes until bedtime. It was absolutely magical, rediscovering each other and falling in love again and again.

¤ ¤ ¤ ¤

No matter how busy life became, David thought about Max Jr.. One afternoon, he grabbed a sheet of stationery and wrote:

Dear Max Jr.,

I served with your father in Afghanistan. We were brothers, and your dad
was one of the few bonafide heroes of
the war—not because he fired on the
enemy or took fire, but because he
would have offered his own soul to a
dying Afghan child. No matter where
life may take you, keep your chin up
and be proud. Few people can say that
their father was a real hero!

When we were in Afghanistan, your
dad saved my life. I've always felt I
owed him one (though he would have
argued it). In any event, as I never
got the chance to pay your dad back,
I now owe it to you. So whenever
the day comes that you need someone—for whatever reason at all—just
call on me and I'll be right there for
you. It's a promise that your father's
already paid for.

Your friend,
David

A week later, he received a letter from Laurie, Max
Jr.'s mom.

David,

We received the letter you sent to
Max Jr. It was beautiful. Thank you

for giving my son a great sense of pride and the realization that his dad is a hero. There could not be a more precious gift. Max Jr. is so proud. He's been showing all his little friends, and I think it's great for him. Although I have no explanation for him now, in the long run he will understand why his dad died so young. My heart is broken forever for my son. He lost one of the greatest men I've ever known.

Max Jr. will always treasure your letter, and so will I.

Thank you again,
Laurie

David dropped the letter and wiped his eyes. He quickly replied:

Laurie,

I pray that Max Jr. understands his dad was a great man and loved by many men who also chose to serve a purpose higher than themselves. Tragically, it cost us in the end, but I pray Max Jr. realizes his dad didn't die from a random addiction but was the casualty of war.

David

David started to get up when something stopped him. It was the strong, familiar feeling of needing to be there for a brother. He looked up and smiled. *Okay, Max,* he thought, *let's up the ante and go all the way with this.*

Moved by an incredible spirit, David wrote Joyce Reney. She was a premiere advocate for suffering war veterans and hosted two national radio shows, *The Power Hour* and *The Reney Report*. David had dealt with her several times and not only considered her to be the hardest fighter for suffering veterans but also knew her to be a living saint. He wrote:

> Hi Joyce,
>
> It's been a while since we last spoke. I hope life is treating you well. The reason I'm writing is to ask a small favor. I have a comrade from the Fourth Ranger Battalion that died. He was ill for much too long and could not find relief at the VA. As a result, he self-medicated until he silenced his pain with an overdose. His name was Max Essington (Sgt.). He was a very honorable man and one hell of a soldier. Not to mention, he saved my life over in Afghanistan.
>
> Tragically, he left behind a son named Max Jr. My brothers from the Fourth Ranger Battalion and I will ensure that the boy knows his dad was an honorable man, but we could use some help. I fear that Max Jr. may grow up never

fully understanding why his dad died the way he did. This boy should take pride in his dad's service to America. Max was one of the few heroes I met. He did everything he could to save a dying Afghan child who tripped a roadside bomb. He would have given his own soul if it were possible. Unfortunately, it didn't work that way. Instead, the boy died in his arms, and Max was haunted terribly over it.

Would you please send a medal to our young friend Max Jr. to remind him that his dad was—and always will be—a hero? Perhaps even a brief note from you would help. Anything would be appreciated. I promise I'll never forget it.

Thank you and God bless!

David McClain

¤ ¤ ¤ ¤

Stretching out their honeymoon for as long as possible, David and Lindsey spent as much time as they could snuggling on the couch and watching movies. They sat out on their porch and made out like two teenagers, eventually making love beneath the stars—their eyes never once leaving each other's gaze. And when neither could take any more, David wrapped his love in a soft, fluffy robe and carried her off to bed where he held her for the night.

On weekday mornings, they'd awaken to music blaring in the background. One morning as David reached over her for the third time to swat the snooze button, Lindsey chuckled aloud and realized that he needed more than the alarm clock. She kissed him, giving him the strength he needed to take on the world. Lying on top of him, she whispered sweet nothings and her dreams for their future. With a final kiss on his neck, she shook him. "You need to get up," she whispered.

While David took his shower, she packed his lunch—including a brief love letter. It was nothing elaborate, just something that would make him smile and keep his thoughts with her, where they belonged. He got dressed and headed for the world that surrounded their dream. "Be careful and hurry back," she said at the door and sent him off to work with a soft, wet kiss.

¤　¤　¤　¤

At noon, David opened his lunch bag to find a folded love letter. It read, *Your kisses are everything I've ever dreamed of. Please don't ever question my feelings for you. I ache for you and always will. I love you. Lindsey*

David read the note two more times and smiled.

A co-worker at Luna Bella passing by his desk stopped and asked, "What are you so happy about?"

"Life," he said. Minutes later, David held the telephone close to his ear and listened.

"You owe me a soft, wet one," Lindsey said.

"You've got it," he whispered. "You know, even after two years the sound of your voice still melts me."

"Trust that I feel everything you do. And that's what makes us so amazing."

"I could kiss you for hours," he said.

"I'm going to hold you to that. Now get back to work. I'll see you tonight at Courtney's for supper."

"That's right. What's she making?"

"She said she's trying a new recipe tonight, an Italian dish with chicken and artichokes."

"I'll be the first one there," he promised. "I love that girl."

"And what about me?" Lindsey asked.

"You, I worship," he whispered.

"You'd better," she said, and hung up the phone.

¤ ¤ ¤ ¤

David was thrilled to email Laurie the good news:

> Laurie,
>
> I have great news, so please pass it on to Max's mom and the whole family. I just got word from Joyce Reney, a radio host for a couple of veteran shows. She's going to read my plea on the air to ensure that Max Jr. lives his life with pride. She told me that she will have people send in letters of support to Max Jr. and that she'll forward them to me. She says that there may only be a handful, but they'll be from Afghanistan war vets like his dad, and that they should make a big difference. Also, Joyce will be sending Max Jr. his own medal for the great sacrifice he's made in the fight against terrorism.
>
> David

The hour David spent interviewing on *The Power Hour* was one of the most difficult of his life. To a national audience, he explained who his friend Max Essington was and what the man meant to others. "When we got home," David said, "besides a list of physical ailments, Max suffered from PTSD with nightmares, flashbacks, depression, and terrible insomnia. But he was told by the VA that none of his problems were service-connected; therefore, they couldn't help him." After a brief pause to compose himself, David explained, "As U.S. Army Rangers, we were taught to value loyalty above all things except honor, yet those who called us to serve have shown neither. Because my friend Max couldn't find relief from his pain, he eventually died."

Joyce asked David, "Why are you so committed to helping young Max Jr.?"

"The difference between my life and Max's death is nothing more than a whisper. Besides, I am obligated through honor. I owed a favor to the father. I'm just paying it back to the son."

Callers phoned in from around the country. Listeners from New York, Kentucky, Wisconsin, Ohio and Texas said "Hi" to David through cracked voices and then told Max Jr. to "stay strong."

At the end of the show, David directed his final words to Max Jr. Though they applied to thousands of other orphaned children just like his little friend, David explained, "Your father's death was not the result of some careless drug overdose. He suffered so terribly from the war that his invisible wounds eventually claimed his life. And because of his premature death, you too have been forced to sacrifice a great deal for the fight against terrorism. You are one of us now, Max Jr. Do not be haunted by silence. Be proud of what your father gave to his country and understand it was that noble decision that took his life. If anyone ever questions who your father was, you have thirty *uncles* who you can call on to help explain. I'd be insulted if you didn't. Be proud, Max Jr., and always keep your chin up. Your dad was a bonafide hero!"

An email immediately followed the show. David opened it.

> David,
>
> You are an angel! I just know all of this is going to help Max Jr. when he gets older. He is truly blessed to have the gift of your friendship. I enjoyed the show very much, though I'm sure it wasn't easy for you to do it since you experienced so much pain. You continue to make sacrifices, but now for your friends—Max, his son and their entire family. I hope God blesses you every day of your life with health and happiness.
>
> Laurie

David replied:

> Laurie,
>
> It was tough at times. In fact, I had to take a moment once because it was getting really emotional for me. When I think back, though, I'm happy I did it. Max Jr. can't ever question whether

it was sincere. He'll be able to hear it in my voice. Joyce called me right after the show and raved about the power she felt from it. She also said there were a few callers who called in to comment. I pray it helps.

David

It will, Laurie quickly replied. *Thank you for your endless generosity and kindness. You're an angel from heaven.*

David vowed to continue to look after his fallen brother's son. As such, Max Jr. was silently inducted into the Fourth Ranger Battalion to take his father's place. At future parades, the boy would march with them. David would do all he could for the boy, but he still didn't consider he and his deceased comrade even. *There's no such thing*, he decided.

◻ ◻ ◻ ◻

The following day, David went to the beach to run laps, while Lindsey sat on their park bench and watched him. Every time he passed, their eyes searched each other out and the excitement built. Without a word, they engaged in an intense foreplay that had both of them hoping for the sun to go down a little more quickly. Soaked in sweat, David stole a kiss from her each time he passed. Her smile eventually turned to laughter.

At home, Lindsey bathed after David, while he sneaked a peak and a kiss. "David, I want you to make love to me until the sun pays the world another visit," she told him.

They never made it to the bedroom.

Chapter 13

□ □ □ □

Another year passed—filled with love and ongoing therapy and laughter and interventions with Lindsey's dad—and the trees were starting to shed their leaves once again. At their house lot a few streets west of North Beach, David and Lindsey shared a bottle of champagne and watched as the contractor poured the foundation for their new home. The day proved symbolic of their relationship. David broke out the house plans for him and Lindsey to go over.

"There will be skylights located in each bedroom," he pointed out.

Lindsey was giddy. "To count the stars to sleep."

He nodded. "And a wraparound porch to face the lighthouse."

"So that we'll never feel lost again."

"Anything missing?" he asked.

"Maybe someone to occupy the other bedroom," she blurted.

"What?"

She never embellished. Instead, she kissed him and poured out another glass of champagne. She then took a drink herself, avoiding the topic for the time being.

David raised an eyebrow and smiled but didn't question it further. They returned to the house plans.

◻ ◻ ◻ ◻

In the morning, David awoke with Lindsey's head on his chest. Just as he started to snore again, she leaned over for a sweet kiss. "I really love you," she whispered and then told him what she was hoping for their future. "What do you think about having a baby?" she whispered.

"A *baby*?" he repeated.

She nodded. "Not just *any* baby," she said, kissing him hard. "I want *your* baby." Her kisses were strong and deep.

David broke free for a second to peek at the alarm clock. "Then we'd better get started," he said grinning—and pulled her onto him.

◻ ◻ ◻ ◻

Saturday morning finally rolled around. Waking in the same position brought a smile to Lindsey's face. She and David lay quietly in each other's arms. While he held her tightly, she still thanked God for having this second chance.

After many playful kisses, they were up and out the door, heading for the beach. Although the radio remained turned off in the car, there was never any silence. Her hand was nestled in his for the entire ride. They talked, laughed, kissed and planned for the future.

At the beach, they took a long walk until he carried her on his back, never once complaining. They stopped somewhere along the way to kiss. "Want to take a swim?" he asked her.

"Either that or we can make love in the water?"

He sprinted toward the surf.

Laughing like a little girl, she took chase.

¤ ¤ ¤ ¤

On Sunday morning, David awoke to find Lindsey's face inches from his. He spent a few precious moments staring at her angelic face. "How did we take so long to find each other?" he whispered. Pushing the thought from his mind, he kissed her gently, sweetly. She stirred and smiled. With the world in the palm of his hand, he tiptoed out of the room and left her to her dreams of a joyful future.

After preparing a tray of eggs and coffee, David picked a wildflower from the yard and placed it into a small crystal vase. He sneaked back into their dark bedroom, placed the breakfast tray at her feet and lay beside her again. He then started kissing her everywhere, inhaling the intoxicating scent of the previous night's love that covered her.

When her eyes slowly opened, he gently rested himself on top of her and kissed her with all the love that made his heart beat.

And as she eagerly returned the passion, the eggs grew cold.

¤ ¤ ¤ ¤

Several full moons had come and gone when David returned home from work and was greeted by Lindsey at the door. She was beaming and held her hands behind her back. He smiled, curiously, and kissed his wife. "What are you hiding?" he asked.

"A gift for you," she answered playfully.

"A gift for me?" He held out his hands. "Well?"

She kept her hands behind her back, while a mischievous grin worked its way into the corners of her mouth and tears formed in her sparkling eyes.

David was persistent. "I can't have it now?"

She couldn't take it anymore. She pulled her arms out from behind her back and revealed two empty hands. He was baffled. She wrapped her arms around him and kissed his neck. "In nine months," she whispered into his ear.

It only took a moment before it registered—before he hugged her tightly. As if he might be hurting his child, though, he quickly pulled away and bent to kiss her belly. "Oh, Linds," he said.

She pulled him to his feet. They embraced tightly and cried together.

The months ticking off Lindsey's pregnancy were a magical haze. They shared the joyous news with loved ones at Cappricio's Restaurant. And it didn't take long for David to spoil Lindsey something fierce. Night after night, she took to the couch and ate ice cream, while he rubbed her feet.

Before long, David and his swollen wife picked out baby furniture and tiny clothes. They set up the baby's nursery, while family and friends gathered to inspect and nod their approvals.

They took the childbirth classes at the hospital.

And each night, as they lay in bed, both sets of hands massaged her belly.

¤ ¤ ¤ ¤

Seven months into the miracle in progress, David visited Max's gravesite to talk to his friend on bended knee.

"Hi buddy. Lindsey's pregnant. The ultrasound says it's a boy, and I couldn't be any more thrilled. But I'm a little scared too," he said. "I'm praying hard that the baby's born healthy." He shook his head. "I just hope that if God's going to punish me for what we did in Afghanistan, that he'll punish me and not my son."

He sighed. "I've been looking in after Max Jr. He's a good boy. You'd be proud." His eyes filled. "I hope you've found peace, brother. I pray every night for it."

David pulled a sealed envelope out of his pocket. "Listen, I need you to do me a favor." He kissed the envelope and carefully placed it at the base of Max's headstone. "It's a message to my son." He nodded. "It's important that I become the dad I always wanted for myself." He shrugged. "And my greatest obstacles and achievements will lie in raising my boy. The person he becomes will be the measurement of success in my own life." He stood. "Can you please deliver it for me, Max?"

David stood, looked up toward the sky and whispered, "Please hear my prayer, Father."

¤ ¤ ¤ ¤

It was a random Monday morning when Lindsey tried to shake David from his sleep. He was dead to the world. "Come on, hon," she moaned. "You have to get up."

He mumbled something incoherent and rolled over. She leaned into his ear and whispered, "Wake up, *Daddy*. It's time."

He lurched up and looked at his wife through squinted eyes. "It's time?" he said.

She smiled. "Yep. My water broke an hour ago. We'd better get going."

He jumped out of bed and searched frantically for everything they needed, periodically stopping to kiss her during the chaos. Leisurely, she slid out of bed and calmly got dressed.

David loaded the new caravan, helped her in and sped down the road toward the hospital. The whole time, she took deep breaths and held on for dear life. "Oooooh..." she moaned.

David was a wreck, while Lindsey was breathing like a freight train right on schedule for a head-on collision. "Take deep breaths," he reminded her.

"You too," she huffed with a grin. "We'd like to make it there in one piece."

They screeched into the hospital parking lot. The car hadn't even stopped rocking when David had the passenger door open. One body part at a time, Lindsey got out. She was huge. As if he hadn't seen her like this for months, he gawked in amazement.

A nurse hurried out with a wheelchair and swept Lindsey into it with one smooth motion. As they raced toward intake, she asked, "How far apart are the contractions?"

"I think they've become connected," Lindsey grunted. The woman chuckled at the candid response.

While Lindsey got carted away, David stayed downstairs for what felt like a few decades to take care of the insurance information.

When he rushed into the maternity ward, Lindsey was already wired for sound, her belly hosting a twisted labyrinth of cords and hoses. She was panting like a dog.

"She needs ice chips," a young nurse commented and handed David a cup of them. Another nurse approached. "The baby's going to be delivered right in this room, Dad," she told David.

He nodded.

"Code croon, rome tee ton four," the PA suddenly called out. The message was barely audible, the announcement mumbled and incoherent. But the staff must have understood. A parade of medical personnel raced past Lindsey's room to assist someone who must have been in trouble. *Oh no*, David thought.

All in one motion, an older nurse with the shoulders of a football player entered the room and snapped on a rubber glove, positioning a rolling stool between Lindsey's legs. She took a seat, squeezed a glob of petroleum jelly onto the glove and dove in. Lindsey panted through another unbearable contraction. "You're eight centimeters dilated," the linebacker announced.

Not two seconds later, the doctor arrived and stuck out her hand. "Mr. McClain," she announced, "I'm Dr. Shobi Sundar." David fumbled through the chaos and managed to shake the woman's hand. The doctor then received the latest update and sighed. "The bad news is, Mrs. McClain," she told Lindsey, "is that it's a little late for an anesthesia." She smiled. "The good news is, you should be ready to go very soon. But don't start anything until I get back." She winked.

Lindsey smiled, but not for long. As she released another horrid groan, David instinctively rushed to her side.

One moment, the room was filled with people, and the very next David and Lindsey were alone. Chaos was replaced by silence. David smiled at his beautiful wife and grabbed her hand. "I'm here, babe," he whispered. "And I love you so much."

When she wasn't huffing and puffing, Lindsey screamed out in pain. Without reclaiming his hand, David managed to feed his tormented wife half a cup of melting ice chips. And through it all, he held her hand.

After what seemed like an eternity, Dr. Sundar entered the room again and took a seat at the foot of the bed, positioning herself between Lindsey's legs. Reaching a hand beneath the sheet, she said, "Okay, let's see what we've got."

David was amazed at how natural the whole experience felt. He looked back. People were starting to pour back into the room, each one gawking at his wife's swollen genitalia. But nothing could have bothered him less. *Perspective is everything*, he thought.

"Ten centimeters," the doctor announced joyfully. "It's time for you to push, Mom."

Lindsey looked over at David. He nodded. She bore down hard. David positioned himself by Lindsey's head. She crushed his hand with each push. While he stood and watched, he felt a mix of helplessness and respect for his wife.

After a supernatural effort on Lindsey's part, the baby's head crowned, its black hair soaked and matted with blood and mucous.

"Here's the head," the doctor announced. "Just a couple more pushes, Mom."

David peeked down and saw his little prince's dark-haired crown. He gasped and fought back the squeal in his throat, while tears began rolling down his face.

Lindsey pushed again and again, but the baby crept out a centimeter only to return a centimeter each time. Suddenly, the baby's heart monitor beeped rapidly. The child was stuck in the birth canal and laboring hard. The doctor remained calm and placed both hands into Lindsey's vagina under the baby's head. She nodded and asked the nurse for an instrument that looked like a large turkey baster. "The baby's umbilical cord is wrapped around his neck. He's fine, but I need to get him out right now." She looked at Lindsey and winked. "Mom," she said, "I'm going to help you, but the baby and I need you to push as hard as you can, okay?"

Lindsey gritted her teeth and conviction glazed over her pupils. David looked up to find two postnatal surgeons waiting. His legs went weak at the knees, and he lost his breath. *I need to be strong for Lindsey and the baby*, he thought. *Of all times, I need to be strong now.*

Lindsey grunted and groaned, while everyone in the room cheered her on. Three pushes later, the head popped out to the neck. The baby was blue, and David felt like crying. Lindsey looked at him. He smiled.

"Everything looks great. He's almost out!" the doctor said.

Lindsey let out a shriek and pushed one last time. The baby's shoulders crossed the breach, and his limp body shot out into the doctor's bloodied hands. A swollen plumb stood out between his legs. *It's a boy*, David confirmed. For a moment, the newborn lay still and lifeless. David held his breath and began to die inside.

Medical personnel swarmed the newborn, while David silently asked God, *If You must, please take my life instead of the baby's.* And then, the baby's cry pierced the room. David couldn't hold back any longer. He cried harder than his boy.

With the newborn in her hands, Dr. Sundar announced, "Congratulations, you have a healthy baby boy."

David kissed Lindsey. She was exhausted but smiling. Dr. Sundar cut the cord and placed the child on Lindsey's chest. "Okay, little guy," she whispered, "It's time to meet your mom and dad."

All three were crying. David hugged Lindsey and wept. "Thank you for my beautiful son."

Between sobs, Lindsey told David, "Oh my God, babe. He looks just like you. Let's name him David Jr."

David kissed her once more and then lifted his newborn son into his arms. "Happy Birthday, D.J.," he whimpered. "It's nice to finally meet you."

After the tiny miracle was cleaned up and checked thoroughly, a blue knit cap was fitted over his pointed head and he was carried to his mother's bosom. David and Lindsey wept over their son's new life.

David stared at his new son, his chest swelling with pride. He bent down, kissed the baby and whispered, "Even with all the darkness, you're going to love it here." His eyes filled again.

"And your dad and I will be right by your side through all of it," Lindsey added. "Always."

¤ ¤ ¤ ¤

That afternoon, the hospital room was filled with flow-ers. Both families had visited the baby and were leav-ing. Though exhausted, Lindsey and David were grate-ful for the time alone with their child. Lindsey cradled the tiny boy in her arms. They stared at the perfect little gift for a long time. D.J. opened his eyes, yawned once and offered a slight smile. They laughed, joyously.

"He seems so happy," Lindsey said. "Do you think he knows something we don't?"

"Maybe he's just remembering where he came from?" David suggested, kissing his son.

"Maybe," Lindsey whispered, glowing with joy.

The new family held each other tightly.

David looked at Lindsey lying beside him and then at D.J. who was sleeping peacefully. *Life is better than good*, he thought, smiling wide.

Epilogue

◻ ◻ ◻ ◻

Eric Holloway and his two boys, Blaize and Flynn, were leaving the cemetery when they found a dirt-stained envelope lying on the ground. Eric bent down and picked it up. It was addressed to *My Son.* "That's odd," he said and opened it—never realizing that the sealed envelope contained a message of hope from a healing soldier to his unborn son.

Dear Son,

First and most importantly, I love you—more than I could ever explain in a simple letter.

Know that I will always be here for you, my son. No matter the circumstances or the situation, I will be right by your side until my final breath. You have my solemn word.

I must admit that this is not a perfect world that we live in, but it's all we have, so it's important to make the most of it. Attitude is everything. If you can adopt a positive attitude and find hope in each day, then your life will be filled with joy—I promise.

No matter where you live, family and friends are your home. Value education because it's the key to opportunity. And although I never want you to start a fight, I never want you to run from one either. Courage is the only thing that guarantees you can keep your word and stand for your beliefs—and you'd better do both because that's where your character is forged. Also, try to give people the benefit of the doubt. We're all human and we all make mistakes—even you and me. Wearing another's shoes is a good practice.

Make sure you laugh a lot and, although it's good to plan for the future, remember to live in the present. Your life will be a string of moments. Don't waste any of them. Be forgiving of others, as well as of yourself, and strive to have no regrets. As far as we know, we only get one shot at this.

You're responsible for your own life, so please make it a great one. Dream big and never let anyone tell you that you can't do something. You CAN do anything... ANYTHING!

Be good to yourself. Believe me, it's not as easy as it sounds. Say your prayers and lean on your faith when things get tough—and unfortunately, things will definitely get rough at times. But remember, it doesn't rain forever. And please be a gentleman. Your life will be the true measure of success for mine. I'm counting on you to be a good man.

Never be selfish. It's a true weakness. Give more than you take and know that you have my heart.

All My Love, Always,
Dad

Eric wiped a single tear from his cheek and placed the envelope back on the ground where he'd found it.

"What did it say?" Blaize asked, looking down at the envelope.

"Yeah, what did it say?" Flynn asked, echoing his older brother.

Eric grinned. "It says that there is no love like a father's love..." He stopped and looked them both in the eye. "And that we should do our best with the gifts God's given us."

Both boys nodded, and they walked away.